MAXWELL'S FLAME

A thrilling murder mystery with plenty of twists

M.J. TROW

A Schoolmaster Murder Mystery Book 2

JOFFE BOOKS

Revised edition 2024
Joffe Books, London
www.joffebooks.com

First published in Great Britain in 1995

This paperback edition was first published
in Great Britain in 2024

Cover art by Imogen Buchanan

ISBN: 978-1-83526-430-0

A NOTE TO THE READER

Please note these books were published in the 1990s, when social attitudes were different.

CHAPTER 1

It's quite easy really. To kill somebody. All you need is nerve. All right, in a perfect world, planning too. In a perfect world, you'd take a leaf out of Hitchcock's book and kill a stranger — perhaps the man sitting opposite you on the train, or the woman walking her dog on the common. But then, you'd have to be Robert Walker — and remember, with all his planning, he didn't get away with it.

But it's not a perfect world, is it? And each man, they say, kills the thing he loves — not a stranger. That's for celluloid and serial killers. Most of us, if we kill at all — and we all have it in us — kill somebody we know. And we do it for a reason.

So there was a victim, that dull Thursday in May, wandering through the dark passageways that ran the width of the building, looking for the photocopying room. Had you been there — and perhaps it's best you weren't — you'd have made out that she was short and rather dumpy with straight dark hair. It was that straight dark hair her murderer aimed for, on the corner as she turned left. A pity really, because the photocopying room was to the right. Anyway, there it was. Her murderer had just enough light here from the stairs to see what he was doing. She didn't see him, didn't hear him until it was too late. She couldn't even find the bloody light switch.

He'd hit her, a little before lunchtime, a crippling blow horizontally across the head. Under that long, dark hair, her parietal bone had shattered, the largest fragments slicing into her brain. She'd buckled and fallen to her knees and he'd hit her again as she'd gone down. The third time, the top of her skull caved in and blood was trickling like some ghastly crimson mask over her upturned face.

For a moment, he caught his breath. She was staring at him, her mouth open, both arms outstretched. He always wondered afterwards whether she could see him, what with the blood and the trauma to her brain. She probably could, because she tried to speak. Perhaps they made perfect sense to her, the guttural, choking grunts that came from her throat. She was bleeding from the nose now and her whole body was quivering, rather like a wasp you kill in summer.

So he'd hit her again. Well, he couldn't leave her like that, could he? What could she hope for if he left her? A few weeks or months tethered to a machine in some off-white hospital ward, where nurses would come to regard her as part of the furniture before somebody decided to switch her off? What sort of life was that for anybody? And this time he used both hands, demolishing her forehead until her lifeless body jerked backwards and the arms flopped uselessly at her sides.

And that was where the planning bit came in. Or rather the lack of it. How do you get rid of a nine-stone human being whose blood is spreading like a black puddle over the corridor tiles? And when you've found somewhere, some niche hidden from the world, what then? Do you just wipe the floor, the walls, the heavy object and go back about your business?

Can it really be that easy?

* * *

They say that everybody remembers where they were the day it happened. It was one of those momentous events of the twentieth century — a scene of horror that would be etched for ever on those who witnessed it. As though time, for those nine seconds, stopped. And the repercussions of it — the ripples on the darkling waters of life — spread outward for ever too.

One of the first to know was Margaret Vincent, peering into the green screen of her word processor and glancing back again to try for the umpteenth time to decipher the Head's memo. She swore afterwards that her begonias shook and trembled on the shelf overhead and the cursor leapt in panic from the screen. It was probable that Heather Robotham heard the same tremor and felt it too. She was on one of those errands foisted on Head Girls from time to time, just to remind her that the post that carried no privileges at all, had responsibilities too. And her errand took her past the Head's office at the crucial time when the balloon went up and the world stopped turning. She thought it best to hurry on.

'Doc' Martin, the school caretaker, was also on an errand. Amazing how easy it was to look busy, with a clipboard in one hand and screwdriver in the other. He remembered checking his watch seconds before he'd heard it. Nine twenty-eight. Tens-es soon — a welcome tea break. Where had he left his kettle? He'd seen Heather, tight little bum swaying ahead of him, down the corridor. Well, there weren't many perks to being a school caretaker in the '90s, but ogling sixth-formers was one of them and bearing in mind Mrs Martin had all the allure of a school pizza these days, he'd settle for that.

Unlike Heather Robotham, though, he had the nerve — and the time — to listen at the Head's door. If anybody else passed, he could always scrutinise the door frame suddenly, looking for those bloody ants. They didn't have very strong doors at Leighford High School — veneer and cardboard to save money now that the school was responsible for its own finances — so he caught most of it.

'GNV what, Headmaster?' Martin recognised the stentorian tones of Peter Maxwell, Leighford's Head of Sixth

Form, a cantankerous old bastard who looked as though he'd been in teaching for a hundred years.

'Now, come along, Max,' the caretaker heard his Headmaster wheedle. It was a Friday and the term was six weeks old. For James Diamond, BA, MEd, it was the worst possible combination. The honeymoon period of the start of term was over. People were not yet all-forgiving in the warm glow of the end-of-term knees-up and by Friday, tetchiness had always developed into a fine art. 'Roger did brief you on this last term, you know.'

Peter Maxwell had gone a rather curious shade of purple, contrasting oddly with the iron grey of his side-whiskers. He raised a quizzical eyebrow. 'Brief to the point of non-existence, Headmaster. If our illustrious Second Deputy mentioned it, I, to quote Trevor Howard in *The Charge of the Light Brigade*, am a Turk's arse. Take my word for it — Deputy Heads will roll.'

Jim Diamond looked at his Head of Sixth Form. It was rather like looking at Medusa — Maxwell's tangle of barbed wire hair coiled like snakes. Not that a classical training brought the similarity to Diamond's mind, for he had the misfortune to be a biologist. No, he had once seen *Clash of the Titans* and the image of Ray Harryhausen's repellent monster had stayed with him.

'Roger handles all the INSET provision,' the Headmaster said patiently, 'and GNVQ is upon us, Max, whether we like it or not.'

Maxwell took in the figure across the desk from him as he had so often in the past few years. As ever, the desk was empty — the mark of a man who delegated. As ever, the perfectly horrendous blond, buck-toothed children grinned at their daddy from Boots frames, just to remind the world that the grey-suited anonymous bugger at the helm was a human being too.

'And who runs the sixth form in my absence?' Maxwell asked.

'Well, I know it's difficult with Alison on maternity leave, but I thought . . . perhaps . . . Deirdre?'

Jim Diamond had never seen Maxwell's knuckles whiten like that before, not even when that HMI had rather cruelly christened him a dinosaur. Even more bizarre was the spectacle of Maxwell's mouth opening and no sound coming out.

'Deirdre?' The Head of Sixth Form forced his vocal cords into action. 'You threaten me — my sixth form — with Deirdre Lessing, the Typhoid Mary of West Sussex?'

'Now, Max—'

'I'm sorry, Headmaster,' Maxwell leaned back, his hands clasped on his shirt front, 'but it's out of the question.'

'Mr Maxwell . . .' The worm that was Jim Diamond, BA, MEd, had turned, as he did about once a term when pushed beyond endurance. 'In-service training is now a recognised part of a teacher's life. It has been arranged, quite properly, though perhaps a little belatedly, by Roger Garrett, as part of his job description. This school needs to attract more students to its sixth form in September in order to survive. And in order to do that, we must embrace the General National Vocational Qualification package. And someone must oversee that. That someone, Mr Maxwell, is you.'

All this had been delivered in one breath, rather as Pat O'Brien and Jimmy Cagney talked to each other in the '30s and '40s — at the rate of two hundred words a minute. It occurred to Maxwell that Diamond daren't have stopped for fear he would not have the bottle to continue.

'I see,' he said, putting his fingers together and tapping them on his lower lip. 'Well, since I find that I am once again indispensable to Leighford High in its upward quest for academic excellence, what can I say?'

'It is only for one week, Max.' Diamond had subsided, still quivering internally. He couldn't quite believe it. He'd stood toe-to-toe with 'Mad Max' and the old bastard hadn't bitten through his windpipe. Perhaps there was a God.

'And Deirdre?' Maxwell riveted the Headmaster with the eyes of the Basilisk. Try as he might, Jim Diamond was powerless to back away. He'd won one round, or thought he had. He wouldn't risk another.

'Oh, I'll keep an eye on things,' he flustered, 'with Deirdre, I mean. How much harm can she do in one week, Max?'

Maxwell smiled and lifted his rickety old body out of Diamond's knobbly office furniture. 'Unchained,' he said, 'that woman could have destroyed the Roman Empire in a single day.' He paused at the door to hear the Head say, 'I promise you, Max, there'll be no changes.'

Maxwell turned to him from his vantage point of a loftier IQ and centuries of culture and smiled again. 'Ah, Headmaster, all History is change. But Deirdre Lessing merely teaches Business Studies, so we'll be all right, won't we?'

* * *

Lieutenant John, Viscount Fitzgibbon was turning in the plastic saddle of his plastic charger, scanning the half-formed line of cavalrymen behind him with his one good plastic eye. A flick of paint from Maxwell's brush and the Lieutenant's face assumed a more human flesh tint, in stark contrast to his white busby and jacket.

'What do you think happened to this one, Count?' Maxwell asked, squinting to paint the hands. 'Eyewitnesses say he was hit in the chest by two bullets shortly after the Brigade moved off. There is a story, however,' he slipped the slim brush between his teeth as he eased the scabbard up a little, so that it rested nonchalantly against Fitzgibbon's left leg, straight in the stirrup, 'that he survived, was captured by the Russians and returned home in 1870. Despite appeals in various newspapers, though, he didn't come forward. Now, why was that, Count, eh?'

Count Metternich, as usual, offered no solution, shed no light. When you're a potentially raunchy tom whose master has had you neutered by a sadistic bastard in a white coat, the last thing you intend to do is give said master the time of day. The flick of a right ear was all Maxwell had a right to and a flick of the right ear was all he got.

'Perhaps he couldn't stand his wife.' Maxwell resumed his painting of the plastic hero. 'Perhaps it pissed him off no end when the Russians released him. What do you think?'

Nothing.

Maxwell looked at the feisty feline, curled on top of his linen basket, a languid tail swaying a little, as if irritated by Maxwell's constant questions.

'Well,' Maxwell went into his Mandy Rice-Davies routine from the '60s, 'you would say that, wouldn't you? Oh, shit!'

The door bell had interrupted his reveries. And Christine Keeler's sidekick, sixteen, blonde, voluptuous, on the game, smiled at him again from the faded newspapers of his memory as he gingerly put down Fitzgibbon at the rear of the left-hand squadron of the 8th Hussars. Why was it, he asked himself as he parked his paintbrush behind his ear and made for the stairs, that someone always rang that bloody bell just as he started work? At the entrance to the hatch into his loft, he stopped and surveyed, as he did most days, the panorama he had been working on now for nearly fourteen years — Cardigan's Light Brigade drawn up on that fateful October afternoon, ready to ride into legend down the Valley of Death. Briefly, Lord Cardigan caught his eye, sitting impatiently on his chestnut, Ronald, hand on hip, as if to say, 'I'm waiting, Mr Maxwell. My Brigade can't start without you.'

'Yes, yes,' Maxwell muttered, 'just as soon as I can. Bugger!' and he hit his head on the hatch as he went down. He scowled at the pile of washing left untended in the corner. 'So many undies,' he sighed, 'so little time.'

The bell rang again. 'Yes, yes, I'm on my way. This is a town house, you know. I do have four storeys to negotiate.'

Through the lumpy glass of his front door, where the purple sunset of the May day was giving way to the orange artificiality of the street light, Maxwell made out a mop of frizzy blonde hair and a green shapeless body.

'Sally Greenhow.' He opened the door to her. 'You've come to seduce me. How nice.'

‘It might be for you,’ she said and swept past him. ‘Max, is that a paintbrush behind your ear or are you pleased to see me?’

‘Ah.’ He flicked the thing out of his barbed wire curls. ‘That’s where I put it. Go on up, oh wise Second in the Special Needs Department. Coffee to the left. Southern Comfort to the right. Do with me what you will.’

‘I’m turning right,’ she called down to him, ‘and stop looking up my skirt, you warped old bugger.’

‘Heaven forfend.’ Maxwell feigned outrage and held an upturned hand across his forehead. ‘I’ll move into a bungalow immediately.’

She hovered in his lounge while he poured them both a Southern Comfort from the bottle in his Arts and Craft Movement drinks cabinet. She crashed into his Oxfam sofa and all but disappeared in its clapped-out centre.

‘Here’s looking at you, kid,’ he snarled in his best Bogart. And he did. And she was. Sally Greenhow hadn’t changed for twenty-eight years now. And she was nearly twenty-nine. Old enough to be Maxwell’s daughter. Her face was round and soft, with large, blue-grey eyes and a perfect pair of matching dimples. Maxwell wondered again if she smelt of baby oil, but that whole image gave rise to cries of ‘warped old bugger’ again in his brain and he sat down opposite her.

She raised her glass in response to his toast. ‘May all your Ofsteds be successful ones,’ she said.

‘Ah,’ he beamed, ‘so you’ve heard the word.’

‘I have,’ she nodded. ‘Next term for definite. We are to be inspected by a team of a dozen or so Ofsted inspectors on or about the third week in.’

‘Oh, goody!’ Maxwell clapped his hands, careful to have put down his drink first, and drummed his heels on the mock Berber.

‘It’ll mean lesson plans, Max,’ Sally warned, ‘but I’m sure you’ve got them all up together.’

‘My dear girl,’ Maxwell crossed his legs, as far anyway as his fifty-three years would allow him to, ‘I haven’t made a lesson plan in thirty-one summers. And if Ofsted intend to try to make me, I'm afraid it'll be a case of Off-fuck. You'll excuse my French, of course.'

'Ah,' she waved a dismissive arm at him, 'you'll come through all right. Something to do with shit and roses.'

'I thought that was a pop group,' Maxwell frowned. 'Now, to business. You didn't come here just to warn me about Ofsted. Or even to drink large quantities of my Southern Comfort. And,' he sighed, 'I suppose I shall have to come to terms with the fact that you aren't after my body after all. So . . .' He saw her rummage in her capacious bag for her ciggies. 'Lovely though it is to see a colleague I only grunted goodbye to not . . .' He checked the large clock, '. . . five hours ago, I suspect an ulterior motive.'

'Sussed!' She clicked her fingers. Maxwell was impressed. Not all women could do that. He slid a glass ashtray out from under his chair with a deft flick of his slipper. 'No, I keep meaning to see you about this INSET business.' And her dimpled, baby face lit up momentarily with the flare of her match.

'Remind me,' said Maxwell, straight-faced, 'what does that rather silly acronym mean again?'

'It's not exactly an acronym,' she told him, inhaling viciously; 'it means In-Service Training . . . Max, you absolute shit!' and she threw one of his own cushions at him. She'd been caught out again. Why was it, having known Mad Max Maxwell for four years, she still fell for set-ups like that?

'All right,' he chuckled, 'what's afoot?'

No, she wouldn't say it. Wouldn't say 'Twelve inches' when the puppet master dictated. In her way, she loved old Maxie, but by God, he was an infuriating bastard at times. 'Next Friday,' she said, 'that's the day after tomorrow.'

'Well done,' Max commented. 'Coming on in Special Needs, then?'

'That's Learning Support to you, Mr Maxwell,' she countered. 'Do try to stay with the jargon.'

'Oops,' Maxwell retracted. 'Pardon me all to hell, I'm sure.'

'We have to be there on Friday. By twelve noon. Didn't you get the bumf through?'

'Oh, I expect so,' he said, 'but you know how it is. It's probably in my in-tray somewhere under requests for references and last term's reports. It's a commonplace of office work that if you leave something in your in-tray for long enough, it becomes obsolete and you can bin it. What are we supposed to do, exactly?'

'Well, we have to be at the Carnforth Conference Centre by twelve. Check into our rooms, lunch, ice-breaking sessions and then into the nitty-gritty, as they say.'

'Yes,' Maxwell rubbed a thoughtful chin. 'What is the nitty-gritty of GNVQ exactly?'

'That's what we're going to find out,' Sally said. 'I really called by to offer you a lift.'

'A lift?'

'Well, surely you're not going to cycle?' Her eyes widened. 'Good God, Max, it's the best part of seventy miles.'

'Kent, isn't it?'

'That's right.'

'Garden of England.'

'It's just off the A259 before you get too lyrical about it.'

'So what are you proposing?'

'Well, how if I pick you up, say, ten?'

'Ten is fine,' Maxwell nodded. 'What does Alan think of all this?'

'Oh,' Sally groaned, 'my dear husband is up to his eyes in some vital contract or other. I've barely seen him for two weeks. I doubt if he'll notice I've gone.'

'Now then,' Maxwell growled sternly. 'I won't have any lip-quivering in chauffeuses in my employ. Alan's got a wife in a million. You know it. He knows it. Come to think of it, now we all bloody know it. Let's forget husbands, and wives and whatever the hell GNVQ is and do what we enjoy best.'

'Oh?' She raised a searching eyebrow. 'And what might that be?'

He leered at her, winked, then dropped the smile entirely. 'Why,' he said, 'character assassination, of course. Now, take that bastard Roger Garrett for instance. Do you know what he had the brass neck to say to me this morning?'

* * *

Jim 'Legs' Diamond passed Peter 'Mad Max' Maxwell in the corridor the next day. Maxwell was feeling fairly flippant. He'd had a nice long chat with Sally Greenhow the night before and he'd finished all the dark blue bits on Lieutenant Fitzgibbon's uniform after she'd gone. Every time he had to mix the blue and black, he cursed whatever bugger it was who chose that colour for the Light Cavalry over a century and a half ago. Whoever it was, he was clearly no respecter of Humbrol paints. And as Maxwell was feeling flippant, he thumped his left breast with his right fist as Roman soldiers were wont to do to their superior officers. It was the only token of respect that Peter Maxwell ever showed to Jim Diamond.

In his turn, Diamond had had a sleepless night. Whenever he looked at the electronic green digits on his bedside clock, it seemed to say only ten minutes later than when he'd looked the last time. And whenever he felt himself dozing, he saw the hair-fringed face of his Head of Sixth Form smiling at him, like Death in The Seventh Seal. Why had he given in? Roger Garrett, Diamond's Second Deputy, had warned him that Maxwell appeared not to have noticed the INSET week. And the content of that week — the introduction of a new vocational course for sixth-formers — was bound to be so alien to Maxwell's outlook as to be unbelievable. It was rather like introducing a plesiosaur to an Apple Macintosh. Yet, the Great Man, after an initial outburst which did some structural damage to the Head's office, had backed down. Acquiesced. And here he was, this Thursday morning, beaming and bashing his chest for some reason.

Only then did it occur to Diamond that perhaps his Head of Sixth Form wasn't well. It was increasing, wasn't it? The stress factor? You heard stories all the time. So-and-so at Weldon High bursting into tears in a French lesson; Whatsisface from Burnside taking all his clothes off and wandering the Physics labs. Well, why not Maxwell? After all, there had been all that unpleasantness last year when Jenny Hyde had been murdered. And Jenny was one of Maxwell's own sixth form. It was bound to take its toll, a thing like that. And Jim Diamond found himself glancing back at the retreating figure in the lightweight Italian suit and the desert boots, watching for any further signs of impending insanity.

* * *

'Hectorina . . .' Maxwell waved a small sheaf of papers at the gawky girl whose gaze never met his. 'Not a bad effort, dear, but I think you'll find that the affectionate name for the British Army's musket was Brown Bess. Black Bess on the other hand, which you have here in your otherwise tolerable essay, was Dick Turpin's horse.'

The Upper Sixth guffawed. 'Not to worry, Hectorina dear. Colour-blindness comes to us all. Richard . . .' He fixed his grey gaze on a rugger-hearty slouched in the corner. At least he would have been a rugger-hearty if Leighford High School had boasted a rugger team. 'Your conceptualisation is inherently cogent. Unfortunately, you haven't the first bloody clue what a paragraph is. Still, such niceties never severely challenged Jane Austen, so what the hell. And,' he held aloft the final few sheets, having thrown Richard's attempts back to the boy, 'talking of hell, Miranda, your . . . thing.' He held it between disdainful fingers. 'You will write out twenty million times, "Apostrophes do not occur before every single letter's' in the English language." Apart from that, I've never seen Wellington's problems in the Peninsula outlined so succinctly. Bravo. Now, my children, list to me,' and he swept past the photo of A.J.P. Taylor he'd stuck up in the corner years ago so that the Upper Sixth could throw darts at it. 'Your revered A level teacher is going away.' There were cries of 'Shame' mixed with 'Hooray'. 'Going away into that sweet good night — actually to the Carnforth Conference Centre, Lydd. Now, I know what you're thinking, dearly beloved. Why is the old fart buggering off for a week when we've only got — how many contact days is it, Zak? You are, after all, doing A level Maths?'

'Er . . . including today . . .'

'No,' Maxwell stopped him, 'never include today what you can put off till tomorrow.'

'OK, then. Twenty-six.'

'Precisely. Twenty-six. Minus the five I'll be away. Twenty-one. The European legations at Peking held out for over twice that time against the Boxer hordes. You'll be all right. And who better to conduct you through the labyrinths of Napoleon's domestic policy but your own, your very own, Mr Paul Moss, the Head of History.'

Maxwell's rapturous build-up fell on stony ears. After all, this group had the rising star that was Paul Moss for British History. The thought of having him for European History as well, even for one week, raised thoughts of suicide in their young breasts.

'When I come back, however,' Maxwell warned, 'you'd better be ready for the most intensive three weeks of your young lives. Now, Hectorina, what part of Napoleon's anatomy went on sale — and failed to reach its reserve — at Sotheby's a few years ago? Let me give you a clue — it was about an inch long and had turned rather black.'

CHAPTER 2

The A259 takes you most of the way, with the sea on your right and the sweep of the downs to your left. You pass within an arrow shot of that gentle rise where Duke William beat the hell out of the English on a misty October afternoon a long, long time ago; near Bodiam with its fine, fourteenth-century castle reflected in its emerald moat; through Guestling Thorn and Icklesham to Winchelsea.

'Cinque port,' Maxwell yelled above the wind and rattle of Sally Greenhow's 2CV. 'Of course, the medieval town lies out there, in Rye Bay. Rather like drowned Lyonesse, isn't it?'

'Did anyone ever tell you, Max,' the girl said, crunching her gears badly, as she negotiated her way past a geriatric in a Rover, 'that you are something of a Town Bore? How do you know all these things about places? You've only got a bike.'

'Ah, but White Surrey and I have been places together you wouldn't believe. Is it me, or are we a touch tetchy this morning?'

Sally shook herself. 'Oh, I'm sorry, Max,' she said. 'PMT I suppose. That and Friday.'

'Ah, yes,' Maxwell nodded. 'PMT. It used to mean Penge Mean Time in my day.'

'When was that, exactly?' she humoured him.

'The 1840s,' he said, 'when men were men and women weren't. There's a Martello tower up the road a bit.'

'Where do we go then? After Rye, I mean?'

'Er . . .'

'No, Max,' she rummaged with the crumpled paper on his lap, 'you're reading it upside down.'

'Oh, Sussex,' he said, as though he'd been visited on the Damascus road. 'Well, you either keep to the A259 across Walland Marsh or you hug the coast along Camber Sands. That way you come to the delightful sewer system of Jury's Gut.'

'Mmm, nice. And where's Carnforth in relation to that?'

'On the Lydd Level, mercifully just outside the bit marked "Danger Area" on the map.'

'Dangerous for what, do you think? Bastard!' and she raised a sudden middle finger to a meandering agricultural vehicle driver.

'Woman driver, I shouldn't wonder.' Maxwell smiled smugly.

She scowled at him behind her tinted glasses. 'You're looking early retirement in the face,' she said, pursing her lips, 'what with the injury and all.'

'What injury?'

'The one I'm going to do you if you make that sort of sexist comment again.'

And apart from the crashing of Sally's gears and the odd stifled chuckle from Max, the rest of the journey was silent, like the 'p' in Bath.

* * *

It was an odd place perhaps for a conference centre, out of the way of the world, off the Dengemarsh road. To the north-east stood the low, rather menacing pile of Camber Castle, one of the ruins that Cromwell didn't knock about, even a bit, but time had done more damage. English Heritage had got their worthy little hands on it however and in time, no doubt, its great Henrician gates would open to a rather bored world once again and the Japanese would have a field day with their cameras. To the south-west, the flat expanse was dotted with standing water and the newly opened holiday camps, with their trickle of May Bank Holiday visitors who had the leisure to stay on. Beyond the levels of the RSPB reserve, stretching to the shingle and the sea, where curlews, little terns and tiny firecrests nested in the open weather, the huge sinister blocks of Dungeness A and B loomed over the little lighthouse that Samuel Wyatt built there in 1792. The nuclear power stations stood like invading aliens on a submissive, battered landscape, crisscrossed and scarred with war.

'Very H.G. Wells,' mused Maxwell, but Sally was already taking them around the broad sweep of the drive into Carnforth and she missed the significance of it.

Maxwell was glad to stretch his legs. They'd stopped for half-past tens-es in Bexhill, at a rather pretty little place with hanging baskets, but what with Maxie's old trouble and Sally's upturned pram of a car, standing upright again was pure joy. She helped him with the luggage — her three Samsonites to his one battered old case marked with a torn P&O label — and they staggered inside.

The place was brand-new. There was no doubt about it, West Sussex Education Authority had coughed up splendidly. Wall-to-wall carpeting, electric sliding doors, plush leatherette furniture. If the rooms were as good as the foyer, they were in for a marvellous week — 'Don't forget to fill in your forms for subsistence every day,' Margaret the school secretary had said. It certainly beat the hell out of the staff room at dear old Leighford High, with its ashtrays and plastic trophies and piles of photocopying.

'Good morning,' a painfully breezy young thing hailed them both across the counter. She looked as though she had been taught the art of make-up by Pablo Picasso, in that her eyeshadow had missed her eyelids by several inches. 'I'm Tracey. Welcome to Carnforth Conference Centre. We hope you have a nice stay. Will you sign the book, please?'

Now Maxwell had a cleaning lady on his floor at Leighford High, the redoubtable Mrs B. (real name unknown), who had a similar habit of conducting conversation in blocks like this and Maxwell was a fair hand by now at handling it.

'I knew you would be,' he smiled. 'Thank you so much. So do we. I'd be delighted.' He held the pen, the one on the little chain anchored to the counter, out to Sally who flashed a smirk at him and signed.

'You are?' Tracey looked up in her pencil-pleated skirt.

'Mr and Mrs Smith,' Maxwell said. 'I trust we have a south-facing room.'

Tracey was still running her elegant, crimson-nailed finger up and down the visitors' list when Sally came to her rescue. 'It's just my colleague's little idea of a joke, she said. 'A very little idea, you'll agree. I'm Mrs Sally Greenhow and my grandfather here is Mr Peter Maxwell.' She stabbed him with the pen. 'Sign, Max. And do try the joined-up writing this time.'

'Ah, yes.' Only the essentials of Sally's conversation had reached the innermost recesses of Tracey's mind. She'd found them both on the list. 'From Leighford High School. For the GVNQ Conference.'

'Something like that,' Sally said.

'I think she knows more about it than I do,' Maxwell whispered out of the corner of his mouth.

'Would you like some tea or coffee? You will find it in the Whittingham Suite to your right. Is it?' Tracey faltered. 'Yes, I think it is. Sorry, I'm new.' And she giggled.

'That's all right,' Maxwell smiled. 'I'm old.'

'I'll have your bags taken to your rooms,' Tracey said. 'Mrs Greenhow, you're in 306. Mr Maxwell, 101.'

'Oh, Christ no!' Maxwell staggered at the bar.

'Are you all right?' Tracey looked at the old codger in some alarm. 'Oh, no,' she laughed. 'It's that telly programme, isn't it? That bloke what has a different celebrity every week. That's quite funny, that is.'

Maxwell frowned at the girl. '1984,' he said, softly, 'George Orwell. And let me assure you, Tracey, there's nothing remotely funny about Room 101.'

Then he felt Sally dragging him away into the Whittingham Suite. Here was instant Victoriana. The windows were stained glass, the walls festooned with velvet and flock wallpaper that would have put a Chinese restaurant to shame. Plush furniture beckoned all around the room. Only the coffee and tea urns screamed 1990s — that and the spotty youth in the white jacket standing beside them.

'What'll it be, Mrs Greenhow?' Maxwell asked in his best W.C. Fields. 'What's your poison?'

'I'll have a coffee, Max, black.'

'Two coffees, please, one black. The other one normal,' Maxwell beamed at the boy.

Sally Greenhow was about to join the throng of coffee-drinkers milling in the centre of the room when someone clapped his hands and called them all to order.

'Ladies and gentlemen. Ladies and gentlemen. Hello . . . I'm Gary and I'd like to welcome you to the Carnforth Conference Centre.' Sally thought the young man something of a male clone of Tracey in Reception. To Maxwell, what with the short back and sides and a pale grey double-breasted suit, he looked like a Mormon.

'We're . . . nearly all here now, so could you make sure you wear these name badges and have a little chat before lunch, which will be served in the Hadleigh Room. We look forward to our ice-breaking session after lunch. Oh, just one thing. Could the vegans among you see Antonio, who is your chef for the week.'

'Vegans!' muttered Maxwell in horror. 'God, Sally, what have you brought me to?'

'Hello!' A rather mannish lass in lace-up brogues and a severe fringe spun round with hand extended. She'd already pinned her badge to her lapel. 'I'm Valerie, Richard de Clare School, Birmingham.'

'Oh, bad luck.' Maxwell shook her hand and felt his tarsals scrinch. 'Peter Maxwell, Leighford High.'

'Leighford? Where's that?' Valerie's lipstick had somehow smeared itself over her front teeth.

'Just follow the yellow brick road,' Maxwell beamed, 'straight on till morning.'

'Please ignore him, Valerie,' Sally cut in. I'm Sally Greenhow, regrettably from the same madhouse as him.' She jerked her head in Maxwell's direction. 'Max is here, you might say, under duress. I'm not sure you'll get a co-operative word out of him all week.'

'What is it you do, Valerie?' Maxwell asked.

'I teach,' she said, rather surprised by the question.

'Yes, quite,' Maxwell humoured her, 'but what?'

'Oh, Business Studies,' she said.

'Would you excuse me?' Maxwell enquired. 'I've just seen a girder out there in the grounds and I do believe it's rusting.' And he wandered away.

'I'm sorry,' Sally said. 'He's a cantankerous old sod, but he's not usually so rude.'

'Oh, that's all right,' Valerie grinned. 'I know what men are.'

'Are you married?'

Valerie turned rather a strange colour. 'Oh, dear me, no,' she said. 'Are you?'

'In a manner of speaking,' Sally told her. 'So you're introducing GNVQ at your school in September?'

'Well, we're seriously thinking about it. Of course, it's all about funding these days, isn't it?'

'It certainly is.'

Similarly pointless conversations such as these were going on all over the Whittingham Suite. It was always the same at educational conferences. Everybody talking rubbish either to impress somebody else or just because they were briefly free of that peculiar hell that most people call a classroom.

Maxwell found himself gazing out of the window where the sun was sharp on the newly planted roses and a sprinkler system was already sparkling on the lawn. It hadn't rained for a week. There was bound to be a hosepipe ban soon.

'And we, who trespass now in Echo Fields,
Called out and, heartless, broke the spell,

And all the wounds which time has healed
(As heal they can in Echo Fields)
Reopened by us and the morning bell.'

Maxwell almost dropped his cup. He stood there with his mouth open staring at the dark-haired woman who stood at his elbow.

'For God's sake,' she laughed, 'tell me you're Peter Maxwell or I'll just die of embarrassment.'

'Yes,' he said at last, 'I'm Peter Maxwell. And you're Rachel Cameron. Or were when we last met.'

'King,' she told him, 'Mrs King.'

'Ah.' He found himself grinning stupidly. Then he felt her hand on his. 'Max,' she said. 'Battling Maxie from all those years ago. Remember Midsummer Fair?'

He nodded. 'Strawberries and cream at Grantchester?'

'You fell out of the punt.'

'Only because some stupid punt pushed me in.'

'That was me.'

And their laughter caused heads to turn in the room.

'Well,' Valerie said to Sally, 'your Mr Maxwell seems to have made a friend.'

'Yes,' Sally said, more surprised than she cared to let on, 'it would seem so.'

'How is it,' Maxwell asked Rachel, 'that you can remember a poem from . . . what? Thirty-one years ago?'

'You wrote it, Max,' she said. 'That's why.'

For a moment, the briefest of seconds, the crusty old Head of Sixth Form with the battered heart was there. Back there in that ghostly dawn, with the mist like a shroud over the lake the first Elizabethans had built at Kenilworth. His fingers were linked with a girl's; the girl who stood before him now.

'Tonight I walked with ghosts in Echo Fields,
And heard their footsteps swishing through the dew,
And stars fell on their ancient shields
(The shields that shone in Echo Fields) . . .'

'"And I was glad,"' she interrupted him, '"that we were there and you were you."'

'Unbelievable,' and he shook his head.

'I still am, Max,' she said softly.

'What?' he had to ask.

'Glad that we were there and you were you.'

'Your parents?'

'Long gone,' she smiled. 'I haven't been back to Warwickshire in years.'

He put his cup down on the nearest table. 'Would it be an appalling cliché to say, "You haven't changed a bit"?' he asked.

'Not only an appalling cliché,' she tapped his arm, 'but a downright lie. The last but one time I saw you was in 1963, Max. It was the spring. You had the top floor of mum and dad's guest house.'

'Did I?' he smiled.

'Well, let's just say you were supposed to have.' She raised an eyebrow at him. 'Though I do seem to remember you found your way down to my floor quite often.'

'Hmm,' he remembered, frowning. 'Well, that must have been because it was dark.'

'Hello.' Sally Greenhow had extricated herself from the manly Valerie and was hovering expectantly at Maxwell's shoulder.

'It was all the Profumo case, wasn't it?' Maxwell was years away. 'Didn't Stephen Ward kill himself that July? Funnily enough, I was just thinking about Mandy Rice-Davies the other day.'

'Someone else whose room you kept stumbling into?' Rachel smiled.

'It was a great time for speeches,' Maxwell remembered. 'Martin Luther King had a dream. Kennedy was claiming to be a Berliner.'

'I had a dream too, Max,' Rachel said.

He looked into her eyes and felt something he hadn't felt in a long time. There was a rising in his heart, a pain in his throat and his head. But at that moment, he wouldn't have been anywhere else in the world.

'Hello,' said Sally Greenhow again.

'Ah, Sally.' Max snapped out of it. 'Sally, this is Rachel. She's . . . an old friend.'

'Oh, good,' Sally said, looking sourly at Maxwell while managing to smile at the same time. 'I thought perhaps old Mr S. had come a-calling.'

'Old Mr S?' Rachel didn't follow.

'Old Mr Senility,' Maxwell explained. 'Apparently, there's a secret book in our staff room on when I'm going to go ga-ga in a big way.'

'Sally Greenhow,' Sally smiled, shaking Rachel's hand.

'Rachel King,' the older woman said. 'What school are you both at?'

'Leighford High,' Sally told her.

'The comprehensive from hell,' Maxwell qualified it. 'And you?'

'St Bede's.'

'What, Bournemouth?' Maxwell asked.

'The same,' Rachel said.

'Good God. That makes us virtual neighbours. St Bede's opted out last year, didn't it? But . . . you aren't Catholic, Rachel. Or did you take the veil after . . .' And he paused. If he'd had the guts he'd have bitten his tongue off.

'No.' She managed to smile. 'No, I'm not a Catholic. About half the staff aren't. There's quite a contingent from St Bede's here. Our Head believes it's time four hundred and fifty nice Catholic girls were brought kicking and screaming into the twentieth century.'

'Oh, our Head doesn't believe anything,' Maxwell shrugged, 'at least, nothing I tell him.'

'I think we're going into lunch,' Sally said, noticing the coffee-drinkers wandering off in knots of two or three. 'May I join you two, or will I be a gooseberry?'

'Well, actually, Sally . . .' Maxwell began.

'Of course, Sally,' Rachel said. 'Max and I have all week to catch up on old times.'

'Rach?' A rather cadaverous churchman with loose spectacles was wringing his hands at Rachel's elbow.

'Yes, Jordan? People, this is Jordan. He's our chaplain.'

'Hello, Jordan,' Sally and Maxwell chorused.

'Hello,' the chaplain beamed, his upper lip almost disappearing up his nose. 'Rach, have you seen Liz Striker? She's got all the photocopying stuff.'

'No,' Rachel said, 'I skipped breakfast this morning.'

'She wasn't there,' Jordan said, 'at least, not while I was. I'll have a word with Michael, shall I?'

'I should,' Rachel nodded. 'Michael Wynn, Deputy Head,' she explained to Sally and Maxwell, 'our Protean Hercules.'

'Your what?' Sally asked.

'Superman,' Maxwell explained. 'You know, the bloke who has so little time to change that he does it in telephone kiosks and then ends up with his underpants on over his trousers.'

'Oh,' Sally said.

'You'll have to forgive each other,' Maxwell said, crossing his hands over his chest to point to the two women currently in his life. 'Rachel went to Homerton and Sally's in Special Needs.'

'Learning Support,' Sally hissed at him.

'Poor Jordan.' Rachel shook her head at his retreating, scurrying figure. 'He's an absolute darling, but couldn't, I fear, run a bath by himself. God, I'm starving.'

* * *

'I'm Valerie Marks,' Valerie was saying, standing on the podium in the Huntingdon Suite. 'Head of Business Studies at Richard de Clare School, Erdington.'

'Strongbow,' growled Maxwell, imitating the advert, and proceeded to make the noise of crossbow bolts thudding into the wood of a bar.

'What are you talking about?' Sally hissed, trying to keep the old idiot quiet, while the rather lacklustre woman was droning on.

'Richard de Clare,' Maxwell explained. 'Thirteenth-century big enchilada. His nickname was Strongbow. As in the cider of the same name.'

'Thank you, Valerie.' Gary headed the desultory clapping around the room. 'Er . . . Rachel. I think you're next.'

The dark-haired woman at Maxwell's side stood up and took her place on the podium. He looked at her again, as he'd been looking at her over lunch. Why, he asked himself — and not for the first time — why did he ever let her go? Her eyes were deep enough for a man to drown in. They always were. And most of the poetry he'd scribbled at Cambridge, he'd scribbled for her.

'I'm Rachel King,' she said. 'I'm Senior Mistress, for my sins, at St Bede's School for Girls, Bournemouth. I have a daughter, Helen, who's married to a solicitor and lives in New Zealand. I like opera, nougat, white wine — oh, and I like walking in fields near castles with strange men.' She was looking straight at Maxwell when she said it. But he didn't hear the laughter. All he'd heard was what she hadn't said. There was no mention of a husband. No mention at all.

'Thank you, Rachel,' Gary piped up. 'Thank you for your candour. Er . . . Peter, isn't it?'

'No.' Maxwell stood up. 'It's Max to those I reckon,' and he crossed purposefully to the podium while Rachel resumed her seat. When he'd got the circle's attention he introduced himself. 'I'm Peter Maxwell,' he said, 'and I'm an alcoholic'

There were murmurs and an inrush of breath. Sally covered her face with her hands, but Rachel was giggling.

'Oh, sorry,' said Maxwell, clicking his fingers, 'wrong conference. That must have been last week. Er . . . I'm the wrong side of fifty, Head of Sixth Form — I suppose that's Years 12 and 13 to anybody under twenty-seven — and I have the privilege to teach at Leighford High. My ambition in life is to be better known than Godfrey Bliss . . .'

In the pause that followed, Gary fell right into the trap. Sally should have called out a warning, but she didn't until it was too late. 'Er . . . who's Godfrey Bliss, Peter?' he asked.

'At last!' Maxwell clapped his hands in joy. 'I've done it! I've made it! After all these years! Thank you, Gary, you've made an old man very happy. By the way, by an incredibly curious coincidence, I too like walking in fields near castles, with women who can be as strange as they like.'

There was a chorus of 'oohs' that Maxwell didn't hear. He was only looking into the smiling face of Rachel King. And she hadn't heard it either. No mention of 'wife', 'better half', 'dearly beloved'. Could there really be no Mrs Maxwell?

'Yes, well, thank you, Peter,' Gary said. 'Er . . . Andrew?'

A slightly stooped man in glasses and corduroy jacket ambled nonchalantly on to the podium. 'Andrew Moreton,' he said.

'Loved your book on the Royals,' Maxwell shouted.

Moreton scowled amid the laughter. 'Dr Moreton,' he continued, 'Head of Science at John Bunyan School, Luton.' And he sat down.

'Oh. Um, Michael, I believe, penultimately.' Gary Leonard was thrown by the man's taciturnity.

'Michael Wynn.' The next speaker brushed past the returning Maxwell. 'Deputy Principal of St Bede's. I'm afraid you've all heard rather a lot of us this afternoon. The trouble is, mention a week of INSET in a plush conference centre on the coast and the queue among the staff goes half-way round the building. It's a difficult decision to make, of course, but as the man who runs INSET, I want you to know it's the merest coincidence that I am here today.'

There were guffaws all round.

'I have a wife, Gwendoline, two children and a dog. I like to fish, have an embarrassing golf handicap and I'm looking forward to working with you all this week.'

There was applause as the big, bearded man sat down.

'Did I detect a certain Welshness there?' Sally asked Maxwell.

'Hmm?' Maxwell was whispering something to Rachel.

'I said,' what with her PMT and all, Sally's patience was not as thick as it might have been, 'do I detect a certain Welshness there?'

'Geordie.' Maxwell shook his head.

Rachel leaned across him. 'He's from Newcastle.'

'Told you,' Maxwell nodded smugly. 'Spender country. You know, Jimmy Nail on the telly. Tall bloke. Looks as though the midwife trod on his face.'

'And last, but by no means least, I'm sure,' Gary said, checking his clipboard, 'Liz.'

There was no one left. They'd been through the complete circle. All twenty-four of them. Maxwell looked at the space for the twenty-fifth.

'"There will be",' he murmured, '"one vacant chair."'

'Don't tell me,' Sally said, 'a line from Spender.'

'No, a line from an American Civil War song,' he told her. 'Before your time, really.'

'Thanks.'

'Er . . . has anyone seen her? Liz Striker?' Gary was still asking.

'Well,' Jordan was on his feet, 'I've done my best.' He looked as though he was going to burst into tears. 'There's no answer from her room and she's got all our photocopying.'

'Well,' Gary said, 'I'm sure she'll turn up. She's probably gone swimming or for a walk along the estuary. Is she a keen ornithologist?'

Everybody looked at each other. Nobody seemed to know.

'Well, never mind. Now, it's nearly time for tea, which will be served in the Whittingham Suite downstairs. After that, Dr Brownwood from the University of Kent at Canterbury will open the formal proceedings in the Huntingdon Suite with a lecture entitled "The Entitlement Curriculum". Thanks everybody. Great stuff.'

'Great stuff?' Maxwell growled. 'This great differencing machine I call a brain computes that this will be the eighty-sixth time I've heard a lecture on the Entitlement Curriculum. Tell me, Rachel, do you still drink Southern Comfort?'

'Good Lord,' she laughed, 'I haven't touched the stuff in years.'

'Well,' Maxwell held out his elbow to her to link her arm with his, 'I believe I saw a bar on the ground floor, somewhere near the Inebriate Suite. Shall I reacquaint you?'

And they sauntered off.

Sally Greenhow stood by herself. 'I drink Southern Comfort,' she said softly, but the only person who heard her was Valerie Marks.

'Of course you do, dear,' she said, 'but let's you and me have a nice cup of tea, now, shall we? Do you crochet at all?' And she led the tall, frizzy-haired kid away.

CHAPTER 3

They wandered along the shingle, Maxwell and his lady, in the cool of a May evening. The sun was an orange fire behind the purple bars of cloud, reflected in the chiselled surface of the sea.

The tall grasses brushed her bare legs under her dress and she felt his hand in hers. It felt good after all these years. And safe. She liked to feel safe. Needed to feel safe.

'It's not much like Midsummer Common,' he said, watching the dying sun gilding the granite blocks of Dungeness A and Dungeness B.

'No,' she said, 'it's better.'

'Better?' He stopped her. 'I seem to remember you spoke out against all that. All that nuclear stuff. Don't I remember you in a duffel coat at Aldermaston?'

'That was Michael Foot,' she laughed. 'Or was it Bertie Russell?'

'I don't know.' He walked on with her, trampling the stems of the sea pinks as he went. 'It might have been Jane Russell for all I know.'

'Whatever happened to Clive?' she asked him suddenly.

'Clive? If you mean of India, it's likely he committed suicide.'

He felt her empty cardigan sleeve slap round his shoulder. 'Clive Spooner. Your old oppo at Jesus.'

'God, yes.' Maxwell threw his head back and saw the high clouds and the last vapour trail spreading out towards the gathering night. 'The class of '63.'

'I've got this abiding memory of him in the Arts Cinema. *Psycho*, wasn't it?'

'It was. He was all right in the shower scene, a little quaky when the detective got his — you remember, that overhead shot — and by the time we saw mother in the fruit cellar, he was hiding behind my seat. Or was it yours?' And he sat down with her in the grass.

'I don't think Clive had a lot to do with women's seats, if my memory serves.'

'Ah, now that's a gross calumny. Clive was nearly as other undergraduates.'

'And who put the gross calumny about, Maxie?'

'Er . . . me,' Maxwell confessed, 'purveyor of gross calumnies. As to what he's doing now, God only knows. You lose touch.'

'You do,' she said, gazing out to the chiselled sea. 'Tell me . . .' He sensed it was the question he hadn't dared ask her. 'Is there a Mrs Maxwell?'

He looked at her, the breeze blowing her hair and her eyes shining. 'There was,' he said, 'once upon a time.'

He could detect no change in her mood, no different light in her eyes. 'It didn't work out?'

'No,' he said, playing with the grass between his hooked-up feet, 'no, a ton of police car saw to that on a tight bend one wet morning. I like to think my wife never knew what hit her.'

She turned to him, her face a mask of pain. 'Oh, Max, I'm sorry,' she said. 'I didn't know.'

'No,' he shrugged, patting the hand that held his, 'there's no reason why you should. What about you? Mr King?'

'Ah, yes.' She took her hand away and rested her chin on her knees, wrapping her long summer skirt around her ankles. 'Jeremy. One of life's gentlefolk, Max. He first hit me on our wedding night. I'd made some silly remark about . . . God, I can't remember now — his father, I think. The daft old duffer got over-merry at the wedding. He was harmless and so was whatever I said, but that wasn't how Jeremy saw it. I'd never actually seen anyone's colour drain before. He went completely white. And rigid. I thought he was about to have a fit. Or a fainting spell at least. Instead, he hit me.' She buried her face quickly in her dress, then she was looking at the sea again. 'He was sorry again in seconds, but that wasn't the point. He'd broken my cheekbone. I was in hospital for over a week.'

It was his turn to try to hold her hand, but he couldn't reach it so he held her arm instead. 'I'm sorry,' he said.

'We've both been saying that all day.' She smiled at him.

'You left Jeremy?'

She shrugged. 'We left each other, really,' she said. 'But what about you, Max? How did you manage? After your wife, I mean?'

'History,' Maxwell tried to sum it up, 'and kids. It's funny, I buried my wife and child and I buried myself in work. A bit of a cliché, I suppose.'

'Child? Oh, Maxie,' and she turned to face him, taking both his hands in hers.

'Jenny,' he said. 'She was not quite sixteen months. Ah, we had such plans for her.'

'They'd have come true, too,' Rachel said. 'I know you, Peter Maxwell. Do you still write poetry, Max?'

He laughed, throwing back his head. 'No,' he told her. 'I left all that behind years ago. It's odd, I thought I had so much to say then, when I was actually so comfortable and so cushioned from the world. A staircase at Jesus was hardly a walk on the wild side.'

'Yes,' she chuckled. 'I always rather envied Timmy. You remember Timmy?'

'Your ghastly little brother? Yes, I do.'

'He was, wasn't he?' she admitted. 'Ghastly is the only word for him. He grew up into a rather fine man, really, something incredibly big in Anglo-American geology.'

'What? That little shit who wouldn't go away even when I'd slipped him the odd half-crown?'

'That's the one. Well, Timmy went to university in '70, when it was all flower power and beads and barefoot in the park. His girlfriends had daisies between their toes.'

'And grass between their ears,' Maxwell smiled. 'Yes, I remember. I was in my first teaching post, not all that much older than some of the sixth form.'

'Well, they invented the word "student", didn't they?' she said. 'Us, well, we were just big schoolboys and girls — or young men and women — depending which side of the fence you were on.'

'Ah, the pre-permissive society,' Maxwell boomed, eyebrows akimbo. 'Good days.'

'Strange days,' she mused, 'looking back.'

'Looking back,' he told her, 'days always are.'

'Yes,' she smiled at him, 'I suppose they are.' She glanced at her watch. 'Shouldn't we be getting back? Supper at eight, didn't they say?'

'Supper at eight,' he said and helped her up. 'May I have the pleasure?' and he bent his arm for her.

She slapped it with her cardigan sleeve. 'Possibly, you filthy old man, but first you can lead me in to dinner.'

* * *

Sally Greenhow stared up at the Artexed ceiling. For some reason her feet were killing her. She hadn't learned much from the good Doctor's introductory lecture on the Entitlement Curriculum, but that was to be expected. You didn't get to be a Professor of Education by being witty, avant-garde or even relevant. In fact, she'd noticed that 90 per cent of the courses she'd attended over the last five years were, to say the least, tangential.

Where was that book she'd bought? Oh, God, yes. Page thirty-one. She opened it, refreshed her memory on the last paragraph she'd read and closed it again.

'Anthea Westinghouse,' she said aloud, 'with the antique pistol because George had foully abused her daughter.'

The room was a witness now to her brave stab of logic at solving the murder puzzle in the book. It watched, breathless, while she rummaged. Where the hell was it? A frown darkened her pretty, kiddy's face and she threw the thing down. 'Well,' was all she was prepared to tell the room, 'one out of three ain't bad.'

Her sentence was punctuated by a knock at the door. That would be that noxious little turd Gary with some organisational/administration bollocks for the morning. Only it wasn't, she realised as she opened it. It was that noxious little turd Jordan, God's vicar on earth.

'Er . . . hello,' he said, 'Sally, may I . . . er . . . may I have a word?'

He'd had several words over dinner. It was one of those unfortunate things. Margot Whoever — Sally hadn't caught her name in the ice-breaking session, but she remembered she was an Art teacher from Maidstone — looked like fun, but she'd been buttonholed by Michael Wynn. Maxwell was off mooning with his lost love like something out of Lochinvar and that lesbian shortarse Valerie Marks was making a beeline for her, probably to discuss the vagaries of needlepoint. So she'd ducked down a table to find herself wedged between a stand of artificial flowers and Jordan Gracewell.

'Well,' Sally's arm crossed her portico diagonally with a rigidity of its own, 'it is a little late, Jordan,' she told him.

'Oh, yes, yes. I know. Only, it's Liz. Liz Striker. I still can't find her.'

This was the B side of Gracewell's record of life. The A side was the altogether more gripping theme of the place of incense in the modern Catholic Church.

'You've tried her room again?'

'Oh, yes. It's directly above this one, funnily enough. I know because there's a strange little kink out here in the corridor.'

'Yes, I know,' said Sally, stone-faced, but the *bon mot* was lost on the young chaplain of St Bede's.

'It's identical with the one upstairs,' he told her.

Sally was on the point of expressing amazement that Jordan had a twin, but suddenly thought better of it and dropped her arm. 'Well,' she sighed, 'you'd better come in, then.'

He almost ducked under her flat chest in an effort to avoid touching it as he swept past her. No, swept was too strong a word for it. Crawled would be better. How did this man survive in a girls' school?

'Oh, it's rather like mine,' he said, surveying the bed, the wardrobe, the en suite.

'Fascinating,' and she snatched up the discarded knickers she'd worn earlier, throwing them into a drawer. 'Er . . . can I offer you some coffee?' Ever regretted anything instantly? Like putting your foot on a garden rake? That was how Sally Greenhow felt at that moment as the padre parked himself like a coiled spring on the arm of her chair. 'Oh, please,' he said.

'Let me guess.' She looked at him. 'White. Two sugars.'

'No, no, indeed.' He fluttered his hands around. 'One.'

'Oh, you old dog!' she chortled, regretting that instantly too, and busied herself with the kettle.

'It's just that . . . well, I don't want you to think I'm paranoid or anything.'

Sally raised her eyebrows. It was as well perhaps that he couldn't see her face.

'. . . but not only have I not seen Liz since yesterday, but no one else has either.'

'Thursday?' Sally checked. 'But I thought the course started today, Friday?'

'Yes, it did,' Gracewell explained, 'but a group of us got here the previous day to set up our presentation. We're on second. Tomorrow afternoon. And we knew we'd have no time today, what with the ice-breaking and Professor Brownwood. Brilliant, wasn't he?'

'Dazzling,' lied Sally. 'Careful, it's hot.'

He took the cup from her, one of a fairly nasty set that had Carnforth Conference Centre written on it, to make absolutely sure that it had no resale value whatsoever to a would-be nicker of other people's crockery. 'Thank you, Sally,' he said, as though he'd just uttered the dirtiest word in the English language.

'So what's your presentation on, specifically?' she asked him.

'Well, the others are doing theirs first; that lot from Luton.'

'Ah, yes, the Adolf Eichmann Comprehensive. Didn't they strike you that way, a little? That Head of Science with the scowl and the attitude. God, I thought my colleague was to the right of Genghis Khan.'

'That's Mr Maxwell, isn't it?' Gracewell said. 'He seems very attached to Rachel King.'

'Yes, doesn't he?' Sally threw herself down on the bed, her head resting against the wall. 'Is there a Mr King?'

'Oh, no. Well, there was, but they say there was mental and physical cruelty. The rumour is she just packed her bags and her daughter one day and left him.'

'Hmm,' Sally nodded, 'that's men for you,' and she grinned cheesily at him.

'No, I enquired at the desk about Liz — Liz Striker. They hadn't seen her go out. Or come back in. I even asked Gary to unlock her room for me. I don't think her bed had been slept in.'

'Really?' That struck Sally as rather odd, too. 'Well, there's bound to be a logical explanation. She's not . . . er . . . she's not having a little flingette with some bloke on your staff, is she?'

'I beg your pardon?' Gracewell seemed horrified.

'Well, I just meant, you know — two head shapes on the pillow, that sort of thing?'

'I think I shall have to be going,' Gracewell said, standing up sharply. 'Thank you for the coffee.'

'Look,' she took the cup from him, 'if I've said anything out of turn, Jordan . . .'

'No,' he said, but he didn't glance back as he made, rather decisively she thought, for the door. 'No, you haven't. I expect I'll get to the bottom of it somehow. Good night, Sally.'

And he was gone, moving off down the dimly lit corridor on silent brothel-creepers, his coffee barely touched in Sally's hand.

* * *

It's always the same with courses. After the ice-breaking session comes the problem-solving session. Maxwell's first problem was how to swap groups. They'd been picked at random by Gary Leonard, the course co-ordinator, and Maxwell was reasonably miffed, though not surprised, to find that he and Rachel were in different groups. He was in A and she was in D. He was still wondering whether a simple crossing out and rewriting or grovelling to a stranger to agree to a swap would be better when breakfast was over in the Hadleigh Suite and the intrepid little bands moved off.

'Catch up with you at lunch,' was all Rachel King had time to say. She winked at him and vanished into her team and the persona she wore for the world.

On their way to the beach, Maxwell took in his team. In a weak and wandering moment, they might have been the A team, although their similarity to the Dream team was rather more striking. And if Maxwell was Hannibal Smith, it was most unlikely that any of their plans would come together, whether he loved it or not. They were a pretty ericaceous mixture, one way or another. Leader-designate was Gregory Trant, a rather reptilian creature whose eyes positively refused to travel in the same direction. He seemed a lacklustre bastard, but teaching in Luton probably does that to people. Should he go down fighting, Michael Wynn, the bearded darling of St Bede's, was in post as Number Two. Then there was Lydia Farr, who taught Textiles in Tenterden and who appeared to have been the model for the

Skexis in The Dark Crystal; Alan Harper-Bennet, who got Maxwell's prize for daring to have a double-barrelled name and still teach in a comprehensive; Phyllida Bowles, a wall-coloured woman who was a positive martyr to hay fever; Margot Jenkinson, whose main loves were ceramics and Sir Andrew Lloyd Webber; and of course Maxwell himself, the only normal one. They took to the heather just before the weather changed and trudged over the slippery shingle with the sweep of the bay to their left.

'Well, there's no shelter at all,' Lydia was saying, holding her hair as if the eddying wind might take it off. 'How are we supposed to construct a shelter if there isn't any?'

'You haven't read your instruction sheet, dear,' Trant patronised her. 'It doesn't say it'll be easy.'

'There's a rubbish tip over here,' Wynn shouted. 'Let's see what we've got.'

'Oh, please!' Phyllida wailed, thrusting her hands resolutely into her jeans pockets. 'I did not enrol on a GNVQ course to catch something from somebody's old mattress.'

'Needs must,' Wynn told her coldly, 'when the Devil drives. Peter? Will you join me?'

'If I must,' sighed Max, 'and that's Max, by the way. Not Peter. Max.'

'All right, Max,' Wynn grinned. 'Funny things, nicknames, aren't they? I knew a bloke at school called Arthur. Arthur Gries. A complete vegetable was Arthur and known to us all as Cret, short, obviously, for Cretin. You're my vintage, give or take a few years, you know how it is. You don't consider how cruel kids can be. It was only when I met him years later at some big Rotary thing and I had to call him Arthur. It just didn't ring true. The man's name was still Cret really, in that you are of course one for life. Shame we can't be more honest, isn't it? Fancy a rummage in the rubbish?'

Gregory Trant, Alan Harper-Bennet and Lydia Farr had wandered off in search of driftwood as a frame for the shelter they had to make. The wind was in the wrong direction for them to hear the shouts of the others and before long, two groups had formed, each out of sight of the other. It was then that the heavens opened, reminding Maxwell of that sudden storm that had appeared from nowhere in the Battle of Evesham, 1265, when Simon de Montfort had been caught napping in that murderous loop of the Avon. Maxwell was reminded of that because he was an historian, first and foremost. Maxwell's kids thought he knew it because he'd been there at the time.

The rain positively hurt with its big spring drops and the unofficial rubbish heap was a quagmire of sludge over which the foraging party scrambled to the shelter of a clump of stunted cedars.

'Oh, bloody hell!' Margot Jenkinson fumed. 'It takes a downpour to winkle out the little fact that you've a hole in your shoe, doesn't it? Wet tights are a bitch, Mr Maxwell, aren't they?'

'They are,' Maxwell bridled in his best John Inman, 'and clean on this morning.' He licked his finger and slicked down his eyebrow with it — not a gesture many single men would have the nerve for.

'Well,' Michael Wynn stuck his head out of cover for a moment, 'looks like the session's rained off. Shall we wait for a bit or make a dash for the house?'

Alan Harper-Bennet and Lydia Farr had made a dash for the house when it started, followed by Gregory Trant. Except that they were on the wrong side and screened from the main drive by a dense privet hedge. Lydia was even more concerned about what the rain would do to her hair than she had been with the vagaries of wind direction and, seeing a side door, she wrenched it open and dashed in. Harper-Bennet collided with her in trying to close it and was mumbling his apologies when he realised Lydia wasn't moving. Couldn't move, in fact. He'd never seen shock before, but he saw it now. Her mouth hung open, her eyes were wide. Every muscle in her body felt like iron.

'Lydia?' Harper-Bennet's voice had a curious sound to it, as though he didn't trust it in the darkness of the corridor.

He followed the woman's stare ahead of her. There was an open door, apparently into a store room. And there, behind a collapsed pile of buff-wrapped stationery, a woman stared back at the pair. It was an odd moment because the woman's eyes were dull and half-closed. Her mouth was open too, like Lydia's, but there was a dark brown something caked around her nose and lips. In the strange light from an aperture in the roof, her hair was plastered to her forehead. And there was no doubt about it. The woman was dead.

* * *

Anywhere can become the scene of a crime. In fiction, of course, it's the west wing or the library of a country vicarage. But that's just English cosies. In the States, it's somebody's swimming pool or a drug-ridden alley in the Bronx. What makes an ordinary, everyday store room into a murder scene is that someone chose to hide a body there. And from that moment, the scene is transformed. From the moment the body is found, it is changed, changed utterly. A terrible beauty is born, as Yeats said, except that Yeats wasn't talking about a corpse.

Father Jordan Gracewell had never seen so many policemen in his life. And he certainly never expected men in white boiler suits and surgical gloves. There was an ambulance and umpteen squad cars, big and white. There were yards of fluttering tape marked continuously with the word 'police', but there was no flashing blue light, no scream of tyres. In fact, the Kent Constabulary had excelled themselves in the speed and efficiency of their response. From the time the call had come from Gary Leonard that a suspicious death had occurred at the Carnforth Centre, eight minutes had elapsed until the first officers had arrived. They were both armed, though no one knew it but them, and the scene of crime officer had followed minutes behind.

So it was not until nearly midday that Chief Inspector Miles Warren stood in that darkened corridor in the centre's sub-basement, surveying somebody's handiwork. He'd been considered too short for the police at one time, but he either fiddled the measurement somehow or the force was desperate, because here he was, a man in mid-life who had never known a crisis. Or if he had, he never showed it. His lads called him 'Stony' because none of them had ever seen him smile.

'What have we got, John?'

Inspector John MacBride was losing his hair already. It was curly and blond, but it had been steadily deserting him ever since he'd left school. He didn't really like Stony Warren, if the truth were known, but he knew the man knew his job and that would have to be good enough.

'Mrs Elizabeth Striker,' he told his superior. 'Married. Age thirty-eight. She was on a course here.'

Warren looked behind him. Uniforms. Cameras. No bloody doctor.

'Do we have a police surgeon in this county?' he asked anyone who cared to listen.

'Dr Anderson was telephoned nearly two hours ago, sir,' someone said. 'His wife took the message.'

'Really?' Warren was unimpressed. 'That's about as helpful as somebody taking the piss. John? Care to chance your arm on this one?'

Warren believed in giving his subordinates experience. Anyway, it took him off the spot. Stony only took chances on his own terms. He saw no reason to expose his inadequacies so early on a case.

'Cause of death is likely to be a fractured skull,' MacBride conjectured. 'She was hit from behind, I'd say, though how often I don't know.'

'Murder weapon?'

McBride shrugged. 'Nothing yet. I've got men out in the grounds.'

Warren had seen that on the way in. Ragged rows of uniformed coppers on their hands and knees in the shrubbery, like some strange primeval ritual. When a body is found, men in blue suits form lines and crawl forward, like a bizarre Tai Chi.

'She didn't die here, then?' Warren took in the wall behind the dead woman's head. There was no space in that tiny stock cupboard to crack an egg, let alone someone's skull.

'No, sir.' McBride was sure. 'Out in the corridor would be my guess. Then she was dragged in here.'

'Why?'

'The old problem,' McBride shrugged. 'It's all very well to put somebody's lights out, but you've then got the perennial puzzle of what to do with the body.'

'So you store it in a store room?'

'It's not good, is it?'

'Not ideal, no,' Warren nodded. 'Perhaps just a temporary hiding place, until our man had time to think. Time to arrange something more permanent. You wouldn't care to hazard a time on any of this, I suppose?'

A smile flitted across McBride's face. 'Well, the body's cold and loose. That means rigor mortis has come and gone. At least forty-eight hours, I'd say.'

Warren nodded again. 'Allowing for temperature variations, state of the body and so on.' He glanced around him. 'That's odd,' he said.

'What, sir?' McBride hated being upstaged, even by Warren. 'The door. It opens outwards.'

'It would have to, wouldn't it?' the Inspector asked. 'Seeing as the store room is so small.'

'Possibly,' Warren said, 'possibly. Bit of bad luck on our man, though.'

'Sir?'

'Well, I assume that Mrs Striker was walled in behind those boxes of paper. They must have fallen and their falling forced the door open. If the door had opened inwards, that couldn't have happened.'

'Still,' McBride reasoned, 'that would only delay the finding of the body for a while.'

'Possibly,' Warren said again, narrowing his eyes.

McBride hated it when that happened. He could never read his boss's mind. And because of that, he would never be one step ahead. Always one behind.

'Tell me,' Warren said, 'have we got everybody still on site? The guests, I mean? Staff?'

McBride nodded. 'All except a few teachers who are somewhere out on the bay, problem-solving.'

If Warren was a smiling man, he'd have done it then. 'Well,' he said, 'when they get back, they can solve a few problems for me. I'd better have a word with the guests. Don't want any of them doing a bunk. It'll cost an arm and a leg to track them all down. Oh, John . . .' He turned in the corridor. 'Let me know when Graham Anderson arrives, will you? And when you've taken Mrs Striker out, build up that wall again.'

'Sir?'

'The boxes. The wall of boxes he stashed her behind. Build it up again. I want to see the room as it was before the stationery toppled. OK?'

* * *

Maxwell had been this way before. Or nearly so. Two of his own sixth-formers had died in mysterious circumstances, so he was no stranger to police enquiries. Even so, he'd never actually crossed a police cordon before. Now, he had no choice.

'Good God,' Phyllida Bowles said, taking in the ambulance, the squad cars, the crowd of holiday-makers parked along the road. 'They must have found Whatsername's body.'

'What?' Wynn asked.

'Thing. You know. Your colleague. That funny little vicar chap was pestering everybody about her yesterday.'

'Mrs Striker,' Margot Jenkinson remembered. 'Do you know, Michael, that gin and orange before we left has really affected my swim bladder. I really must take more orange with it.'

It was then that they were stopped by the long arm of the law in the form of a particularly officious WPC who reminded Maxwell of Helen Mirren in that television cop programme — forty but desirable. They each gave their name and it came as no surprise to Maxwell when Margot Jenkinson's cliché, 'What is all this about?' elicited an irrelevant statement from the girl in blue. 'The Chief Inspector would like a word.'

* * *

Miles Warren had his word in the Trevelyan Suite on the first floor, away from the prying eyes of sightseers at the gate, on the little raised dais built for some third-rate jazzman who still haunted England's south coast every summer. He had done this once, already, to everybody else, guest and staff alike, at the Carnforth. Now he did it again, to the returned rump of problem-solvers.

And as he told them that the body of a woman had been found on the premises and that she had been murdered, he watched each one of them intently. Because Miles Stony Warren knew what every detective knew. That information like this was a two-way process. Tell somebody there's been a murder and they'll react. Some gasp. Others scream. Still others cry. Some won't move at all. There's just a tightening in the neck, a flick of the fingers, a bat of the eye. And you watch it. You watch it with the two-way mirror that is your trained eye. And you note it. And you remember it. And in the good old days, it was little things like that that sent men to the gallows.

CHAPTER 4

'You can't actually do this, you know.'

It was a phrase, with variations, that Chief Inspector Warren was to hear a lot in the twenty-four hours that followed the discovery of Elizabeth Striker's body. But Chief Inspector Warren had a certain way with him. When he spoke to you, he made you feel that his suggestions were so reasonable that it would be unreasonable not to comply.

And anyway, Chief Inspector Warren had the Carnforth Centre's inmates by their short and curlies.

'You know why he's done this, don't you?' Alan Harper-Bennet said, cramming his pipe with something dark and gruesome.

'Do tell.' Margot Jenkinson was on her second G and T of the evening.

'He wants to see who runs.'

There were murmurs of agreement in the plastic opulence of the Whittingham Suite.

'How do you mean?' It had not been a good day for Lydia Farr. She was still trembling slightly from her experience earlier, and the sedative she'd been given was beginning to wear off.

Harper-Bennet leaned forward, as though talking to an idiot. He was good at that. He'd been teaching now for sixteen years.

'He's set up his incident room, or whatever it's called, here at the centre and he's asked us all to stay. OK, the staff go home when they're not on duty, but they're all local. If we go home, we scatter the length and breadth of the country, and that means expense, co-operation with other forces, et cetera. This way, he's got us cornered. And if anybody expresses a wish to leave, wham! The full rigour of the law is up his jacksie before he can say GNVQ.'

'Somebody has.'

All eyes turned to the tall, frizzy-haired woman lounging in the corner, a Carnforth courtesy copy of *Marie-Claire* spread on her lap.

'Who?' came the chorus.

'Who else but my dear old colleague,' Sally Greenhow shrugged. 'Who else but Mad Max?'

* * *

Mad Max had been in an incident room before and he didn't cherish the memory. This one of course was different. It was the Trevelyan Suite at the Carnforth Centre. Mucked about with, granted. The plastic opulence had gone, the plants had been removed. From nowhere had come a warehouse full of desks, chairs, filing cabinets, telephones and VDUs. There were black and white photographs of the murder scene plastered over display boards against one wall, and, well out of sight of the window, of the dead woman herself. Somehow, in black and white, they looked even worse than the real thing.

It was in Stony Warren's ante-room, off the Trevelyan Suite, that Peter Maxwell sat now, watching the evening rain trickle the length of the windows and bounce on the UPVC sills. There was a scrape of the door and the Chief Inspector entered. For a fleeting, nostalgic moment, Maxwell found himself wishing that the guv'nor might wear a trilby hat and trench coat, have an impeccable Oxford accent and very probably the plummy tones of Jack Hawkins. The reality was different. Miles Warren was losing his hair, was of less than average height and had the rather grating whine that characterized the Lea Valley through Hertfordshire to Gravesend. The nearest he'd probably come to Oxford was watching re-runs of *Morse* on the telly.

'Mr Maxwell?' He slid back a chair and sat down. 'Inspector McBride tells me you wish to leave. Is that right?'

'Let's say I had no wish to come in the first place.'

'Oh, really? Why was that?'

Maxwell sighed. 'You've never been in teaching, I take it?' he asked. Warren shook his head.

'But I presume that in your job you have come across a certain quantity of what we in education call bullshit?'

A more demonstrative man would have smiled. As it was, Warren just nodded. 'Cowsheds full,' he said.

'This course I am on is a classic example,' Maxwell told him. 'Another inspired set of letters that educationalists have been bombarding us with for thirty years. Old wine — new bottle. May I ask how old you are, Chief Inspector?'

'I'm forty-three,' Warren said.

Maxwell nodded. 'So you left school . . . ?'

'When I was fifteen.'

'Wise,' Maxwell commented. 'Very wise. Got out while the going was good.'

'I don't know,' Warren said. 'It's hard on the force these days. So many bright young things coming up at your elbow. Degreed. Pushy. You know the sort.'

Maxwell knew.

'How well did you know the deceased?' Warren had suddenly changed tack.

There was a little red light flashing quietly in Maxwell's head. He had to respond to it. 'Shouldn't there be another officer with you?' he asked. 'And a tape recorder?'

Warren leaned back, clasping his fingers behind his head. This was one of those times when, on his own terms, in his own way, he was prepared to take a risk; throw caution to the winds. 'PACE?' he said, twisting his lips. 'Done more damage than the Luftwaffe. This is just a little chat, Mr Maxwell — a sort of tête-à-tête. We could have it in the bar, if you'd prefer.'

'All right.' Maxwell got to his feet.

'Except that . . .' Warren dropped his relaxed position, his body upright, his head rigid. 'Except that you might want to tell me things here you wouldn't want to say in a crowded bar.'

'Might I?' Maxwell asked. 'Such as?'

Warren leaned forward. 'Such as why you and you alone have asked to go. Such as why you have not answered my questions about Mrs Striker. Things like that.'

'Am I right in saying,' Maxwell asked, 'that I don't have to talk to you at all?'

'Perfectly right,' Warren nodded, 'but that wouldn't get us anywhere, would it? Now, you're a reasonable man, Mr Maxwell, I can sense that. I'd hate for us to have got off on the wrong foot. Shall we start again?'

'Why not?' Maxwell sat down. 'I'm sitting comfortably.'

'Elizabeth Striker,' Warren persisted. 'How well did you know her?'

'Not at all,' Maxwell said. 'Never met the woman.'

'Really?'

'The first I heard of her was when the padre was wandering around asking everybody if we'd seen her.'

'By the padre, you mean . . . ?'

'Jordan Gracewell, Chaplain of St Bede's.'

'Ah, yes. A young man who worries a lot, I'd say.'

Maxwell looked at the Chief Inspector. If he read the man aright, here was one who gave nothing away, let nothing slip; whose face was a mask of inscrutability for the world. Miles Warren made Fu Manchu look like an ingénue. Yet he was dropping little gems about Carnforth's clientele. That must be for Maxwell's benefit; to see how far he'd go, which way he'd jump.

'Would you?' Maxwell had seen all the Fu Manchu films — he'd even read the Sax Romer. Inscrutability was his middle name.

'Tell me a bit about yourself, Mr Maxwell,' Warren said, sensing a brick wall.

Here we go again, thought Max. Ice-breaking part two. 'Little old me? Well, let's see. I'm fifty-three. Head of Sixth Form at Leighford High School.'

'Near Chichester?'

'That's right.'

'And what exactly do you do as Head of Sixth Form?'

'Well, this and that,' Maxwell hedged. He'd been equally vague writing his own job description some years before. 'The school prospectus says I am responsible for the academic and pastoral guidance of two hundred sixth-formers. That means I do everything from writing their university references to wiping their bottoms — metaphorically, of course.'

'Of course.' Warren's eyes narrowed. 'And this course you're on this week?'

'Is yet another attempt to weld the disparate worlds of education and industry. To provide some cohesion where actually there is none. The problem is that employers can't make up their minds what they want. Are you an historian, Chief Inspector?'

Warren sighed, shaking his head. 'I've got too many problems in the present,' he said, 'without worrying about the past.'

'Hmm,' Maxwell smiled. 'The reason I ask is that when Britain was at its greatest — the workshop of the world making more goods and more money than anyone else — the education system was a shambles and attendance non-compulsory. Now we've got the little buggers chained to desks for thirty-nine weeks of the year, in practice until they're seventeen, we're fourteenth-rate, a rather feeble satellite state of Brussels. Ironic, isn't it?'

'So you don't approve of vocational education?'

'In the right place, of course,' Maxwell told him, 'but that place is not the school. We're about the business of enriching young minds, not telling them how to plonk their fingers down on keyboards and teaching them to spread sheets or base datas.'

'What about your private life? Are you married?'

'No,' Maxwell said. 'Actually, I'm a widower.'

'I'm sorry.'

'Thank you, but it was all a long time ago.'

'Some wounds never heal,' Warren observed. 'You live alone.' It was a statement, not a question.

'Apart from my cat, yes.'

'Interests? Hobbies?'

'All human life,' Maxwell said. 'I am fascinated by the cinema, by history of course. And I collect model soldiers.'

'Fascinating,' Warren said flatly. 'Tell me, Mr Maxwell, is there anybody on this course that you know? Knew beforehand, I mean?'

'My colleague, Sally Greenhow.'

'Ah, yes.' Warren consulted a typed list on his desk. 'Anyone else?'

'Yes,' Maxwell said, 'Mrs Rachel King.'

'Also of St Bede's,' Warren said, 'as was the dead woman.'

'That's right,' Maxwell nodded.

'May I ask how you know her?'

'We were . . . we knew each other many years ago, Chief Inspector. Before I came into teaching.'

'That's rather a coincidence, isn't it?' Warren asked. He was not a man who believed in coincidences.

'I suppose it is,' Maxwell shrugged. 'Synchronicity, perhaps. Fate.'

'Perhaps,' Warren nodded, searching Maxwell's honest, open face, boring into the twinkling grey eyes. 'So, you'd still like to leave, Mr Maxwell?'

'Well, the course can't continue now, surely? My Upper Sixth, not to mention my GCSE classes, have exams in a month. I'd like to be back there with them.'

'Very laudable,' Warren nodded. 'But you see my problem, Mr Maxwell. Someone in this building killed Elizabeth Striker, smashed in her skull like balsa wood. That someone might be you, mightn't it?'

'It might be,' Maxwell said, 'but I hope that isn't an accusation, Chief Inspector.'

It looked for a moment as though Miles Stony Warren would break the habit of a lifetime and smile, but it was only a trick of the light. 'Don't worry, Mr Maxwell. If I accuse you of anything, believe me, you'll know it. Now, will you stay? Just for a day or two? It would make my job a lot easier.'

Maxwell pondered awhile. Then he stood up. 'All right,' he said, 'just for a day or two. But I'm off on Monday whatever happens.'

'Absolutely. Thank you for your co-operation.'

And Maxwell left.

Warren pressed the intercom button on his desk and John McBride came in, jacketless, tieless, shirt-sleeves rolled. 'Well?' Warren asked.

'Glib bastard,' was McBride's considered opinion.

'And educationally a dodo,' Warren agreed. 'Can we use him?'

'Sir?'

'Switch him on. Wind him up. See what he stirs up, among the others, I mean.'

'I think so,' McBride nodded. 'But we'll have to watch him like hawks . . . He's not our man, then?'

'Good God, John,' Warren picked up his sheaf of papers, 'if I had second sight, I'd be the Doris Stokes of the '90s. I've drip fed him a little today — pointing the finger at Gracewell, mentioning cause of death. Let's see what he does with that first. Tomorrow, bright and early, we'll start the interviews. Lydia Farr is first — assuming she's more collected than she was today. And talking of cause of death, nothing from Anderson, I suppose?'

The Inspector shook his head.

'Right,' Warren sighed. 'That's one for you. I want his report on this desk by nine tomorrow. How you get it is up to you.'

* * *

How John McBride got Dr Anderson's report was to knock the old duffer up at six thirty the next morning. McBride had always known that doctors did all right for themselves, driving TR7s when he rattled around in a clapped-out Montego. He wasn't quite prepared for the palatial pad of the police surgeon however. In the past, the old boy had always presented his findings at the station in the incident room, but the guv'nor was in a hurry and no one had time to stand on ceremony. A woman was dead. It was time to move.

The torrent of abuse he received from the medico didn't quite square with the refined-looking gent who opened the door to him in dressing-gown and slippers.

'Do you realise,' Anderson wanted to know, 'what the fucking time is?'

'Six thirty, sir.' McBride was a young man who was going places. Punctuality was the politeness of policemen.

'Six fucking thirty!' Anderson repeated as though he couldn't believe his ears.

'Chief Inspector Warren was wondering if your report was ready.'

'Wondering, was he?' Anderson snapped. 'Miles Fucking Warren couldn't fight his way out of a paper fucking bag on his own. Have you had any breakfast, McBride?'

'No, sir. My shift doesn't start for another hour.'

'Well, you'd better come in, then. Gladys won't be stirring for hours yet. It's her bridge night on Fridays and it always takes it out of her. However, my coffee is legendary and I can still toast a mean slice of bread.'

'That's kind, sir, thank you,' and the Inspector went inside.

At the door, Anderson paused to deliver a well-timed kick to the ginger torn mewling at his feet. 'Why don't you fuck off out of it?' he snarled. It seemed a good idea to the cat and he roamed off in search of Anderson's tabby in order to comply.

Over coffee, MacBride listened while Anderson gave him the gist of his experience, the Inspector rattling off the notes he knew his guv'nor would want to see.

'There were three blows,' the doctor said, spreading his marmalade with a sure hand. 'The first was delivered from behind and to the right, horizontally, while the victim was still standing. I would say the killer is right-handed and a little taller than the late Mrs Striker, but I can't be sure on that point. This first blow would have caused a radial fracture of the parietal area of the skull and almost certainly extensive haemorrhaging. She was probably still standing when the second blow fell.' Anderson slurped his coffee. 'Bugger, that's hot. Marmalade?'

'No thanks, sir,' McBride declined.

'The second blow was like unto the first, but from a different angle, probably because the victim was falling to her left. This one wasn't quite as powerful, but it struck the top of her head, the occipital. Mrs Striker must have been nearing unconsciousness now and probably kneeling when the final blow was delivered. This one was the most powerful of all, probably two-handed, and it came from directly above, shattering the top of the skull. There was a hole about two centimetres in diameter. I couldn't reassemble the bits, they're too fragmented, scattered in the hair. That clinched, it, of course. You don't get up again after a smack like that.'

'Would there have been a lot of blood?'

'Oh yes. The head bleeds like buggery, of course. Our man would be fairly covered in it.'

'And the attack didn't happen in the store cupboard where she was found?'

'Lord, no.' Anderson blew again on his coffee. 'No room. I'd say she was battered in the corridor and dragged there. Your boys will be able to pinpoint that forensically.'

'Time of death?'

'Ah, now that's not easy.' Anderson rose to attend to the toast slowly smouldering in his toaster. 'Fucking thing!' he snapped and hit it to retrieve his burnt offering. 'Laymen think a thermometer up the bum says it all. It doesn't. My guess — and that's all it is at this stage — is that she died sometime during Thursday afternoon. I can't be more accurate than that.'

'That'll do me,' McBride said, swigging back the last of his coffee. 'Thank you, doctor.'

'Going so soon?' Anderson had sat back to wrestle with another pack of butter. 'You've only just got here.'

'Needs must,' McBride winked, 'when Mr Warren drives.'

Anderson snorted. 'Man's got a fucking clock for a heart,' he said. 'Can you find your own way?'

'Of course. Thank you, sir. I appreciate your time.'

Anderson scowled. 'Time, young man, is my least precious commodity. Years of experience, pearls of wisdom, keenness of eye, steadiness of hand — these things I'm paid for and you should be grateful for. Now, off you fuck. I've got to try to spread this fucking butter.'

* * *

Breakfast at the Carnforth Centre took place a little later than it had at Dr Anderson's. Maxwell got there a fraction after eight and felt his eyebrows singeing as he leaned over to point to a particularly delicious-looking fried egg. The floozy behind the brightly lit counter then ruined it all by slapping it down on the fried bread and breaking the yolk. The sausages looked palatable, but even Maxwell's constitution rebelled at the black pudding and he wandered with his tray into the Hadleigh Suite.

There was an edge to the hubbub he hadn't noticed yesterday. But that was then. Before they'd found her body. Now, between the enforced bonhomie, there were little darting glances; small, almost imperceptible swivels of the eye. And when there was a lull, it seemed to Maxwell to be full of sound — the sound of everybody watching everybody else. So much for the team-building exercises planned for later. If anybody intended to ruin a conference like this, a murder was the best way to do it. For a moment, Maxwell thought he might have killed Liz Striker himself.

An arm was waving to him from the window side of the room. Rachel King sat with Michael Wynn, drinking coffee. Maxwell nodded and shuffled his way past the knot of plain-clothes policemen who sat apart at a table of their own, apparently eating breakfast; actually observing the Carnforth clientele.

'Morning,' Maxwell said, sitting opposite the pair from St Bede's. 'Doesn't this remind you of an old George Raft movie? With the guards over there and us cons in our striped suits. It's about now that some ox tips his slop over somebody, and in the confusion, Raft slips Cagney a file. Then somebody says, "Give me a break, warden," and the young Elisha Cook goes over the top in all sorts of ways.'

'Good morning, Max,' Rachel said, leaning forward and smiling at him over her coffee.

He paused in mid-raconte. 'I'm sorry,' he said, 'was I rambling?'

'Just a threat,' she nodded.

'Bit on edge, I suppose.'

'We all are,' Wynn sighed. 'I just can't get over this.'

'Are you leaving today, Max?' Rachel asked.

'No,' he told her, sugaring his coffee. 'I told Warren I'd stay till Monday.'

'You know they're going on with the course, don't you?' Wynn asked, passing Maxwell the salt.

'You're not serious?'

'I'm a Deputy Principal,' Wynn winked. 'We're always serious.'

Maxwell guffawed. It was a little out of place perhaps and he had the grace to grimace to the top table. An inscrutable-looking WPC glowered back at him.

'Been at St Bede's long?' Maxwell asked Wynn.

'Ten years,' Wynn told him, 'though in the silent watches of the night it sometimes seems for ever.'

Maxwell knew that feeling.

'I was Head of Geography before that.'

Maxwell didn't know that feeling at all. To Maxwell, being Head of Geography must be rather akin to being a leper. The news certainly killed that conversation outright.

'Been at the budgie seed again, Rachel?' he asked his old flame, peering into her nearly empty bowl.

'That's muesli,' she said. 'I just wasn't very hungry.'

'I never remember you eating that in the '60s.' He tackled his bacon manfully.

'I'm not sure it was around in the '60s. Besides, I wore jeans then — and I had a beehive hairdo.'

'Da Doo Ron Ron!' Maxwell winked at her.

'Of course,' Wynn said, leaning over his coffee, 'you two go back a way, don't you? Rachel said something about it yesterday.'

'Ah,' she smiled at Maxwell. 'Dear dead days.'

He looked at her and nodded. Why on earth did that still happen? Why did he have that churning feeling inside? That catch in the pit of his stomach? That flutter of the heart? He was fifty-three years old, for God's sake, crustier than a Coburg. But it did still happen and he couldn't help it.

'What sort of woman was she?' he asked Wynn.

'Who?' The Deputy Principal of St Bede's seemed oddly inattentive. But then, Maxwell remembered, he had been Head of Geography.

'Elizabeth Striker.' Maxwell realised he'd better explain.

'Liz? Oh, salt of the earth,' Wynn said. 'She was Head of Family Studies.'

'Is that cooking?' Maxwell looked to Rachel for help. He caught the light in Michael Wynn's eyes. It was one he'd seen before. Often. The light of a member of the establishment being appalled by Maxwell's political incorrectness.

'Not exactly,' Wynn said. 'Liz was very keen to establish GNVQ. She's done all the spade work herself.'

'Known her long?'

'All the time I've been at St Bede's.'

'Part of the furniture, was Liz,' Rachel nodded, gazing into the middle distance. 'We'll miss her terribly.'

Wynn nodded. 'That we will,' he said. 'It's Jordan I'm most worried about.'

'Jordan?' Maxwell echoed him.

'I passed him in the corridor last night. He didn't seem to see me at all. I said hello . . .'

'As you do,' Maxwell nodded.

'As you do,' Wynn agreed, 'and it was as though he didn't hear me either. I felt like a bloody ghost.'

'He was the one who was looking for Liz,' Maxwell said. 'He asked me.'

'He asked us all,' Rachel remembered.

'Were they close?' Maxwell asked.

'I think they were,' Rachel said. 'You'd certainly see them in the corner of the staff room locked in some deep, meaningful conversation.'

'Jordan had his problems,' Wynn said, 'when he first joined us, I mean. Couldn't cope with Class 3B — that sort of thing. Liz — and I don't think this is too strong a word — Liz saved him. Or saved his sanity at any rate.'

'He's all right now?' Maxwell said.

Wynn raised his eyebrows. 'Well, it's all relative, Max, isn't it? Let's say he can teach the Catechism like a good 'un. There've been fewer complaints, let's put it that way.'

'Is there a Mr Striker?'

'Leonard, yes,' Rachel said. 'Works for a computer firm. Such a nice bloke. He'll be devastated.'

* * *

Leonard Striker held his wife's hand for one last time. She was covered in a green sheet and there was another one over the top of her head. Only her right hand trailed beneath the cover. Only her face lay pale, so pale on the mortuary pillow. Her eyes were closed, but puffy and purple with the bruising. They'd cleaned her up for him, of course. So that he couldn't see the shattered cranium or the work of Anderson's disc saws.

'Yes,' he said in a voice stronger than he'd hoped, 'yes, it's her.' Somehow he couldn't bear to say her name. Because saying it would have sent him over the edge. And he would have cried. Broken down. And it wasn't in Leonard Striker's nature to do that. Least of all in front of strangers. And for the first time in his life he was grateful for the fact that he and Liz had not been able to have kids after all.

He turned away. Out into the corridor where a balding police detective shook his hand, muttering something to the effect that he would get him, however long it took. Out into the car-park where the rain was already falling on the tarmac and forming puddles on the uneven surface. Out into the rest of his life.

'What a bloody miserable world,' McBride muttered, watching him go.

'It's a formality.' Warren watched him too. 'That's all. Just one more little step in the right direction.'

McBride threw a sideways glance at his guv'nor. There were times when he didn't want to be a Chief Inspector at all.

CHAPTER 5

Lupine was how Peter Maxwell described Lydia Farr. Not to her face, of course. Nor indeed to anyone else's. It was one of those inner pronouncements that crusty old bachelors make to themselves and stick with because there is no one to qualify, no one to contradict. She wasn't lupine in character; on the contrary, Maxwell wasn't aware of her until he'd heard she'd fainted at the sight of Liz Striker's corpse. It was just her face and her weird, yellow eyes. When she smiled, Lydia reminded Maxwell of 'Mad Jack' Nicholson, just before his axe came crashing through the door in *The Shining*. She had that aura of insanity about her, that mask of mania.

In fact, Lydia Farr was a tangle of emotions and she always had been. The fat kid had been laughed at and teased by the boys and even when the puppy fat left her and puberty raised its ugly head, they laughed at her acne. There was no Mr Farr. Yet Lydia had not given up. Now in her thirty-somethingth year, she still joined karate classes and went to singles bars because that was where you found men. And habitually, she took herself down off the shelf of celibacy and dusted herself and put on her bravest face for the world.

It was a long, pointed face, with a long, pointed nose. It didn't remind John McBride of a wolf. It reminded him of the witch in the book that was now compulsory bedtime reading for little Sam. For little Sam McBride wouldn't go to sleep until his dad had read to him the bit about the witch and how she had lured the hapless Hansel and Gretel to her gingerbread house in the woods. But this witch had been crying. She held a handkerchief in her bony hands and sat as still as she could facing the two detectives.

A cold WPC sat at her elbow, compulsory under the new police code of practice, but as much use as a colander in a shipwreck.

'We don't want to distress you,' McBride told her, 'but we need to establish a few things.'

'Yes, of course.'

'Tell us about the finding of the body,' he said softly. John McBride was nearly thirty. He'd done well to get to Detective Inspector, one of those pushy, degreed types his guv'nor had quietly complained to Maxwell about. What was left of his curly blond hair was wreathed in Lydia Farr's cigarette smoke and his eyes were clear and patient.

'I told him,' Lydia said, pointing to Stony Warren beside McBride with a quick jerk of her finger.

'I know,' the Inspector said, 'but you'd be surprised how, if you repeat something, some little fact emerges; something you hadn't mentioned before. It probably won't help, but it might be something vital.'

'All right.' She drew herself up as though facing a walk to the gallows and closed her eyes. Only the cigarette twitched in her endlessly fidgeting fingers. McBride looked at Warren. The tape was running.

'We were on a problem-solving exercise. We had to erect a shelter, a sort of survival hut thing, on the beach, from any bits and pieces we could find. It was to test the ingenuity of the group, I think. Anyway, it came on to rain and Alan and I—'

'Alan?' McBride interrupted, for the benefit of the tape.

'Alan Harper-Bennet. We decided to run back to the centre. It seemed the obvious place. Gregory Trant was there too, although some distance behind.'

'What made you take the side door?' Warren spoke for the first time.

'Er . . .' His interruption threw Lydia for a moment, but she quickly regained her composure. 'I don't know. The rain, I suppose. It was bucketing down. It was the first door I saw.'

'It's down some steps, isn't it?' McBride asked.

'That's right. I half expected it to be locked.'

'But it wasn't?'

'No. No. I opened it.' Lydia's concentration showed now in her face. If she were walking in her mind those deadly paces to the gallows, it was now she saw the noose for the first time. She blinked several times, her throat tightening. The WPC beside her saw the handkerchief tighten in the woman's fist. 'The door ahead of me was open.' Lydia could see it clearly, her head cocked to one side, a quizzical expression on her face. 'I remember . . . I remember there was water in my eyes. Rain. It stung. There was a pile of paper, still wrapped in ream boxes. And beyond them was . . . beyond them . . .'

She felt the touch of a hand on hers. It was Stony Warren's; and no one was more surprised than he that it was.

'I . . . don't really remember the rest. I do remember being taken past . . . it . . . along the corridor. Presumably Alan was leading me away. I think I screamed . . .'

* * *

'. . . the bloody place down,' Alan Harper-Bennet concurred. Miles Warren slouched in his chair, his own cigarette quietly burning in the ashtray in front of him. The blinds were down. The lights were on. It wasn't even eleven o'clock in the morning and already it felt like midnight. Harper-Bennet was a solid, square-faced rugger player with sandy hair. He reminded Maxwell of the young Bill Travers before he had grown a beard, gone grey and got funny about lions. He didn't remind Chief Inspector Warren of anybody, except of course a potential killer. The man certainly had the brawn. Shoulders like sideboards in fact. Games and

Sociology loomed large on Harper-Bennet's CV, probably in that order.

'Tell me,' MacBride said, 'do you work out, Mr Bennet?'

'I do,' the teacher said, 'and that's Harper-Bennet, by the way.'

McBride wrote something down and just sat there.

'Why did you tell Miss Farr not to go that way?' Warren asked. He hadn't moved from his almost recumbent position, his eyes half-closed in the artificial light.

'What?' Harper-Bennet shifted those massive shoulders.

'When you and Miss Farr were running for shelter, when it started to rain, she was making for the side door, the one to the ground floor, and you said . . .' For effect, Warren shuffled Lydia Farr's notes. He didn't really have to. He knew exactly what she'd said. 'You said, "Not down there." Why did you say that? Mr Bennet?'

'Because it wasn't the way in. Not the main entrance, I mean. And the name is still Harper-Bennet, by the way.'

'But she ignored you?'

'Yes,' the games master had to concede. 'But I'm not sure she heard me, what with the rain and our feet on the gravel.'

'But clearly she did, Mr . . . Harper-Bennet, because I've just told you what she said you said.'

'Yes, well, clearly.' Harper-Bennet cleared his throat. He didn't like to be made a fool of. And Chief Inspector Warren was doing a very good job of that.

'Have you seen a dead body before, Mr Harper-Bennet?' McBride asked.

'No. Well, my grandfather, but that hardly counts.'

'All human life counts, sir,' McBride told him.

'Of course,' Harper-Bennet blustered. 'I didn't mean . . . What I mean is . . .'

'What did you think had happened?' Warren cut his man up. 'To Mrs Striker, I mean?'

For a moment, Harper-Bennet just sat there, his mouth opening and closing. 'I don't really know,' was the eventual outcome. 'Some terrible accident, I suppose. I could see the blood.'

'Where?'

'On the woman's head.' Harper-Bennet was holding his hand in front of his own, unsure in his recollection of it if mere words were enough.

'You didn't touch the body?' McBride asked.

'No. No. I got Lydia — Miss Farr — out of there. She was hysterical. Trant didn't look too chipper, either. He'd joined us by this time.'

'You weren't hysterical?' Warren asked.

'Me? No,' Harper-Bennet shrugged. 'No, no. I was fine. Well, you know. I'm a Territorial. I've been around. She was out of it, you know. Screaming blue murder . . . Oh . . . I mean . . .'

'You took her upstairs?' Warren chased his man.

'Yes. Trant and I found the lift and took her to her room.'

'Room 203?' McBride checked.

'That's right. I put her on the bed and telephoned Reception.'

'Where was Mr Trant?'

'He went off saying he'd fetch somebody. I always thought Greg was a cooler customer, but I'm afraid he panicked. No balls in the end.'

'Who took your call?'

'I don't know. A girl. Tracey, was it? You'd have to ask her.'

'We did,' Warren told him. 'Your call was logged at ten thirty-one.'

'Right.'

'Which is odd.'

'Is it?'

'Timing is very important in cases of murder, Mr Harper-Bennet,' Warren said. 'Crucial, in fact. What time would you say you and Miss Farr discovered the body?'

'Er . . . I don't know. About five minutes before, I suppose.'

'Would it surprise you to know it was nearly thirteen minutes before?'

'Nearly . . . ? No. No, it couldn't have been.'

'You were seen entering that side door at ten seventeen. Allowing for the time taken to open it, see the late Mrs Striker, get to Ms Farr's room and lay her on the bed, that's quite a long time, Mr Harper-Bennet, before you contacted Reception.'

'Well, Lydia . . . Miss Farr . . . was hysterical. I've told you. She was in a fainting condition. I had to revive her.'

'Oh? How did you do that?' McBride asked.

'A flannel.' Harper-Bennet's eyes were bulging in his head. Little beads of sweat stood out on his upper lip. 'I got a flannel from the bathroom.'

'Ms Farr's room is en suite?'

'They all are,' Harper-Bennet said. 'Look here, what are you implying?'

'Nothing,' Warren shrugged, unclasping his hands and leaning forward for the first time. 'Nothing at all, sir. I'm just tying up the odd loose end — you know how it is.'

Harper-Bennet looked at the cold-eyed detectives in front of him. 'Can I go?' he blurted. 'I'm late for a lecture.'

'Of course,' McBride said and he leaned forward over the table. 'Interview terminated at . . . eleven sixteen. Thank you, Mr Harper-Bennet.'

The big man grated back his chair. He swayed for a moment, as though about to ask a question. Then he thought better of it and left with a scowl in the direction of the WPC who was already pouring Mr Warren another cup of coffee.

'Who saw him, sir?' McBride asked, when Harper-Bennet had gone. 'Going in through the side door?'

Warren turned one of his stormiest glances in his Number Two's direction. 'His conscience, John,' he said softly.

'Sir?'

Warren got up and stretched his legs. 'Unorthodox policing bothers you, doesn't it, Inspector?' he asked.

McBride glanced at the WPC. He didn't like being put on the spot. And he thought he knew his guv'nor. Warren's latest ploy was indeed bothering him. 'Can you get me the staff list, Sheila?' he asked. 'It's on my desk.'

'Very good, sir.' She smiled and left the room.

McBride knew he didn't have long. And he rounded on Warren. The Chief Inspector was ready for him. 'Call it man's intuition,' he said. 'It was the way Bennet kept sneaking furtive looks up Sheila's skirt. Did you notice that?'

'No,' McBride frowned. 'But that's . . .'

'. . . not unusual, no. Ninety per cent of red-blooded males would cop a crafty look. But not constantly. Not in the way he did. There's something . . . unhealthy about it.'

'So . . . ?'

'So I invented the sighting. For all I know, the whole episode, from finding the body to making the phone call, may have taken seconds. We'll have to check with Gregory Trant. But it rattled him, didn't it? He was edgy, wouldn't you say?'

'Well, yes . . .' McBride conceded. 'But?'

'He went to the bathroom,' Warren said.

'To get a flannel, yes.'

'To get a flannel?' Warren raised an eyebrow. 'Is that what Lydia Farr said?'

'Er . . . no. There was no mention of a flannel because she was hysterical. Fainting. She just didn't remember.'

'And, conveniently, Gregory Trant had already buggered off. The other possibility is that there was no mention of a flannel because there was no flannel.'

'Then why go to the bathroom?'

Warren sipped the coffee Sheila had made for him. 'Warrants,' the Chief Inspector said. 'We need warrants, John.'

'Why?' McBride was nettled. There was no heading 'Intuition' in any police manual he'd ever read. It belonged to crime fiction, not crime fact.

'Because we need to find a few things.' Warren handed his empty cup to the returning WPC. 'Like Ms Farr's used underwear, which was probably in the linen basket in her bathroom.' He paused in the doorway. 'And like some bloodstained clothing. I'd settle for that; wouldn't you, John?'

* * *

There was a lull midday shortly after lunch. The group had been subjected to a mid-morning lecture on 'GNVQ in Practice' during which Maxwell had fallen asleep and had slumped sideways against a pillar. He'd eaten too much at lunch — the quiche, which the Head of Games at Leighford High told him real men didn't eat, was particularly entrancing — and he lay now on his narrow bed in Room 101, facing God-knew-what terrors. He may have been dozing off again, when there was a sharp rap at the door.

A tall kid stood there, in faded stonewash jeans and a skimpy top that showed her navel. 'Are you alone, Max?' She popped her head around the door.

'I'm not sure what that question is supposed to imply, Mrs Greenhow, but yes. How would you like me?'

'Back, Max,' she said solemnly. 'I'd like you back.'

He looked at the girl in front of him, the earnestness on her pretty, dimpled face, the eyes grey and bright behind the glasses. 'I've never been away,' he said.

'Haven't you?' Sally asked him, perching on his bed and plumping up the pillow behind her. 'A woman's been murdered, Max. I want your brain.'

'Vincent Price,' Maxwell clicked his fingers, 'or was it Peter Lorre? It's either *Revenge of the Blood Beast* or *Secret Seven Discover Satanic Abuse*. I'll remember in a minute.' Both take-offs were lost on Sally Greenhow. The only lorries she knew had eight wheels and turned into side streets.

'I'm serious, Max,' she said. 'Sometimes you just make me want to scream.'

'All right,' he chuckled, collapsing into the easy chair by the desk. 'What are you suggesting?'

'That we solve this ourselves.'

He looked at her, then shook his head.

'Why not?' She bounced forward on the bed so that her breasts jiggled.

'It's none of our business,' he said.

Sally Greenhow's mouth flopped open. 'Can you hear yourself?' she asked. 'Is this the same Mad Max who solved Jenny Hyde's murder last year?'

'That was different,' Maxwell said. 'Jenny was one of mine.'

It was and she had been. Jenny Hyde was in the sixth form at Leighford High. When she was found, Maxwell had felt responsible. There were members of the West Sussex CID who felt he was responsible too. But it was a painful memory for Maxwell. He had no wish to be reminded of it.

'Liz Striker was somebody's,' Sally argued. 'Rachel King told me she was married. What's her husband going through about now, I wonder?'

'It's not the same.'

There was another knock on the door, more furtive, doubtful.

'Well, well,' Maxwell said, rising. 'I am in demand today.'

He opened the door to the hunched, rather unprepossessing figure of Jordan Gracewell. He was glancing nervously up and down the dimly lit corridor.

'Selling the *War Cry*, padre?' Maxwell asked.

'Mr Maxwell,' Gracewell blurted, 'I was wondering if I might have a word?'

'Be my guest.' Maxwell threw the door open.

'Oh!' The chaplain caught sight of the long legs of Sally Greenhow across the bed and hesitated. 'I'm sorry, I didn't realise you had company.'

'No, no.' Maxwell closed the door and ushered Gracewell into the room. 'Not company, exactly. Just Mrs Greenhow. We were discussing the role of Intermediate Level GNVQ, weren't we, Sally?'

'Bollocks, Max!' the girl snorted and rummaged in her bag for her ciggies.

'Before she joined us,' Maxwell explained, 'Mrs Greenhow was at the Ernst Rohm School of Charm.'

'I . . . shouldn't really be here,' Gracewell said. 'I'd better go.'

'Why?' Maxwell stopped the man with the edge in his voice. 'What have you got to hide, Mr Gracewell?'

The chaplain looked so utterly vulnerable at that moment, so totally alone, that Sally wanted to pick him up and run with him.

'Nothing,' Gracewell said. Then he wandered into the corner of Maxwell's room and stared out of the window, across Carnforth's manicured lawns and rose-beds. 'Everything.'

Maxwell then took another sexist offensive step. Well, why not? He'd been taking them all his life. 'Sally,' he said, opening the door, 'would you mind?'

Sally Greenhow would and did. She sat there with a cigarette clinging to her lower lip and her lighter flickering in her left hand. 'Maxie?' was all she could manage.

'If I were you,' Maxwell took her arm and lifted her off his bed, 'I'd concentrate on your strategic intent. I particularly like your concept of the exercise book — archaic, but somehow, in this day and age, innovative. Do keep in touch. Remember, synergise to maximise.' And he slammed the door in her face.

He waited for the furious knock. All he got was a strangled cry as Sally Greenhow dashed off down the corridor. Not a bad Greta Garbo, he mused as he turned to face the back of Jordan Gracewell.

'Are you a drinking man, padre?' he asked.

'Er . . . no.' Gracewell had not turned. Only his hands fluttered convulsively to his sides.

'No.' Maxwell raided the courtesy bar again, looking for Southern Comfort. 'Unfortunately, I am. Running up quite a little bill here, one way or another. I'm sure County will accept eight Southern Comforts as necessary subsistence; what do you think?'

There was a pause. 'I think I know who killed Liz Striker, Mr Maxwell.' The chaplain had turned to face his man. Jordan Gracewell was nearly thirty. He'd been a priest for three years, a teacher for two. The great love in his life was God. God and Elizabeth Striker.

'Really?' Maxwell said. 'Perhaps you should talk to the police.'

'I can't.' Gracewell sat down heavily in Maxwell's chair. Maxwell sat down more gently on his bed. Ever the master of body language, he didn't want to be higher than Gracewell. Not now. The last thing he wanted to appear was an authority figure. And he leaned forward, giving an air of concern without invading the young man's space.

'I can't talk to Warren. He frightens me.'

Maxwell nodded. 'That may be part of his job,' he said. He felt the warm, dark gold nectar hit his tonsils. 'Distilled on the banks of the good ol' Mississippi,' he said. 'Are you sure you won't . . . ?'

Gracewell was already shaking his head. Not once did he look Peter Maxwell in the face. 'I'd like to talk to you, Mr Maxwell,' he said. 'I feel I can trust you. I can't trust anyone else here. But you, you're different . . .'

'Mr Gracewell,' Maxwell warned softly, 'perhaps you need a priest . . .'

Gracewell turned away, suddenly, savagely. 'No,' he said, his voice like gravel, 'that's the last thing I want. Will you . . .' He turned back, looking into the steady, grey eyes of Mad Max Maxwell for the first time. 'Will you hear my confession?'

Maxwell spread his arms in supplication. 'I'm not exactly qualified,' he said.

'Please?' Gracewell was on the chair again, this time perched on its arm, staring at Maxwell with pleading eyes.

'All right,' Maxwell said.

Gracewell took a deep breath and launched himself. 'For two years now, I've been . . . in love with Liz Striker.'

'In love?'

'Yes. She was a married woman and I am a man of the cloth.'

There was a silence.

'Is that it?' Maxwell thought he'd better ask.

'Isn't that enough?' Gracewell bellowed, tears welling in his eyes. For Maxwell, it wasn't. He'd half suspected something about sniffing the saddles of little girls' bicycles or at least a little ragged breathing over the phone to the local convent. It was all rather tame, really.

'Did you have an affair with Mrs Striker?' Maxwell asked. 'Anything physical, I mean?'

'No, no,' Gracewell shuddered. 'Although I often thought about it. Often imagined . . . Sometimes, when we were alone together, working late on marking or preparation, the temptation was strong.' He closed his eyes. 'Appallingly strong. I . . . I will have to resign.'

'As my lately departed colleague said, if my memory serves, bollocks, padre.'

'What?'

'It's a euphemism for testicles,' Maxwell explained.

'I have committed adultery in my heart,' Gracewell sobbed, the tears starting to trickle down his cheek and splash on to his black cuffs.

'Yes, well,' Maxwell fished out a relatively respectable hanky, 'better there than somebody's bedroom. Now, come on, old chap, buck up. I can't stand to see a grown chaplain cry.'

'I'm sorry,' Gracewell sniffed, accepting the handkerchief gratefully. 'I actually feel a lot better now. Now it's off my chest.'

'Oh, good,' Maxwell smiled, 'good.'

'Thank you, Mr Maxwell.'

He suddenly felt his hand being shaken warmly, by both of Gracewell's. 'Not at all,' Maxwell beamed. 'The pleasure's been mine. Now, who did you say killed Liz Striker?'

'Oh, I don't know,' Gracewell said, 'but I'm making an educated guess, with all the information at my disposal.'

'Yes?'

'Rachel,' Gracewell said, as if he'd just ordered chips. 'Rachel King.'

CHAPTER 6

It was Peter Maxwell's turn to rap on Sally Greenhow's door.

'Why, Max,' she did her Southern Belle to perfection, 'Ah declare, you've come to escort me tuh the lecture.'

'Sod the lecture!' Maxwell brushed past her and slammed the door.

'Oh well,' sighed Sally. 'Looks like I'm not going to the ball after all.'

'Cheer up.' Maxwell had flung his heavy carcass into the girl's chair. 'Some day your prince will come.'

'Yes.' She looked him up and down. 'Some day. Can I rustle you up a coffee?'

'You can.' He sat fuming, his grey whiskers standing even more on end than usual. 'White. Three sugars.'

'Three?' She fiddled with the kettle on the bedside cabinet. 'Max, you're regressing. That's nursery food. You'll be angling for spotted dick next.'

'I don't know what I'm doing here,' Maxwell said, wiping his hands down his face as though to wipe away his features.

'Not for my scintillating company, then?' Sally professed. 'Or the opportunity to apologise for throwing me out of your room so unceremoniously no more than half an hour ago? I was tempted to go and play Mummies and Mummies with Valerie Marks.'

'I've just heard the most ludicrous load of guff in my life,' he told her.

'That was this morning, Max.' Sally found the sugar packets. 'This afternoon — "Experiential Learning" — could have been even better.'

'I'm not talking about the lectures, dear girl,' Maxwell said, hauling off his bow-tie. 'I'm talking about the cock-happy clergyman.'

'Who?' Sally's eyes widened as she looked at Maxwell over her glasses.

'Jordan "Superstud" Gracewell, that's who. Tell me, Sallance, in your quieter moments, when hubby's at the office, or the squash club or waxing his CD player, do you ever read whodunnits?'

'It has been known,' she confessed. 'Ruth Rendell, that sort of thing.'

'Motives,' Maxwell ruminated, bending himself oddly to take off his jacket and flinging it on the floor, 'do they ever feature? In this Rendell person, for instance?'

'Often,' she told him.

'Right. Let me try you with this one. Are you sitting comfortably? Only you'll need to, I think. A has such a goddammed powerful sex aura that women just flock to him. He has to fight them off. That's not that difficult, because A happens to be a Catholic priest, so he's had the training. Undergone the Bell test or whatever where they tie electrodes to your nuts then show you photos of Sharon Mammothtits to curb your natural testosterone levels. Unfortunately for A, B and C are so crazy for his body that they come to blows — behind the scenes, that is. And B ends up stoving in C's head in order to gain unimpeded access to the aforesaid body beautiful. And if you haven't guessed it by page two, I'm a Chippendale.'

Sally had been about to pour Max's coffee. Now she sat down on the bed instead. 'All right,' she nodded, 'apart from the body beautiful bit, A is Jordan Gracewell. C must be Liz Striker . . .'

'Got it in one.'

'Who's B?'

'It's obvious.' Maxwell waved his arms in the air. 'And I could have kicked myself for not guessing it sooner, Watson. B is none other than our old friend Professor Moriarty, otherwise known as . . . Rachel King.'

Sally blinked at her old colleague in disbelief.

'Well, say something,' Maxwell said. 'Most people are quite impressed by my Basil Rathbone.'

'Oh, Max,' Sally frowned, shaking her head, 'is that what Gracewell told you?'

He looked at the girl. It must be all those years teaching in Special Needs. 'Do you think I made it up?' he asked.

'What does Rachel say?'

'Rachel?' Maxwell laughed. 'Do you think I could tell her? My dear girl, that's why I came to you.'

'Well,' Sally resumed her housewifely duties at the coffee front, 'Max, I'm flattered.'

'Don't be,' Maxwell rumbled. 'Yours was the first room I passed after I ran out screaming.'

Sally ignored him. Underneath that bluff exterior was a core of solid, molten gold. She knew it. And in her own way she loved it. 'Three sugars.' She handed him the cup. 'And the Lord have mercy on your arteries.'

'We have an understanding, the Lord and I,' Maxwell told her. 'He won't let me go of the cholesterol and I won't sing in any of his churches. It's a fair deal, I've always felt. Ta,' and he took the cup.

'Gracewell wasn't serious, surely?' Sally said.

'Oh, but he was,' Maxwell nodded. 'He genuinely had to confess to stirrings under his cassock for the late Mrs Striker.'

'And the current Mrs King? Oh, sorry, Max.'

'Look,' Maxwell said, 'Mrs King and I were a long time ago, Sally. She was Miss Cameron then and I hadn't celebrated my eightieth birthday — at least, not quite. You don't have to talk about her in hushed tones, you know.'

'But still,' Sally shrugged, grateful that it was Max who had said it, 'you can't believe that she's a murderer.'

'I don't believe it,' Maxwell said. 'Gracewell does. Good God, girl, I don't believe Belgium exists, but it's there on the bloody map. I don't believe Bill Clinton's the President of the United States—'

'He isn't,' Sally said straight-faced. 'Hilary Clinton is.'

'Oh, ha!' Maxwell slurped his coffee. 'I got the impression, while we're on American Presidents, that if I hadn't kicked Gracewell out when I did, he'd have confided in me that he thinks Rachel shot Kennedy.'

'What are you going to do?' she asked him. Sally Greenhow had seen that light in Maxwell's eyes before. Somehow it excited her.

'Prove the egotistical befrocked bastard wrong,' Maxwell said, eyes narrowing as he planned. 'I think we owe it to Rachel to sort this out before Father Dowling out there blabs to the fuzz.'

'We?' Sally exploded. 'When I asked you, not an hour ago, to undertake just that, you virtually told me to piss off.'

'Did I?' Maxwell paused in mid-slurp. 'Dear lady, I think you must be confusing me with somebody else.'

Then, suddenly, Peter Maxwell was deadly serious. 'Sally,' he said, 'this is not going to be a game. We can expect no help whatever from the boys in blue. In fact, if once they find out we're snooping, we'll probably be up before the beak ourselves. And, more importantly,' he held her hand, 'there is a murderer somewhere in this building.'

'Why are you squeezing my hand, Max?' she asked him.

'Freudian substitute,' he grinned gappily at her. 'If I told you what I'd like to be squeezing you'd have me committed to the Home for Repulsive Old Roués. And who'd catch a murderer then?'

'Max,' her face was close to him, 'Max, I think I'm scared. Do you know, I check these locks a dozen times a day. Catch myself looking round corners before I walk down corridors. Daft, isn't it?'

His eyes locked on hers as he shook his head. 'Keep feeling that way, kid,' he gave her his best Bogart. 'That's the way you know you're still alive.'

* * *

Little Sam McBride discovered Playmobil that Sunday. It was his fifth birthday and his mum and dad had bought him the boxed set of knights at a tournament. Peter Maxwell, had he known, would have been proud. Parents with foresight — the Middle Ages was part of the National Curriculum's History Key Stage 2 — educational toys, if ever there were some.

If the truth were told, John McBride already hated his son's birthday. Nothing to do with the lad himself, who was very much the apple of his father's eye. No, it was the dozen or so other five-year-olds who descended on the unsuspecting semi that killed it for John. By the time night came and a sort of peace returned to the estate, Inspector McBride had lost track of the crimes perpetrated by the vile little monsters. Only his inordinate self-control had prevented the addition of another crime to theirs — he had not quite committed infanticide.

Cathy McBride was five months pregnant. She sat that night still surrounded by the debris of the day, slowly twirling the little plastic knights in her fingers. 'Thanks, daddy,' she said.

John looked up from his notepad, and laughed. 'How many more of these have we got to do?'

'Well,' she said, adjusting the lump that would be little Sam's brother or sister, 'that depends on how you care to calculate it. If you go on throwing parties for Sam until he's sixteen — I expect after that, he'll just want you to pay for them and go away — that's another eleven. Then there are another sixteen for the Embryo here; that's twenty-seven.

Assuming we have no more kids. Then of course, there's your grandparental contribution . . .'

'I don't notice Sam's grandparents very much in the offing, do you?'

'Ah, you're just a rotten old stick-in-the-mud, John McBride. Fancy a drink?'

'I'd kill for a beer,' he said, but his head was back in his notebook and he wasn't really there any more.

'Penny for your thoughts,' she said, nudging him with the cold can she'd liberated from the fridge.

'Oh, it's this bloody case, Cath,' he said.

She'd heard it all before. Every time it was this bloody case. He hated murder. No one ever gained. No one ever won. She'd seen this, even from the outside. She knew he had to tell people their loved ones were dead. It might be a wife. It might be a husband. It might be a son. Everyone had someone. That was how it was. And here they were, with the party streamers of their little boy's birthday still twirling in the air, and they were suddenly talking about death.

'Tell me,' she said, as she always did.

He couldn't, of course. Not really. Not the nitty-gritty of things. He couldn't show her the shattered head of Liz Striker, her cramped little grave of paper packages in that stock cupboard. Nor would he have wanted to.

'It's this woman,' he said, seeing in his mind's eye the black and white photographs of the corpse, the green sheet and the pallid, waxy face. 'The victim, Elizabeth Striker. She's too bloody good.'

'She's dead, John.' His wife didn't need to remind him.

'I know.' He closed his eyes and let his head loll back. For the past few hours he'd sunk himself into his rest day, bitten the bullet that was his son's birthday party, played all kinds of ghastly, exhausting games. But she was still there, Liz Striker, at his elbow. That and the fact that she was dead.

'She taught Family Studies, whatever the hell that is, at St Bede's, a Catholic comprehensive in Bournemouth. She was married to Leonard, two years her senior. He's in computers in a local firm. They seemed happily married. No obvious financial worries.'

'Was the attack sexual?'

He sipped his beer. 'No. At least, no signs of it. St Bede's might give us a clue, of course. The guv'nor's going over there tomorrow.'

'Aren't you going with him?'

'No,' her husband told her. 'The natives at Carnforth are getting restless. One of them's threatened to go tomorrow. My job is to try to stop him.'

'Can you?'

'Of course not,' McBride shrugged. 'The guv'nor's stuck his neck out keeping them all there this long. I didn't expect that kind of thing from Warren. I hope he hasn't overreached himself. Three days. I think he expected somebody to crack after three days.'

'No sign?'

McBride shook his head. 'What did you think of your teachers at school, Cath?'

His wife laughed. 'They were all right, I suppose. Except old Pearson. Used to get the girls to stand on chairs if they got things wrong in Maths. I think they took him away in the end.'

'Hmm. More than one weirdo at the Carnforth Centre, I shouldn't wonder. The problem is deciding which of them wanted Liz Striker out of the way. Good old Liz, about whom nobody has a bad word. But somebody didn't like you all that much, did they, Liz? Somebody snuffed you out like an altar candle.'

* * *

The lights burned late in Room 101 that Sunday night. Peter Maxwell had seen more Agatha Christies and police procedurals than Sally Greenhow had had hot flushes. Accordingly, he knew how it was done. On the plasterboard wall of his room, Supersleuth had pinned dozens of bits of paper.

'You know, Max,' Sally said, between puffs, 'that lot is almost a flow chart. We'll make an energetic go-ahead teacher of you yet, storming, norming and so on.'

'Wash your filthy mouth out,' Maxwell growled, putting the finishing touches to his deductive reasoning. 'I look nothing like the American Commander in the Gulf. There. What do you think?'

Sally looked at the arrows, names, question marks, all of them radiating out from the name 'Liz Striker' in the centre. 'I think it is absolutely incomprehensible, Maxie.' She smiled wide-eyed. 'Are you sure you never lectured in a college of education? Perhaps if you talked me through it.'

'Oh, ye of little brain,' he sighed. 'Watch the blackboard while I run through it.'

She tucked her feet under her bum on the bed and listened carefully.

'The murdered woman, Liz Striker,' Maxwell said, 'what do we know about her?'

'I thought you were telling me,' Sally said.

'Now, come on,' Maxwell wagged a finger at her, 'question and answer. It's a tried and tested classroom technique. I learned it at university, circa 1849.'

'All right.' Sally was game. 'She was Head of Family Studies at St Bede's, Bournemouth. Very keen on GNVQ.'

'That's it!' Maxwell shouted.

'What?' Sally nearly jumped out of her skin.

'Being keen on GNVQ is reason enough for anybody to be murdered.'

'Maxie . . .' Sally growled.

'All right, all right. Keep your bra on. Oh,' he glanced at her pert chest, 'too late, I see. Right. What else?'

'Urn . . . according to Jordan Gracewell . . .'

'Ah, yes,' Maxwell's roving finger strayed to another part of the wall, 'the Gospel according to Gracewell.'

'. . . according to him, she fancied him something rotten.'

'Right. Well, let's indulge his incense-induced fantasies for a little longer. Liz fancies Jordan . . .'

'. . . who fancies Rachel.'

'No, I don't think so,' Maxwell corrected her. 'I think Jordan fancies Jordan.'

'You'll need to talk to Rachel.'

'I know,' Maxwell's face darkened, 'I know. That'll have to wait till morning. When did she arrive?'

'Liz? Thursday.'

'Who with?'

'Sorry?'

'I beg your pardon, heart,' Maxwell apologised, 'it's the emotional strain. With whom?'

'Don't get all grammatical on me, Max,' Sally said. 'What I mean is, how do you mean?'

'Well, was there a minibus from St Bede's? Did they all come by car? Train? Tom Pearce's grey mare? What?'

Sally blinked. 'I don't know.'

'We need to know that. We need to know how she got here and precisely when.'

'Right.'

'Then we need to know who else was here.'

'The lot from St Bede's,' Sally said, 'and the lot from Luton.'

'Indeed,' Maxwell nodded, 'the lot from Luton. That's Harper-Bennet and Co, isn't it?'

Sally shuddered. 'He's revolting,' she said.

'Harper-Bennet?' Maxwell checked. 'Is he? Why?'

'I don't know,' Sally shrugged. 'Call it women's intuition, but there's something decidedly unsavoury about that chap.'

'All right,' and Maxwell wrote 'weirdo' alongside Harper-Bennet's name.

'Oh, now, steady, Max,' Sally protested. 'I mean, it's only a gut reaction. We don't know anything.'

'Relax, Sal, this isn't a court of law. In this room every bugger is presumed guilty until we can convince ourselves of his/her innocence. Come to think of it, that's exactly like a court of law, isn't it?'

'What was she doing in that stock room?' Sally asked, following the various arrows now in Maxwell's mad diagram.

'Beginning to smell, I shouldn't wonder,' Maxwell said. 'A more pertinent question is: did she die there or was she put?'

'How can we find out?'

'"Watch the wall, my darling, while the gentlemen go by."'

'Eh?'

'"The Smugglers' Song",' Maxwell told her, 'Kipling. But instead of five and twenty ponies, it'll be thee and me.'

'Where?'

Maxwell was already on his feet. 'The scene of the crime,' he said.

'Max?' She was still struggling to find her slip-ons.

'Do you want to find Liz Striker's murderer or not?' he turned to ask her.

'Yes,' she told him.

'Then, as Old Blue Eyes would say, we'll do it my way. Come on. Last one in the basement's a suspect.'

* * *

There's something eerie about a new building after dark. The assumption is that only ruins are haunted, only castles have ghosts. But there's something about the echo of a new building, the smell, the total darkness of the unlit stairways. And what was worse, for Peter Maxwell and Sally Greenhow, was that they both knew they were walking in a dead woman's footsteps.

They took the stairs, running their fingers over the polished plastic handrail, and descended the two half-flights from the ground floor. Maxwell was busy mentally preparing his excuses if there was still a copper at the corridor's elbow. None of them convinced him at all. He was pretty sure that Mr Security dozing on the front desk hadn't noticed them. Sally was as lithe as a cat and Maxwell had taken his brogues off, so the collective sound they made was minimalist.

There was no cordon across the corridor that led to the stock room. No sign of a copper on duty. All seemed well.

'Shit!' It was Maxwell's most controlled whisper.

'What?' Sally asked him, equally sotto voce.

'First degree bruising,' Maxwell winced. 'But an inch or so to the left and we'd be talking testicular trauma.'

'It's a little filing cabinet, Max,' Sally hissed, 'though when I say little, it's at least two foot six high.'

'Please.' Maxwell waved his hands as though to make light of the collision. 'Size isn't everything. Here we are.'

'Is this it?'

They were looking in the darkness, to which their eyes had now become accustomed, at a plain wooden door marked 'Reprographic Store'.

'It must be.' Maxwell tried the handle. 'Shit.'

'Locked?'

'Yes.'

'Bugger.'

'Bugger indeed.'

'Not necessarily.' Sally ferreted in the back pocket of her jeans. 'Turn your back if the tightness of my stonewasheds is too much for you.'

'Not at all,' Maxwell whispered. 'I was just wondering if now is the time . . . What the hell . . . ?'

Sally waved something at him in the near-darkness. 'My flexible friend,' she said and proceeded to slide the credit card up and down the door jamb.

'Jesus!' Maxwell was amazed as the girl flicked the handle and the door swung outwards. 'How did you do that?'

'I know your views on Special Needs, Max,' she raised an eyebrow at him, 'but there are times when such training is invaluable.'

'I don't think I need educational flatulence at one in the morning, Sally, if it's all the same to you.'

'All I was going to say was, it's a two-way process. You learn as much from the kids as they do from you.'

'Really?' Maxwell was peering into the stock room.

'Remember Rory Elliott?'

'Do I ever?' Maxwell muttered. 'The only boy I ever felt compelled to drop a pile of textbooks on during his first day at school. Don't think I saw him after that.'

'That's because we had him — in Special Needs. Well, you know who his dad was, don't you?'

'Er . . . Wild Bill Elliott?' Maxwell went much further back than Sally Greenhow.

'Dave Elliott. Spent most of Rory's life in and out of Parkhurst and places.'

'Oh, yes. Armed robbery.'

Sally nodded. 'But a wizard with the old plastic' She wagged her credit card triumphantly. 'And on the rare occasions he was out, Dave passed on this fine family tradition to young Rory.'

'Who in turn passed it on to you.'

'Well, fair's fair,' Sally said. 'I taught him to cope with numbers so he could read the dials on a safe and he taught me the rudiments of lock-picking. Mind you, I think we were dead lucky here.'

'The rumour is that they found her there, behind those packs of paper.'

'Not much room.'

'Very perceptive, Mrs Greenhow.' Max reached as far as he could into the darkness.

'Could we risk a light, do you think?'

Maxwell shook his head.

'I said, "Could we -"'

'No,' Maxwell hissed, 'I don't want to advertise this little sortie. As John Paul Jones might have said, "I have not yet begun to sleuth." We don't want to be taken down town before we've had a good old rummage around. Odd, though.'

'What is?' Sally couldn't see anything in the blackness beyond Max's shoulder.

'That the door opens outwards.'

'Why?'

'Doors don't, these days. Oh, in a twelfth-century long house or a fifteenth-century dower house, anything might happen. To get to one of the bedrooms in the post office in Tintagel, you've got to use a ladder, but now . . . well.'

'Well?'

'Well, I suppose this room was an afterthought. Folks using a conference centre might need to run off copies of things and that means a store. So they had a cubby hole big enough, but to put the door in so that it opened inwards would kill all the space. So it had to open outwards.'

'I don't see what that tells us.'

Maxwell was already closing the door. 'It tells us three things,' he said, feeling his way along the corridor. 'One,' and he wagged an authoritative index finger in the air, 'the guy who built the Carnforth Centre was no Christopher Wren. Two — and perhaps more pertinently — the stock room door must have been unlocked and open for Lydia Farr and Alan Harper-Bennet to have seen Liz Striker's body. And three . . .' He paused and felt Sally bump into him.

'Bloody hell, Max,' she hissed, steadying herself.

'Three,' he'd turned to face her, 'the murderer doesn't work here.'

'How do you know that?'

'Because if he did, he'd have a key — or at least access to one — and would have locked the bloody door. Wouldn't you?'

'I wouldn't cave in somebody's skull in the first place.'

'Well, that's gratifying,' Maxwell said. They'd reached the bottom of the stairs again now and a faint light in the foyer above lit the area. 'Lie down,' Max whispered.

'What?'

'I said—'

'I know what you said.' Sally lowered herself to the floor. 'I just like hearing you talk dirty.'

'Not like that. On your face.'

'Max!'

'Ssh. You'll wake the dead.' That was a one-liner Maxwell instantly regretted.

'What am I doing?'

'You're being Liz Striker. I've just crept up behind you.' He knelt as well as his old trouble would allow him beside her. 'I've bashed you over the head — we know this from the dear old Chief Inspector. Now, I've got a problem. I've got to hide you.' He looked up and down the corridor. 'There's no natural light. Assuming the lights weren't on . . . Where's the switch?'

Sally sat up. 'What do you want me to be — a corpse or Switchfinder General?'

'That's rather good,' Maxwell hissed through gritted teeth. 'In fact I wish I'd said it.'

'You will, Oscar,' she muttered, 'you will.'

'Ah,' he said, 'the switch is over there. So, did she put the light on or not?'

'Does it matter?'

'Don't know. Don't know.' Maxwell was thinking out loud. 'Lie down again. What do you weigh?'

'I beg your pardon?' She sat bolt upright.

'Good God, Sally, calm yourself. It isn't as if I've asked you how old you are. Mind you, I know that one already. You're thirty-two.'

'I'm twenty-nine!' she snapped. 'Would you like to guess my weight too, like a bloody currant cake at the school fete?'

'All right,' he whispered. 'Er . . . nine stone seven.'

'Bloody cheek. I'm eight stone four, in old money.'

'Right. Oh, Jesus.'

'I'm supposed to be saying that,' she hissed. 'Who said you could put your hands there?'

He collapsed to his knees alongside her. 'I'm supposed to be your murderer manhandling you prior to stashing you in the cupboard. I don't suppose chummy asked Liz Striker her permission.'

'Probably not,' Sally conceded. 'But I'm only prepared to take role play so far, you know. How do we know he didn't kill her in the stock room?' Sally asked, wiping her hands.

'No room,' Maxwell said. 'By leaning forward I could touch the back wall. The only possibility is if she'd been looking into the cupboard when chummy struck. And I don't think that's likely.'

'Why not?'

'Because the door would be in the way. That's not a conventional width. It's too narrow. Chummy might hit the door frame in his exuberance and miss his mark completely.'

Sally Greenhow looked up at Peter Maxwell. 'You know, Max,' she said, 'you're either bloody good at this or you're a prize bull-shitter. I can't make up my mind which. Are you seriously saying you can't lift me up?'

'Seriously,' Maxwell nodded. 'But then I am eighty-eight years old with a dicky ticker and three artificial hips so it's hardly surprising. Do we know what Liz Striker weighed?'

'Why is grass?' Sally countered. 'Honestly, Max, you do pose some imponderables.'

'Ah, it's the philosopher in me. The police would know.'

'You aren't going to break into their incident room, please God!'

'No,' Maxwell said. 'It's manned twenty-four hours. We'll just have to ask somebody in the St Bede crowd. In the meantime, let's make the assumption that chummy couldn't lift her either. So . . .'

He grabbed Sally's wrists and began dragging her along the corridor.

'Ow!'

'Ssh!' Maxwell hissed. 'You're supposed to be dead.'

'Much more of this and I will be. Ow!'

'Right.' Maxwell had hauled her to the stock room. 'If that's how chummy got her here, he'd still have to lift her to put her in there.'

'Which means?' Sally was on her feet again. The experience of the floor was altogether too chilling.

'Which means that depending on Liz's weight, we're looking for a strong bloke.'

'Or woman.'

'Woman?'

'Why, Maxie,' Sally grinned, 'it's very sexist of you to assume that our man is a man, if you follow me.'

'I'll follow you anywhere, Mrs Greenhow. Now, that's enough sleuthing for one night. Come on. You can see me to my room. I'm afraid of the dark.'

'We all are, Max,' Sally said, suddenly very cold at that hour, in that place. 'We all are.'

CHAPTER 7

Monday morning brought the sun again. Inspector McBride had missed Peter Maxwell who had in turn missed breakfast. At her door in the wee wee hours, Sally Greenhow had decided to tackle the Luton lot on what they knew. She'd start, over breakfast, with Alan Harper-Bennet. Maxwell would have a go at the St Bede's contingent. It didn't take Sally three guesses to ponder who he'd start with, or, to quote Maxwell, with whom he'd start.

But John McBride pulled rank and got Gary Leonard to open Maxwell's room, just to see if he'd really gone. He hadn't. Despite the fact that Maxwell had been seen driving off into the morning with Mrs King, his bags were still there, and his underwear. And briefly, before an unhappy Gary Leonard relocked the door, Inspector McBride had noticed, on Maxwell's wall, what for all the world looked like part of an incident room. Maxwell was trying to solve Liz Striker's murder by himself.

Sally Greenhow made two mistakes that morning. She tackled Alan Harper-Bennet first and when she finally escaped, some hours later, it was to collide with Valerie Marks somewhere in the labyrinth of corridors that led to the sauna.

'Sally, have you got a minute?' she asked.

'Well, I—'

'Coffee? Let me show you my room.'

'Well, actually—'

But Valerie Marks could be surprisingly persuasive in the leading by the elbow department and Sally found herself sitting primly in the room of the Head of Business Studies from Richard de Clare.

'Did I understand you correctly when you said you were married?' she asked as she busied herself with the kettle and the milk sachets.

'That's right,' Sally said breezily, toying for a moment with confirming it by adding 'to a man'. But she thought better of it and settled for reminding Valerie that she took her coffee black.

'Do you happen to know,' the herring-bone suited woman pointed a plastic spoon at her, 'if Rachel King is married?'

'Rachel? Er . . . divorced, I think.'

'Ah, I wondered,' and she rummaged for the sugar packets.

'Er . . . no sugar, thanks.' Sally craned round to see that the old girl wasn't trying to slip her a Mickey Finn in order to have her wicked way with her. 'Why . . . er . . . why do you ask?'

Valerie Marks turned to face her and smiled. 'No, dear,' she said, 'I'm not making a play for her. Or for you, so you can breathe again. What I didn't choose to broadcast from the podium the other day when we were all ice-breaking is that I have been living very happily with Joan Clark for nearly twenty-five years. Of course, there's nothing formal because this isn't, thank God, America, but we'll have a quiet little do come October, to celebrate our silver. Sally, you've gone quite crimson.'

'Oh, Valerie,' she said, 'I'm so sorry, I feel . . . well, I feel ridiculous.'

'Don't worry, dear.' The older woman patted the girl's hand. 'Here's your coffee. No, I'm used to it. "Old Dyke", "Butch Cassidy", I've heard them all. Children are very perceptive, aren't they? And very cruel. Now, about Rachel King . . .'

'I don't really know her,' Sally said. 'Maxwell does.'

'Ah, yes, I thought I recognised a certain frisson there.'

'They were lovers once . . . Oh, God!'

'Don't worry.' Valerie shook her head, smiling. 'You haven't betrayed him. It's not actually Rachel I'm concerned with, but her husband.'

'Her husband?'

'She didn't say she had one, did she? On the podium during ice-breaking?'

'No. She did mention a daughter, though . . .'

'She struck me as rather more conventional than that.'

'Than what?' Sally asked.

'Than to have a child out of wedlock. I got the impression she was particularly organised. To the point of scheming, in fact. I can't really imagine Rachel allowing her passions to get the better of her.'

'I'm sorry, Valerie,' Sally was searching for a soothing ciggie, 'I'm not very with it this morning. Why are you asking me about Rachel?'

'Well, it's such a small world, isn't it? If indeed I'm thinking of the same person. When I lived in Park Villas, Erdington — Joan and I moved last year — our next-door neighbour was a Jeremy King. Nice bloke. Charming wife. Three delightful children. We got to know them quite well. And one night, I'll never forget it, Jeremy had had a few I suppose, over dinner, and he told me about his first wife. She was unstable. Accused him of beating her, whereas in fact you couldn't imagine a kinder, more gentle soul. He'd divorced her after she tried to blackmail him. Her name was Rachel. Still, it couldn't be the same one, could it?'

* * *

Rachel King drove Peter Maxwell to the ancient town of Rye. On the way, he bored her to death with the town's history.

But she found herself loving the lilt of his voice and chuckling at his wisecracks as they drove, the roof of her Suzuki down and the wind in their hair.

It was quarter to ten as she found a lucky parking space and they heard the gilded quarterboys chiming their cherubic hammers on the bells of St Mary's. Maxwell gave Rachel his best Barry Fitzgerald and they found a coffee place with a terrace overlooking the sparkling brown waters of the Tillingham. Maxwell ordered.

'I don't believe it,' she said. 'How can you possibly remember apple strudel after all these years?'

'Ah, that's not all.' He smiled at her. 'Let's see, now. You had a pony called Tallulah, a dog called Gelert. And didn't you have a pet spider?'

'Georgina had the spider.'

'Georgina!' Maxwell slapped his forehead. 'How could I have forgotten little sister George?'

'Well, I do my best to,' Rachel laughed. 'She's a granny now.'

'Little Georgie a granny?' Maxwell looked agonised. 'Have you a loaded revolver in that handbag, Mrs King? I must put myself out of my misery.'

The young thing who brought their coffee and strudels grinned stupidly at them, not quite believing that some silly old duffer and his wife could have anything left to laugh at after all the years they'd obviously been together.

'Thank you for this, Max,' Rachel said, pouring for them both.

'Wait till you've tasted it first,' Maxwell advised. 'They've been a little over-zealous, I think, with the cinnamon.'

'No, I mean, taking me out of Carnforth. It was beginning to resemble the Chateau d'If.'

'That bad?'

He saw her smile freeze a little and that funny little frown he'd almost forgotten played around her eyes.

'What's the matter, Rachel?' he asked, putting the milk down.

'I'm afraid, Max,' she said, smiling again. 'I'm so afraid.'

He took both her hands, burning one of his on the coffee pot. 'Shit!' he hissed. 'Why?'

'Liz Striker is dead and you ask me that?'

'No, I'm sorry. I mean, why specifically? Do you think there's a maniac loose at Carnforth?'

'Isn't there?' she asked him. 'Isn't anybody who can do that to another human being a maniac?'

'Yes,' he admitted, 'I suppose so. But don't worry. Lightning doesn't strike twice in the same place, you know.'

'No.' She tried to smile again. 'Unless the storm isn't over, that is.'

'The storm?'

'I thought you were going home today,' she said, freeing her hands to drink her coffee.

'So did I,' he nodded, tackling the second mouthful of the strudel. 'I changed my mind.'

'Why?'

'I don't know. Perhaps because . . . because I don't want to be a prime suspect.'

'You?'

'Oh, yes. It was made perfectly clear to me by Warren of the Yard that if I left he'd have me in the frame.'

'He said that?'

'He didn't have to. I know the way the police mind works, Rachel.' Maxwell restirred his coffee. He'd got a sneaky feeling she'd shortchanged him with the sugar lumps. 'It's the way they drive the lighted matches under your fingernails, loop your foreskin to the door handle, things like that.'

'Oh, Max,' and she swiped him with her napkin. 'Well, whatever, I'm glad you're staying.'

'Me too,' he said. 'Me too. Now, to cases. How heavy do you think Liz Striker was?'

He saw that frown again. 'How heavy was she? What a peculiar question.'

'Just humour an old man,' he said.

'Well, all right. Er . . . let's see. She was about five two, I suppose. Thick-set, though. She still wore her hair long as though it were the '60s . . . I'd say she was about nine stone. Why?'

He checked the other tables on the verandah to make sure that no one in earshot wore a tall pointed hat or had a tall, pointed head. 'I've been making a few enquiries of my own,' he said, in his best Jack Warner. 'Chummy would have had to have carried or dragged Liz depending on his relative strength to her relative weight.'

'A dead weight, of course.' Rachel was carried along with Maxwell's reasoning.

'Exactly. If he lifted nine stone with no help at all, he's likely to be Arnold Schwarzenegger's big brother. If, on the other hand, he dragged her . . .'

'There'd be blood on the floor.'

'Precisely.' It was Maxwell's turn to frown. 'You're better at this than I am.'

'Not really.' She poured them both another coffee. 'It's just . . . well, I've tried to imagine how it was. How it must have been. For Liz, I mean. She must have been getting some photocopying done.'

'Really?'

'There's nothing else in that section of the basement.'

'How do you know?'

'I checked.'

Maxwell's senses were beginning to reel. Suddenly, there were two amateur sleuths at the Carnforth Centre. It wasn't the upstaging that bothered him. It was something else. Something he couldn't explain. Couldn't give a name to. But it caused a pricking in his thumbs. 'Did you?' he asked her.

'Max . . .' She searched for the words. 'How can I say this? Liz Striker was a colleague of mine. More than that, a friend. Oh, not a good one, I'll grant you. I'm not going to pretend we were bosom pals now the poor woman's dead. But I did work with her. I feel I owe her something, that's all.'

'Does Jordan Gracewell feel the same way?'

'Jordan? I don't know. Why?'

'What about Michael Wynn?'

'Ah.' A smile crossed her lips as she took the cup in both hands. 'Michael's a real family man. Not to mention a pillar of the establishment. Chairman of Rotary, all that guff. Our Principal's going next year. Barring miracles, Michael will take over at St Bede's. That's good for us all.'

'I wish I could be so up about headmasters. Mine's a callow youth with a timetable for a heart.'

'Ah, the new breed,' she laughed.

'Tell me about Jordan,' he said.

'Jordan? What's to tell?'

'Anything you can.'

'Max,' Rachel put her cup down, 'what's all this about? You're not serious about your own enquiries, are you?'

'Why not? You are.'

'I told you my reasons,' she said. There was suddenly a harshness about her, an edge he'd forgotten. Then it came flooding back. It was the first time they'd gone out together, walking in that grubby little market that permanently litters the square in Cambridge. There was an old man, he remembered, busking on the corner. He was in rags, with wild hair and swarthy face. Between discordant blasts on his mouth organ, he croaked 'Moon River' at passers-by. Maxwell had thrown him some change.

'Why did you do that?' she'd asked him.

'Well . . .' Maxwell hadn't felt inclined to explain his own humanity.

'I don't approve of begging,' she'd said.

'It's not begging,' Maxwell had told her. 'He's singing for his money.'

'Let me have your definition of singing, please,' she'd said. He hadn't liked her then. The look in her eyes, the hardness in her heart.

And for an instant, he didn't like her now. 'I'm not sure I can explain mine,' he said. 'Call it a crusade, if you like; oh, a quiet one, I'll grant you, but a crusade nonetheless. You see, murder is an affront to us all, isn't it? I think we owe it to Liz Striker to do something. And we owe it to ourselves. Now,' he sighed, glad to have got that off his chest, 'what about Jordan?'

She fluttered her hands. 'I don't know what I can tell you.'

'Has he ever made advances to you?'

She almost dropped her cup. 'Advances?' she laughed. 'Max, I don't know whether you've noticed, but Jordan Gracewell has this peculiar little habit of wearing his collar back to front. He is a Catholic priest.'

'So was Thomas Wolsey, but it didn't stop him having at least seven children.'

'Wasn't that rather a long time ago?' She raised an eyebrow.

'To me,' Maxwell chuckled, 'it was yesterday. No, I'm serious.'

'Well, no, of course not.' So was she. 'I'd have noticed.'

He flicked his fingers and ordered more coffee.

'You know something, Peter Maxwell, you are an imperious bastard.' She shook her head, smiling.

'I know,' he beamed. 'You wouldn't have me any other way.'

'I'd like to,' she said.

'What?'

'Have you. Any way you like.'

'Rachel . . .' He was blinking at her, whether with the sun or the suddenness of her suggestion, he wasn't sure.

'Well,' she said, her gaze falling, 'perhaps not a good idea.'

'No.' He reached out for her hand. 'No, it's . . . it's the best idea I've heard for a long time. It's just that . . . well, I am a little rusty.'

She smirked at him, like a schoolgirl again. 'A little WD40 should take care of that,' she said. Then she rapped his knuckles with her spoon. 'But that comes later, you disgusting old man. You've already lured me away from this morning's session. I really must be at this afternoon's. I'm working with Dr Moreton.'

'Who?'

'Head of Science at the John Bunyan.'

'Oh, the Luton lot.'

'Quite. He's rather dishy, don't you think?'

Maxwell could barely picture him. 'Not my type,' he shrugged. 'Am I paying?'

'You certainly are, Sir Galahad,' and she watched him rummage for his change. 'By the way, what on earth prompted you to ask if Jordan Gracewell had made a pass at me?'

'Hmm?' He looked up at her from examining the fluff from his pockets. 'Oh, nothing. It's just that he thinks you killed Liz Striker.'

* * *

By the time Maxwell and Rachel drove back into the sweeping drive at the Carnforth Centre, the paparazzi were there in force. Whenever he saw a clutch of them together, they reminded him inexorably of the rats in Browning — grave old plodders, gay young friskers — following a story for their lives. They swarmed around Rachel King's car as though she were the latest arrival at a Car Boot.

'Are you staying here?' one of them asked her.

'Did you know the dead woman?'

'Why haven't the police let you all go?'

Rachel had never been subjected to this before, but Maxwell had. He leaned across as far as his seat belt would allow and smiled his gappy engaging grin. 'You're quite right to be excited about GNVQ,' he said. 'We at the chalk face think it's a pretty exciting time too. Can't wait to put it into practice, via our team critique.'

'And you are . . . ?' One of the spottier ones pointed a biro at him.

'Incredibly pissed off by the appalling standards of journalism in this great country of ours.'

'Oh, ha,' the spotty youth sneered. 'I'd like your name.'

'I'm sure you would,' Maxwell beamed, 'and my IQ and word-power, I shouldn't wonder, not to mention my taste in bow-ties.' He saw the lad's bemused face and took pity on him. 'All right,' he said, straight-faced, 'John Patten, rather tenuously Secretary of State for Education. Drive on, chauffeuse.'

And Rachel put her foot down.

* * *

'Bastards!' John McBride shook his head, staring out from the lowered blinds of the Trevelyan Suite. 'When the guv'nor gets back, there'll be hell to pay. If I find the shit who leaked all this to the press . . .'

'You can't keep a murder under wraps, sir,' WPC O'Halloran told him. She thought it was something the Inspector ought to have known already.

He looked at her. She was right, of course. Repulsively Christian. Done a lot of work with deprived kids on council estates, that sort of thing, but right, nevertheless. 'Who's waiting?' he asked.

'Michael George Wynn, St Bede's School'

'Right. Bring us two teas, Mavis, in . . .' he checked his watch, 'five minutes.'

'Yes, sir.'

Michael George Wynn sat in the incident room annexe, the sunlight slanting in through the slats to gild his pepper and salt beard. He'd been chatting about this and that with DS Dunn. They'd found common ground in the same golf handicap, so that whiled away the time that McBride kept them both waiting. The Inspector always did this. Any one of the Carnforth guests was a suspect. And waiting rattled them. Even the innocent ones.

'Right.' McBride entered with a brusqueness that even made Dunn jump. 'Mr Wynn, I'm sorry to have kept you waiting.' He nodded at the Sergeant, who flicked on the machinery. 'Interview commenced eleven thirty-eight, Mr Michael Wynn, in the presence of DS Dunn and myself, DI McBride.'

DI McBride sat down opposite the Deputy Principal of St Bede's. 'You knew the dead woman?' he asked.

'Yes, I did,' Wynn nodded.

'For how long?'

'Ooh, let's see. Nine, no . . . ten years.'

'In what capacity?'

'She was a colleague at the school where I teach.'

'That's St Bede's School, Bournemouth?'

'Yes.'

'What did you know about her?'

'Liz? Well, it's difficult to know where to start. She was a warm, genuine person. Do anything for anyone type. She's a great loss. I mean, any human being is, but Liz in particular. As far as St Bede's goes, literally irreplaceable.'

'Not the sort of woman to have made enemies, then?' McBride asked.

'Lord, no. Oh, except among the kids, maybe.'

'The kids?'

'Inspector, you must understand — as a policeman you're dealing with warped psychology every day. I don't know how many thousands of children would have passed through Liz's hands in her career. But the odds are, she'll have crossed some of them. You know how it is. As a teacher, you're responsible for discipline. So you catch some kid misbehaving and you castigate him or her. Ninety-nine times out of a hundred, that's the end of the matter. But that hundredth time . . . well, that's the oddball.'

'The psychopath?' Dunn asked.

Wynn smiled. 'It sounds a little ludicrous stated as baldly as that, doesn't it? But essentially, yes, you're right. So you find your tyres slashed the next morning or your office vandalised or a rather colourful thumbnail sketch sprayed on the back wall of the Sports Hall. It's usually harmless.'

'But in this case it wasn't,' McBride reminded him. 'Are you seriously telling us that a child did this? Battered his teacher to death?'

There was a knock at the door and Mavis O'Halloran stood there with a tray of teacups. Dunn waved her in.

'A child, no,' Wynn went on, 'but children have this infuriating habit of growing up, Inspector. The boy becomes a man. The girl a woman. As far as I know, it's been like that since Adam was a lad'

'That's an interesting idea, Mr Wynn,' McBride narrowed his eyes against the steam of his tea, 'the possibility that someone on this course is a former pupil of Mrs Striker's. But she'd know them, surely?'

'Perhaps she did,' Wynn shrugged, stirring his tea slowly. 'We'd only been here a couple of hours. Perhaps she hadn't had a chance to mention it to anybody.'

'Yes, Mavis?' McBride snapped. The woman was standing there with an empty tray as though waiting for a tip.

'Er . . . the warrants have just come through, sir. I thought, in the absence of the DCI, you'd want to know.'

'Yes,' McBride said quickly. 'Thank you. That will be all.'

Wynn found himself smiling as the girl left.

'Something strike you as amusing, Mr Wynn?' the Inspector asked.

'Interesting rather than amusing,' Wynn said, 'the way in which professions work. I'm not sure I could get away with such blatant sexism in my line. At St Bede's, I usually end up making the tea.'

McBride's face darkened. He didn't like Michael Wynn. He didn't like Michael Wynn any more than he liked Peter Maxwell. They were both the sort who ought to report to the station every week for a damned good smacking. He flicked the intercom switch in front of him. 'Mavis,' he said, 'would I be horribly sexist if I asked you to bring in another sugar lump . . . dear?'

And Michael Wynn chortled anew.

* * *

The pool was empty except for Sally Greenhow. Her backstroke needed work, but it was competent and she trailed through the blue water under the dim lights. Her body looked blue and irregular with the refraction at the water's surface and she came up for air before she touched the side.

Something made her turn. She couldn't say what. It may have been a coat falling in the cloakroom, something like that. But it echoed and re-echoed as small sounds do in an empty, vaulted chamber like a swimming pool. Unlike Peter Maxwell, she wasn't a film buff, but she'd seen one film on telly when she was a child that had frightened her badly and it rushed back to her now. It was a black and white B feature and she couldn't remember who was in it, but the heroine was being driven insane by the baddies and her father's body kept popping up at various points around the spooky old family home. It was the scene in the garden pool that terrified her most. The old boy just sitting there, his long hair streaming out with the weeds in the current, his dead, sightless eyes staring ahead. She shuddered to wipe the picture from her mind and climbed out quickly.

For a moment, she stood dripping by the poolside. The feeling that someone was watching her grew stronger. She looked left. She looked right. No one. The only light came from the pool and from the changing area. She felt her heart thump and saw her breasts heaving under the flimsy bikini top. She walked quickly back to where she'd left her clothes, splashing through the footbath as she went, swinging her head to spray the surplus water from her hair.

She was just reaching for her towel when she heard it again.

'Who's there?' Her voice was stronger than she hoped. 'Who is it?'

'Sally?'

Sally Greenhow relaxed, her shoulders hunching as her heart descended from her mouth. 'Max, you utter bastard!' she hissed.

A bow-tie and braces came round the corner with Peter Maxwell inside them.

'What the devil are you doing here?' he asked her, his voice booming with the echo.

'Skiing,' she said, rubbing the towel through her hair. 'That and shitting myself. Do you always spy on girls in swimming pools?'

'Every chance I can get,' he beamed. 'Sally? You're really frightened.'

'Oh, piss off, Max,' she snapped.

'Later. At the moment, I need to know how it went with the Luton lot this morning.'

'It's . . .' Sally looked at her wet wrist. 'Oh, bugger . . .'

'Nearly half-past ten,' Maxwell helped her out. 'I'm in rather a hurry, I've been summoned to the presence.'

'The presence?'

'McBride sent a rather homely policewoman to ask me to accompany her to the incident room. I said I was busy and would be along shortly.'

'Well, it's too complicated to tell you in a couple of minutes, Max. Trot off to see the constabulary while I change and . . . oh, God.'

'What's the matter?'

'My knickers have gone.'

'What?'

'My knickers. Max, you aren't playing silly buggers, are you?'

Maxwell looked shocked. 'I can honestly say, hand on heart, I have never touched a lady's knickers without obtaining her express permission first.'

'But they're gone.' Sally frowned. 'I left them here.' She riffled through the clothes. 'Everything else is here. Except the knickers.'

'Well, well.'

'Things are far from well, Maxie.' Sally was biting her lower lip, fumbling for her specs. 'Can we go? Can we go tomorrow? I don't like it here.'

'Perhaps it wasn't very sensible,' Maxwell was as serious as the girl now, 'to swim alone. At this time of night. Did anybody know you'd be here?'

'No . . . oh, wait. I may have mentioned it to Valerie Marks.'

'Ah, of Richard de Clare.'

'Now, that's unkind, Max,' Sally scolded him. 'She's just rather . . . butch, that's all. Anyway, even lesbians don't go around pinching underwear.'

'Ah,' Maxwell passed Sally her watch, 'what a little innocent.'

'Will you please bugger off so I can get at least partially dressed?'

'Oh, right . . .' and he padded off. 'Will you be all right? Getting to your room, I mean?'

'I'll be fine,' she told him, but she didn't convince herself.

'See you when I can, then,' he called. 'You'll be awake?'

'Oh, yes,' she promised, 'but make your intentions clear, because I'll have a shotgun under my pillow.'

'That's my girl!' He winked at her.

And she watched his shadow move huge and silent across the wall and around the corner.

* * *

Inspector McBride interrupted Head of Sixth Form Maxwell on his way to the Trevelyan Suite. McBride was tired after four days cooped up in the same four walls. He needed air. He needed space. So he took Maxwell out on to the roof garden that gave off the bar. There was no one out here and McBride relaxed enough to allow Maxwell to buy him a drink.

'Boddingtons, I think you said.' Maxwell put the golden glass down on the white enamel table. 'Lovely night for May, Inspector.'

It was. A full complement of stars studded the heavens, yet, curiously, nothing was right with the world.

'I did.' McBride took a sip. 'I also said a half, but what the hell. Your very good health, Mr Maxwell.'

'And yours, Mr McBride.' The Head of Sixth Form raised his Southern Comfort. 'They're out of peanuts, I'm afraid.'

'They're bad for you,' McBride assured him.

'So,' Maxwell perched on the rail that ran the length of the building, 'how's it all going, then?'

'I hoped you might tell me,' McBride said.

'Come again?'

The Inspector got up and leaned with both arms on the rail. At the edge of the floodlit grounds, the nightwatch of the newsmen stood smoking. 'Love 'em or hate 'em,' he said, 'they're always there. Like sharks in the bloody water.'

Maxwell nodded. Well, well, the rozzer was a lyricist too. 'Tell me,' he leaned to his man, 'are you still on duty?'

'No,' McBride said. 'I should have gone home three hours ago.'

'I hope you have an understanding wife,' Maxwell smiled.

'Cath? Oh, yes.' McBride smiled too. 'It's in policemen's wedding vows. Didn't you know? Their wives promise to love, honour, obey and not mind about the hours.'

Maxwell laughed.

'The rumour is, Mr Maxwell,' McBride had become all confidential, 'that you are something of an amateur detective.'

'Me?' Maxwell frowned. 'Whoever gave you that idea?'

'Oh, a snippet here and there.' McBride was non-committal. He wasn't about to tell Maxwell he'd got Gary Leonard to break into his room. 'Which puts us in a rather awkward position.'

'When you say "us",' Maxwell checked, 'who do you mean exactly?'

'You and I,' McBride told him.

Maxwell decided to overlook the lapse of grammar. 'How so?' he asked.

'Well, to be frank, you could be useful.'

'What, listening at keyholes, you mean?'

'Nothing that unsubtle, Mr Maxwell. I wouldn't insult your intelligence. But people might say things to you they wouldn't say to us, if you get my drift.'

'All right,' Maxwell nodded. 'So long as I'm content to play — excuse the rather unpleasant phraseology — coppers' nark, you gain. What's the down side?'

'The down side is that your metaphorical listening at keyholes could queer everybody's pitch, so to speak.'

Metaphorical? Maxwell looked at John McBride in a slightly new light. Perhaps you didn't get to be a Detective Inspector before you were thirty for nothing after all. 'So your message to me tonight is . . . ?'

McBride finished his drink. 'Lay off.' The voice was harsh, the eyes cold. 'Whatever you think you know, forget it. This isn't a Miss Marple, Mr Maxwell. This is real. Leave it to the professionals.' He put his glass down loudly on the metal table. 'Am I getting through?'

'Yarc, yarc,' said Maxwell.

'You what?' McBride frowned at him.

'West Point slang, apparently. Brown-nosers among the cadets who sit at the front in lectures, agreeing with the lecturer — YARC — "You're absolutely right, commander!" Good night, Mr McBride.'

CHAPTER 8

Maxwell padded down Sally Greenhow's corridor at a little after midnight. As he turned into it, he'd seen the lighted cigarettes of the paparazzi dogwatch darting like fireflies in the trees that ringed Carnforth's entrance way. A police car dithered at the gates then swung left before any of the newshounds were awake enough to give chase. Inspector McBride going home at last.

Maxwell knocked three times and whispered low. 'You and I,' he muttered, 'were sent by Joe.'

'What?' a bewildered voice called from inside.

'It's me, Sally,' Maxwell hissed. 'Old Grey Eyes is back.'

She opened the door a crack then hauled him inside. 'Where the fuck have you been?' she demanded.

'Ssh.' Maxwell held a finger to lips. 'The neighbours.'

'Sod the neighbours.' Sally was in a pink housecoat and had a towel wrapped around her head. 'I'd just about given you up.'

'Not for dead, I hope. Sorry.' He flopped into her armchair, flicking aside the curtains to check the grounds again. 'Inspector McBride was chatty.'

'Really?' She rummaged in her bag. 'I'd got him pegged as a surly bastard. You don't deserve this,' and she brandished a bottle at him.

'Ah,' his eyes lit up, 'Chateau Carnforth. A '43 by its label, not too presumptuous in its precociousness.'

'It's actually bottled for Tesco,' she said, yanking out the cork with her Special Needs Department bottle-opener, 'and if it's older than last Christmas, I'll vote Conservative.'

'Ah,' Maxwell smiled, 'now, there's a rash statement. Found your knickers?'

'No.' She poured for them both. 'I don't think there's much point in letting this breathe — it looks as if it's been on an iron lung for weeks. Cheers.'

'Here's looking at you, kid!' and he took a gulp. It didn't mix well with Southern Comfort, but he wasn't enough of a cad to say so. 'Here's to crime.'

'What did McBride want?'

'To warn me off, basically,' Maxwell told her, loosening his bow-tie.

'Off what?'

'Aren't they the water authorities watchdog?'

'Maxwell,' Sally growled. All in all, she felt she'd gone through enough today.

'Sorry.' He beamed his most endearing beam. 'The case, dear heart. He warned me off the case. Called me Miss Marple at one point.'

'That's ridiculous,' Sally said, lolling on the bed. 'You must be twice Joan Hickson's age.'

'Thank you, seat of my desires,' he grinned acidly. 'But to more important matters. The Luton lot.'

'Ah, yes . . .' Sally jerked her bum forward and reached for the Former Yugoslavian red again. 'Well, "lot" is a rather, shall we say, plural way of putting it.'

'Oh?'

'I began with Alan Harper-Bennet.'

'And?'

Sally wasn't inclined to tell Maxwell about Valerie Marks knowing Rachel. Anyway, it was rather a long shot. It wasn't likely to be the same woman. And she wasn't sure how Maxwell would react to the news. Better let sleeping Heads of Sixth Form lie. 'I got no further. I sat by him at breakfast, intending to sneak in a few searching questions and go on to someone else, Dr Moreton, perhaps. Or Phyllida Bowles. Anyway, Mr Harper-Bennet had other ideas.'

'Fancied you, did he?'

'In an oblique sort of way, yes. It's never happened to you, Max, so you wouldn't understand.'

'Oh, thanks.' Maxwell looked hurt and outraged at the same time. 'That's not altogether true, you know. I've had my flings, sown my oats and other metaphors.'

'No, I don't mean that.' She hunted for her ciggies. 'I mean. . . well, it wasn't me Harper-Bennet fancied, but my body.'

Maxwell looked blank. 'I thought the two were inseparable,' he said. 'He's not likely to fancy your mind, is he?'

It was Sally's turn to look hurt.

'No,' Maxwell knew a raw nerve when he saw one, 'I didn't mean that disparagingly. God, I'd kill for an MEd.'

'Liar!' she threw at him. 'What I meant was that men like Harper-Bennet treat you as a sex object. I got the impression he'd be equally happy with my . . . Oh, God . . .'

'Panties?' Maxwell was way ahead of her.

Sally nodded. 'It had to be,' she said. 'Oh, Jesus,' and she fumbled to light her cigarette. 'The thought of that pallid bastard sneaking into the pool changing-rooms . . .'

'Yes, yes.' Maxwell could be an insensitive bastard at times. This was one of them, dismissing the girl's sense of outrage with a double positive and a swig of wine. 'Now, let's share a few facts. How did the Luton lot get here?'

'Moreton, Phyllida Bowles and Gregory Trant came in the school minibus. Apparently, they've got another one for school teams and so on. And they needed it to bring all their presentation equipment, not realizing that they had all the hardware here at Carnforth anyway.'

'And Harper-Bennet?'

'Brought his car.'

Maxwell flicked aside the curtains again to view the line of vehicles parked under the artificial light. 'Do we know what he drives?'

'No.' Sally blew smoke to the ceiling. 'But I'll lay you odds he's got my knickers in his boot.'

'What time did they arrive on the Thursday?' Maxwell asked.

'Harper-Bennet was here first. The others hit a lot of traffic on the M25.'

'As you do,' Maxwell nodded. 'What did Harper-Bennet do?'

'Found his room.'

'Which is?'

'Oh, yes,' Sally nodded, nostrils flaring to cope with the smoke, 'he made damn sure I knew that. 58 — on the first floor.'

'What were his movements after that?'

'It got a bit difficult then, Max,' Sally said. 'For a start, we were supposed to be initiating change in our respective establishments and had to persuade recalcitrant old bastards like you of the need for GNVQ, and secondly, Harper-Bennet was doing his best to look at my tits.'

'Is there a Mrs Harper-Bennet?' Maxwell asked, out of curiosity.

'There is not. Who'd have him?'

'Who indeed?' Maxwell was elsewhere.

'Mr Maxwell,' Sally said slowly, 'a look of inscrutability has appeared on your otherwise benign features. What's going on in that febrile brain?'

'Ah,' Maxwell smiled, 'if only we could answer that. Try this for size. Alan Harper-Bennet is a weirdo. Into ladies' undies in a mammoth way. Perhaps he has a collection at home in Luton — well, I don't suppose there's much else to do there, really. He makes a habit of adding to the collection whenever he can. He probably got yours today. Did he try to get Liz Striker's last Thursday? Did she object? Put up a struggle? Did he panic and kill her?'

'It's a bit thin, Max,' Sally said. 'Surely, if that's the case, she'd have died in her room, wouldn't she?'

'Not necessarily.' Maxwell said. 'You see, I can't help thinking that Liz died because she knew something.'

'What?'

'I said—'

'No.' Sally shook her head in irritation. 'I mean, what did she know?'

'Ah,' Maxwell's finger was in the air, 'the sixty-four thousand dollar question. If we knew that, we'd have chummy in the frame.'

'How did you make out — no, let me rephrase that — what did you learn from Rachel?'

'Oh, Christ!' Maxwell looked at his watch and gulped down his wine. 'Not a lot, really. Listen, we'll do a swap tomorrow. I'll tackle Phyllida Bowles. You have a go at Michael Wynn.'

'Max,' Sally stood up with him, 'I want to go home tomorrow. Remember?'

He looked at the frightened face under the pink towel, slightly flushed with the wine. He patted her cheek. 'Sally,' he said, 'the day before yesterday you were all set for me to solve this thing. I can't do that if I'm not here.'

'That was then,' she said, 'before . . .'

'Before Alan Harper-Bennet swiped your knickers.'

'Quite.'

He leaned forward and kissed her on the forehead. 'Well, we'll see,' he said. 'I can catch a train, you know, if you want to go. Let's see what the morning brings, shall we?'

And he left her to lock the door firmly behind him.

* * *

It was late. Hustling past the rubber plant at the top of the stairs, he crashed as quietly as he could through the fire-doors and down to the next floor. He caught himself a nasty one on the fire extinguisher on the corner, and then, he was there.

Outside Room 215. He knocked once. Twice. God alone knew what emotions ran through Peter Maxwell's mind as he waited there. He felt like a fumbling student again, in those pre-permissive days of the early '60s, when it was all Elvis and John Leyton and strawberries at Grantchester and the plop of punt poles on the Cam. Her face hadn't changed. Her laugh. The easy way she had with her. But she was older. Christ, he was older. There'd been no grey hair then, no side-whiskers. He'd still been trim from seven years of rugger and cricket. He'd only recently discovered Southern Comfort. What was he doing here? It could be a disaster. But he knocked again, his heart thumping.

No answer. Maxwell checked his watch in the stillness of the corridor. It was nearly half-past twelve, for God's sake. Earlier, they'd made their tryst for midnight. But Maxwell had let this wretched Liz Striker business intervene. He'd put it first. But it wasn't the case, was it? Not really. It was his own inflated ego, that was all. Well, he was paying for it now. Rachel was obviously asleep.

Maxwell quietly drove his forehead silently against the door frame. What an idiot! Still, he'd see her at breakfast and apologise. There was always tomorrow.

* * *

Tomorrow was Tuesday. Maxwell thought, as he shaved in the innermost recesses of Room 101, that he'd normally be having 10CS this morning. Some poor bastard of a supply teacher would be taking them instead. Donna would be putting her lipstick on, Stacey would be doing her hair — or Carla's as the mood took her. Ronnie would be tackling his sandwiches about now. And in front of this hidden curriculum, they were supposed to be discussing the Bay of Pigs. Well, well. Perhaps GNVQ at Carnforth had its attractions after all. One of them was lying in. Maxwell had been doggo after his shower and it was only the sound of cars on the gravel under his window that woke him up.

He chose the spotted tie this morning — the one he told everybody had been given to him by Sir Robin Day in exchange for a few interviewing tips — and padded down in his brothel-creepers to face the world. But there was no one in the Hadleigh Suite. A few scattered pieces of toast and half-finished coffees gave it an aura of the Marie Celeste. Even the red-faced woman who doled out the scrambled eggs had vanished. Maxwell nearly looked out of the window to see if the lifeboats had gone.

'Mr Maxwell?' A female voice made him turn. It was WPC O'Halloran, grim-faced, tired-looking.

'Good morning, my dear,' Maxwell said.

'Everybody's in the Whittingham Suite. Shall we?'

'By all means,' Maxwell said and a difficult few seconds of protocol followed, during which she eventually let him go first.

Everybody was indeed in the Whittingham Suite. They all seemed to be gabbling at once, like the elect crowd invited to the BAFTA award ceremonies they persisted in showing every year on the telly — loads of luvvies congratulating each other while secretly hating everybody's guts. The only one Maxwell couldn't see was Rachel. Perhaps she'd slept in. A rather ashen-faced Inspector McBride stood on the dais at the front, flanked by assorted heavies in and out of uniform. For all it was a Tuesday morning, clearly in shift hours, McBride wore neither tie nor jacket. Something, as Sherlock Holmes might have said, was clearly afoot.

Maxwell sat at the back. He had no hope of reaching Sally Greenhow, flanked as she was by Alan Harper-Bennet on one side and Valerie Marks on the other. Margot Jenkinson moved her bag for him.

'Have I missed the main feature?' Maxwell whispered to her.

'I don't know what's going on,' she said. 'We were all summoned from breakfast. I'd kill for a bit of toast. Camel?' She poked a cigarette packet under Maxwell's nose.

'No thanks.' He waved them aside, unsure whether to smoke them or ride them.

'Ladies and gentlemen . . .' McBride cleared his throat. 'I apologise for calling you together like this.'

Maxwell noticed that there were Carnforth staff members in the audience too. Tracey was there, the counter and reception manned in her absence by God-knew-who; Antonio, the chef for the week, in a less than reputable off-white shirt; and the ever-up Gary Leonard, groomed, as always, to within an inch of his life. The red-faced woman peered over his shoulder.

'I am sorry to have to be the one to tell you that there has been another incident here at the centre. The body of Mrs Rachel King was found a little over half an hour ago.'

* * *

Peter Maxwell sat under one of the cedars that had stood by the road for years. Far, far longer ago than the building of the Carnforth Centre, there had been a house on this site. Three cedars had been planted then. The storm of '87 had claimed one and the branches of the second had been lopped by the council, because they drooped too low over the road.

He saw her coming, a green and stonewashed speck in the strong sunlight that still gilded the centre. He sat in the evening shadows, a little chill in his shirt-sleeves, because the heat of the day was not yet that great, his arms outstretched, resting on his knees, like a model for a Maxfield Parrish.

'I've looked everywhere for you,' Sally said, looking down at him. She sat on the grass by his elbow. 'Max, I'm so sorry.'

'Thanks,' he said.

'I don't know what she meant to you; not really. But all the same . . .'

'That's the irony of it,' he said, staring ahead at the uniformed policemen standing in knots in the front drive, and the big, white cars, 'neither do I. Oh, once . . . Once she was everything. I couldn't open a book or turn a corner without seeing her there — her face, her hair. That musical laugh she had.'

'Max,' Sally played with the grass, afraid to look her old colleague in the face, 'it's none of my business, I know, but . . .'

'I left her,' he smiled. He looked at the frizzy-haired girl who in turn found the courage to look at him. 'Was that what you were wondering?'

Sally shook her head. 'I've no right to ask,' she said.

'No, no.' He patted her hand, and gave her his Bob Hoskins. 'No, it's good to talk. It helps. I've been on my own all day, walking the shingle, the dunes. I don't think I've ever heard the gulls cry so lonely before. Not even when Jenny . . .'

'Your wife?'

Maxwell nodded. 'No, Jenny was taken from me,' he said, 'by the chance of being in the wrong place at the wrong time. With Rachel, it was different. It was a conscious decision. I let her go.'

'Why?' Sally asked.

Maxwell chuckled. 'I'm damned if I know now. Then, when I was twenty-one and my whole life was before me . . . Well, it all seemed so different. I hadn't lived alone for twenty years then. Hadn't sent myself a big, red, India rubber ball for Christmas. Maybe if I had . . . Then, I felt trapped. How does the Bard put it? "Cabined, cribbed, confined." I felt I was being smothered, Sally. And I needed to breathe.'

'How did she take it?'

'Badly,' he remembered, watching John McBride emerge into the sunlight a hundred yards away beyond the sloping lawns. 'We'd gone for a walk along the river, by the Backs. It was an evening like this, the May Ball — which, Cambridge being Cambridge, is always held in June, of course. I'd paid a bomb for the tickets, hired a dinner jacket — I wasn't used to a bow-tie then; the damned thing was killing me. Rachel looked lovely. She'd hired a ball gown, powder blue with sparkly bits. We danced. We sang. We drank. Probably not in that order. I hadn't planned to tell her, to spoil the evening. It was magic. I could see it in her eyes. But along the Backs, just passing King's, it all came out. My pathetic sermonising. Cliches about not being right for each other, not working out. She cried. I cried. I offered to take her home . . . well, back to her digs, I mean. She wouldn't. The last I saw of her she was standing on that little bridge at King's, still lovely, still adorable . . .' His voice tailed away until Sally gripped his arm again.

'She sent me a letter,' Maxwell went on, staring ahead again. 'It was vitriolic, Sal. In all my fifty-odd years, I've still never read anything like it. She said cruel things, untrue things. Hurtful . . . I couldn't blame her.'

'Perhaps you had a lucky escape, Maxie,' she said softly.

'Oh, now,' he smiled, squeezing the hand that held his arm, 'you're not going all dewy-eyed on me, are you?'

'No,' Sally choked back the tears, 'no, you old bastard, you don't deserve it.'

'I thought you were going home today,' Maxwell said.

'Yes,' Sally sniffed, 'I thought I was too.'

'Mr Maxwell.' The voice made them both look up. It was a uniformed constable neither of them recognised. 'Mr Warren would like to see you. In the incident room.'

* * *

Chief Inspector Warren had been missing for two days. No one at Carnforth had seen him on the Monday. And now it was Tuesday evening, it seemed he'd turned up for the first time.

Maxwell was ushered into the pool of light in the incident room. He noticed what looked like the stub of one of Margot Jenkinson's Camels in the ashtray. Warren, sitting opposite him and next to John McBride, looked older. Years older.

'I don't have long, Mr Maxwell,' the Chief Inspector said, looking at his watch. 'John.'

McBride flicked the switch. 'Interview commenced nineteen eighteen between Chief Inspector Warren and Mr Peter Maxwell; Inspector McBride in attendance.'

'Mr Maxwell,' Warren began, 'you know of course that Mrs King is dead.'

'Yes.'

'What was the nature of your relationship with her?'

'We were . . . old friends.'

'Friends?' Warren checked, letting a pencil stub slide through his fingers.

'Yes,' Maxwell said.

'How old?' McBride jabbed in.

'Until this week, I hadn't seen Mrs King for nearly thirty years.'

'That's a long time,' Warren nodded, narrowing his eyes. 'Where did you know her?'

'At Cambridge,' Maxwell said. 'I was at Jesus, reading History. She was at Homerton, down the road.'

'That's a college of education?' Warren asked.

'It was then,' Maxwell told him. 'I believe it's part of the University now, affiliated in some way.'

'Did you know that Mrs King was going to be here? On this course?' McBride asked.

'No. She was Rachel Cameron when I knew her. And in any case, we weren't sent lists of personnel in advance. It wasn't until we were having coffee on the first morning that I realised who she was. Tell me, Chief Inspector, how did Rachel . . . how did Mrs King die?'

Warren flashed a glance at McBride. 'She was beaten to death,' he said flatly, with no emotion at all. 'Just like Liz Striker.'

Maxwell closed his eyes. While he was doing that, Warren looked at his watch again. 'When did you see Mrs King last?' he asked.

'Er . . . yesterday afternoon. At a session.'

Warren consulted the schedule on the desk in front of him. 'That was "Managing the Mechanics of GNVQ"?'

'Was it?' Maxwell said. 'I really couldn't tell you.'

'You were working with Mrs King?'

'No. I was with Lydia Farr. Rachel was with Dr Moreton, I believe. We'd been paired off for that particular exercise.'

'Did you not have dinner with Mrs King?' McBride asked.

'No, I'd gone for a sauna. By the time I got back, she'd been and gone, I was led to believe.'

'What time was this, sir?' McBride asked.

'The sauna? Oh, I don't know, half-six or so. I don't remember exactly.'

'What time did you get to the dining-room?' Warren asked him.

'Ooh . . . about seven fifteen, seven twenty.'

'Anyone else in the sauna?'

'I don't think so. Why?'

Stony Warren leaned forward for the first time. 'Because Mrs King didn't come into dinner last night, Mr Maxwell. While you were soaking away in the steam or tucking into your prawn cocktail, somebody was caving in the skull of an innocent person.'

Maxwell blinked. 'But . . .'

'Yes?' Warren said slowly, moving back from his man, giving him space.

'I was told she'd been in. I asked.'

'Who did you ask?' McBride snapped.

'Margot. Margot Jenkinson.'

'Ah, yes,' Warren said, glancing at McBride. 'Tell me, your . . . er . . . colleague, Sally Greenhow. Spends rather a lot of time in your room. And you in hers.'

'I beg your pardon?' If Maxwell's blood pressure had been any guide, his bow-tie should have been whizzing round by now.

'Do you really think we'd set up an incident room here and not be aware of what's going on?' McBride sneered.

'I think I shall be forced to say something about invasion of privacy shortly.' Maxwell did his best to keep his temper in check. 'Cliché though it may be.'

‘Look!’ Warren slapped the palm of his hand down on the desk so that the Camel stub flipped out of the ashtray. ‘Some bastard has demolished the skulls of two women under this fucking roof inside five days. I don’t give a tinker’s fuck about your pissing privacy.’

Warren stood up sharply, staring down at Maxwell. ‘Luckily for you, it’s not my problem any more. As of . . .’ He checked his watch again, ‘. . . three minutes ago, I handed jurisdiction of this case to Inspector McBride.’ He walked away, out of the pool of light, and Maxwell heard him cross to the door. ‘Unluckily for you,’ the Chief Inspector said, ‘Inspector McBride feels exactly the same as I do.’

The door slammed. And he was gone.

CHAPTER 9

'So what happens now?' Sally was sorting her tops.

'They'll let us go unless I miss my guess.' Maxwell was tapping the walls of Sally's room.

'Why? Why now of all times?'

'Because they've cocked it up,' Maxwell told her. 'Warren had no jurisdiction to keep us here.'

'He didn't force us,' Sally reminded him.

'He made it pretty clear he'd come down like a ton of bricks on anybody who left. I know. I was that course-leaver,' Maxwell reminded her. 'And he must at least count it a likelihood that if he hadn't done that, Rachel would be alive now.'

'Max, what are you doing?' she had to ask.

'Checking for bugs,' he told her.

'Bugs?' She stood back from her laundry pile. 'Are you serious?'

'The fuzz know I've been spending time here. They know you've visited me in my room. Stands to reason they're eavesdropping.' He yelled loudly at the lamp.

'Oh, come off it.' She clicked her tongue. 'You've seen too many Cold War movies. For a start it's illegal and secondly, it costs a bomb. Just because they know we've been cohabiting occasionally doesn't mean they've got a transcript of our conversations.'

'You're right.' Maxwell flopped into Sally's chair.

'How are you now?' she asked him. There were times when Sally Greenhow didn't just look like a little girl, she sounded like one — as a kid might enquire after somebody who'd come off his skateboard.

'I'm fine,' he told her, smiling. Sally looked as if she had troubles of her own. Maxwell wouldn't add his to hers. Anyway, he didn't know how he was. Rachel Cameron had been a long time ago. Rachel King was only four days old. You can't mourn somebody you've only known for four days. And yet. And yet . . .

'Max,' Sally said suddenly, 'I'm going tomorrow. I really am. I stayed today because . . . well, I felt I owed it to you.'

'That was kind,' Maxwell said.

'But tomorrow,' she pulled herself together, 'no more Mrs Nice Girl. As our American cousins would say, "I'm outta here."'

'As I said,' Maxwell got up, 'I think we all will be. Sally . . .'

'Hmm?'

He took her hand. 'When I've gone I want you to lock the door.' She nodded. And for an instant he thought he saw her lip tremble, but it was probably just a trick of the light.

* * *

It wasn't the best of times; it wasn't the worst of times, but Maxwell couldn't sleep anyway, so he thought he'd risk the wrath of the law a little further by paying a call on Margot Jenkinson. Her room was number 63, on that stretch of corridor where the doors were painted green. He wasn't quite sure what colour Margot Jenkinson was painted as she peered round it, but he felt quite sure Laurence Alma-Tadema would have killed for it in one of his Roman canvases, showing the blood and dust of the arena.

'Yes?' She tried to focus, no mean feat at nearly midnight when your liver and you are slowly bidding each other a fond farewell.

'Peter Maxwell, Margot. I'm sorry to inflict myself on you at this hour.'

It was the witching hour, aptly enough. Twenty-four hours since Maxwell had hovered, heart thumping, outside Rachel King's room. He'd never do that again.

'What do you want?' She was a little suspicious.

'Just a chat,' he smiled gappily. 'Are you decent?'

'The question is, are you?' she said. 'Mr Maxwell, two women have died.'

'Not by my hand,' Maxwell said. 'Please call me Max. Everybody does.'

'Well . . .' she dithered. 'All right, then, just for a while,' and she let him in.

The smell of gin hit Peter Maxwell like a wall. A pessimist would have said that the bottle of Gordon's on the dressing-table was half empty. Margot Jenkinson had a sufficiently gin-tinted outlook on life to regard it as half full.

'Drink?' she asked him.

'Why not?' Maxwell smiled.

'Oh, do have a seat.' She whipped her inappropriately named smalls off the chair. 'I've only got gin, I'm afraid. Right out of it.'

'I often feel like that,' Maxwell sighed. 'I wanted to talk to you about Rachel.'

'It's dreadful.' Margot's hand trembled a little as the bottle hit the glass. 'Just dreadful.'

'I must have misheard,' he said.

'Sorry?'

'Last night. I thought you said that Rachel came in to dinner.'

'I'm sorry,' Margot frowned, 'I thought she did. I must confess, Max, my eyes aren't what they were. I get the wobbles sometimes. I'm at a funny age, I think.'

'I have been for years,' Maxwell said.

'You knew Rachel from way back, I understand.' She passed him his drink.

'That's right.' He raised the glass to her. 'From a time before time.'

'That's very poetic, Max,' she smiled. 'Not at all like my Gerald.'

'Your Gerald?'

She waggled a gold-ringed finger at him. 'Other half. Poor dear has a drink problem, I'm afraid. Oesophageal varices the size of submarine cables. But you can't tell him. No, Gerald was never poetic. Now Michael Wynn is poetic.'

'Is he?'

'Well . . .' She looked about her, as though the Spanish Inquisition were about to spring, scarlet-coated, from the wardrobe. 'I shouldn't say this of course, but he was busy chatting up Tracey yesterday something furious.'

'Tracey?'

'The receptionist, you know. Has her make-up done by Dulux.'

'I'd got Wynn down for a family man,' Maxwell said, echoing what he remembered Rachel saying.

'Oh, he probably is. He's very proud of his children.'

'Hmm,' Maxwell nodded.

'No.' She sieved the gin through her teeth. 'I know men. Away from the nest, you're all inclined to spread your wings.'

'Maybe,' Maxwell nodded. 'But one of us has spread a little too far, wouldn't you say?'

'That depends.' Margot pursed her lips as the gin hit her tonsils.

'On what?' he asked.

'On whether you assume the devil in our midst is a man.'

'You interest me strangely,' Maxwell told her.

'I didn't assume, Max, I'd interest you any other way.'

* * *

The thought police arrived at Room 101 at seven sharp the next morning. Wednesday. Maxwell had no time to savour the fact that he would be missing Sixth Form Assembly, nor to worry what a dog's breakfast Deirdre Lessing might be going to make of it in his place. The iron fist of the Kent Constabulary hammered on all the guests' doors at the same time. It was the nearest thing to a dawn raid that Maxwell was likely to experience.

'Could you assemble in the Whittingham Suite, please, sir?' a bobby whose face he didn't know asked him. Another one barged the first aside, waving a piece of paper.

'Is it peace in our time?' Maxwell said.

The constable was unmoved by wit and had a job to do. 'I have a warrant here to search these premises,' he said.

'Do I have the right to be present?' Maxwell asked him.

'You do,' the straight-faced copper told him.

'Then I waive it,' Maxwell beamed. 'But I know exactly how much has gone from that courtesy bar,' and he wagged a finger at the officer as he padded out into the corridor.

'How exciting!' Michael Wynn joined him on the next landing. 'A pyjama party!'

Maxwell couldn't help chuckling. At least Wynn had had time to get a dressing-gown on, even if it was yellow with black spots. A similarly weird array of night attire met them en route to the Whittingham Suite. Only McBride and his heavies were properly dressed.

'I apologise, ladies and gentlemen,' the Inspector had to shout above the hubbub, 'but as of eight o'clock last evening, I have taken temporary charge of this case pending the arrival of Superintendent Malcolm from Divisional Headquarters in Maidstone. As you will know, my officers are now carrying out routine searches of your rooms under warrant. When they have finished, unless we need to detain any of you, you will be free to go.'

As could have been predicted in a stroppiness of teachers, McBride was bombarded with complaints and cries of 'Outrageous!' Only Alan Harper-Bennet seemed happy enough to stand near Sally Greenhow, deep in meaningful conversation while ogling the lace trim of her negligee.

Maxwell was just about to swing into the saddle of his white charger and thunder to her rescue when he was waylaid by Dr Moreton, the over-qualified Head of Science of John Bunyan School, Luton.

'Funny business, this, Mr Maxwell,' he said, rummaging in his pockets for his pipe. 'I don't know, no sooner do you and I have a chance for a chat, but we're being sent home. Funny business.'

'As you say, doctor,' Maxwell nodded, keeping one eye on Harper-Bennet lest his hands should stray. The other eye was trying to focus on Valerie Marks, whose Oriental silk thing-ummie was clashing horribly with Sally's boudoir boutiquerie.

'Who's your money on, then?' Moreton was cramming a particularly repulsive-looking shag into the bowl of his briar.

Maxwell looked him right between the eyes. 'You, actually,' he said.

Moreton paused only briefly in his cramming, then smiled slowly and said, 'Oh, very good.'

'Think about it,' Maxwell said. 'You were here at the Carnforth Centre on the day Liz Striker died. You were here yesterday when Rachel King was murdered.' Maxwell reached out and squeezed the man's right arm. 'Biceps like bidets,' he commented.

'I keep myself in trim, yes,' Moreton agreed, 'but you'll have to do better than opportunity. Logically speaking—'

'You'll have to give me more time,' Maxwell interrupted him. 'And in my experience, murder and logic have very little to do with each other.'

Moreton's face flashed amber as he lit his pipe. 'Had a lot of experience, have you — of murder, I mean?'

'Some,' Maxwell nodded.

'Oh.' Moreton appeared a little crestfallen, but a triumphant look spread across his face in an instant. 'Well, I hate to disappoint you.'

'Oh?' Maxwell raised an eyebrow. 'Now don't tell me you're going to deny you did it? Aw, shucks! Looks like I'll have to pin it on somebody else.'

'I had the opportunity to kill Rachel King, yes, as indeed did you, Mr Maxwell. But I couldn't have killed Liz Striker.'

'Really? Why so?'

'Because I wasn't here.'

'But Sally . . . I was led to believe the Luton lot arrived on the Thursday.'

'The others, yes. But I didn't arrive until Friday morning, shortly before you. You see, I had been on interview the day before.'

'I see. Did you get it?'

'I'm sorry?'

'The job,' Maxwell had to explain. 'Did you get the job?'

'No.' Moreton blew smoke in the direction of Gregory Trant. 'No, it wasn't for me. I pulled out.'

'Ah,' Maxwell nodded. 'Some schools do that to you. Look good on paper, but when you get there—'

'Oh, my dear boy, this wasn't a school.'

'Oh?'

'No, it was rather a plum number with the World Health Organisation. I'm a biologist, you see.'

'Oh, bad luck,' Maxwell frowned.

Suddenly both men were aware of a presence at their shoulders. Or to be precise, the shoulders of Dr Moreton. Maxwell had never seen McBride look so serious, not even when he had announced the discovery of Rachel King's body.

'Dr Moreton,' the Inspector said, 'might I have a word?'

And no sooner was the pipe out of the Head of Science's mouth than he had disappeared into the throng of the pyjama party and beyond, through the door into the Trevelyan Suite marked 'No Admittance'.

* * *

All in all, the searching constabulary had left Maxwell's room in reasonable nick. As he showered, shaved, dressed for the road, he couldn't help wondering why Andrew Moreton should have been fingered. Maxwell had deliberately hung back in the Whittingham Suite until the searches appeared to have finished. Indeed, until McBride reappeared through that deadly door from whence Moreton had not returned. No one else was taken up by the thief takers. So why Moreton? Had they found something in his room? Or was the foulness of his tobacco in itself a civil offence? Maxwell would give his eye teeth to know. But of course, these things only happened in fiction, didn't they? The private investigator had a buddy on the force or a nephew who was running the case and so all kinds of classified information were passed to the hero. How bloody unlikely. McBride might as well take to the Carnforth roof and shout with a loudhailer so that everybody knew. What a bugger!

'I'm not sorry to see the last of that place,' Sally Greenhow said, adjusting her driving mirror as she pushed the accelerator to the floor. 'I suppose we'd better get back to school, Max. Tell Diamond.'

'You tell him what you like,' Maxwell said, only now remembering to put on his seat belt. 'I've still got two and a half days off.'

'What?'

'I can't leave it there, Sal.' He shook his head. 'Two women dead. One of them . . . a friend.'

'But the police have got somebody,' she protested, craning to see if the road was clear. 'Moreton.'

She waved and grinned sweetly at the paparazzi mouthing questions at her.

Maxwell wound the window down and said, 'I am not now, nor have I ever been a Communist,' and he wound the window up again.

'I wish you wouldn't talk to the press,' she scolded him.

'Do you know how many people were arrested on suspicion in the Ripper case?' Maxwell asked her.

'I'm only an honorary historian, Max,' Sally reminded him. 'I'm Special Needs, remember?'

'Learning Support,' he corrected her. 'Over two hundred,' the real historian went on. 'And they let 'em go again.'

'That was a long time ago, Max,' Sally said.

'Ah, but it's the principle, Sally,' he said. 'All right, so we can assume the rozzers found something incriminating in Moreton's room. But he couldn't have killed Liz Striker. He was on interview that day.'

'What?' Sally frowned. 'But I was told . . .'

'What?' Maxwell cross-examined her.

'I was told he was there. With the others in the minibus.'

'Who told you that?'

'Alan Harper-Bennet . . . Oh, Christ!'

'Sally?' Maxwell turned as far as the seat belt would allow. The tall kid had gone a funny colour. 'Sally, what's the matter?'

'Max . . .' She was shaking, her knuckles white on the wheel. 'There's something I've got to tell you. Something I shouldn't have done . . . Oh, God!'

'Turn left!' Maxwell ordered.

'What?'

'Left. The Green Man. They're open.'

* * *

They were. Maxwell thanked his God for the new licensing laws and led the trembling girl into the cool darkness of the snug, out of the unseasonably fierce sun. She took off her dark glasses and when he'd got her safely sitting down, he ordered a Southern Comfort and a brandy and swigged one before he reached her. As he got there, she held out a piece of paper.

'If this is an absence note from your mum,' he said, 'I'm not sure I can accept it . . .'

'I don't know who it's from,' she whispered, though there was no one else in the bar to hear, 'but I know who it's to.'

'To whom it is,' he murmured, unable to stop himself, and he read the note with growing horror. 'Where did you get this, Sally?' he asked.

She took the brandy in both hands and buried her nose in the balloon. She pulled a face as it hit her lips. 'You know, I don't really like this stuff,' she said.

'Have a sip of mine.' He held out the glass, his eyes still on the sheet she'd given him.

'I'd better not,' she said. 'I'm driving.'

Then Maxwell was reading the note aloud. '"Oops, got the wrong one there, didn't you, old boy? Never mind, it's business as usual for us after all. We don't want little Jo to find out, do we?"'

'What does it mean, Max?' Sally asked him, scanning the Head of Sixth Form's face.

'That depends on where you got it,' Maxwell said, smoothing out the paper's folds and staring at it on the table.

'Alan Harper-Bennet's room,' she said.

'When?'

'Last night.'

Maxwell sucked in his teeth. 'Sally,' he said, 'you must never go down to the end of town without consulting me.'

'I know, Max,' she mumbled. 'After you'd gone last night, I was about to lock my door, like you said, when who should turn up but Harper-Bennet. He said he had something to show me.'

'Did he now?' Maxwell's left eyebrow threatened to join his hair line.

'It was in his room,' she said.

'You went to his room?' Maxwell was incredulous.

'Oh, Max, I know it was bloody silly, but . . . well, I thought it might shed some light on this wretched business.'

'It might have got you killed,' Maxwell growled, looking the girl hard in the face.

'I know,' she shuddered, 'I know.' She closed her eyes briefly, then took up the tale, 'Anyway, I went. I thought of the old pervert pinching my knickers and I wanted them back. If I had the chance, I'd find them and confront him. He offered me wine.'

'It was late.' Maxwell was the voice of reason.

'That's what I told him,' Sally said, 'but he poured two glasses anyway. Basically, he took up where he left off the other day. Did I believe in open marriages? How did I know I could trust Alan — my Alan, that is — and so on.'

'So he didn't have anything to show you?' There was a twinkle in Maxwell's eye for all his concern.

'It didn't get that far,' Sally assured him. 'I "accidentally" spilt my drink and while he'd gone for a cloth, I took a butchers in his drawers.'

'You feisty little minx!' Maxwell rolled his eyes. 'And found the knickers?'

'No. I found that.'

'Why did you take it?'

'Stupidity,' Sally moaned. 'Sheer bloody stupidity. Don't the police call it tampering with the evidence?'

'Do they?'

'Don't you see, Max, if I'd left it there, in the drawer, where he'd put it, the police would have found it this morning and Mr Harper-Pervert would be helping them with their enquiries.'

'That's assuming it *is* evidence,' Maxwell said.

'What? Well, surely.'

'What do you suppose it is?' he asked her.

She picked it up as though it had poison smeared over it. 'Well, it's a blackmail note, isn't it?'

'Is it?'

'Oh, Maxie!' she shrieked, then, quieter, 'For fuck's sake, don't be so bloody obtuse.'

He smiled. 'Obtusian is my middle name,' he said. 'Sorry, Sal, just playing devil's advocate.'

'And are you winning?' she asked, straight-faced.

'No,' he admitted, taking the paper off her, 'no, I'm not. ". . . got the wrong one" — that's Liz Striker. "Never mind, it's business as usual for us after all" — that means the blackmail money continues to be passed in the same way. "We don't want little Jo to find out . . .' Maxwell shrugged. 'Obviously a Bonanza fan.'

'Whoever little Jo is, he's obviously the innocent party. It's because of him or rather his need to be kept in the dark that Liz Striker died. By mistake. She wasn't the blackmailer. Somebody else was.'

'That's one interpretation,' Maxwell nodded.

'Max, it's the only interpretation.'

'Where exactly was the note?'

Sally screwed up her face with the effort of remembering. 'Top drawer, opposite the bed.'

'Was Harper-Bennet's room the same plan as ours?'

'Yes, but a mirror image. Bed on the other side.'

'So the drawer you found that in was the first one you'd come to — from the door, I mean?'

'That's right.'

'And it was on top? You didn't have to rummage?'

'No. I intended to, but he came back pretty pronto. Max, you've got that funny look on your face again. What are you thinking?'

'If I was a murderer,' Maxwell said softly, 'and I'd just killed the wrong person and I'd received a blackmail note from the real person, the last thing I'd do is keep it. And the last place I'd put it is in the first place anybody would look.'

'You've lost me.' Sally shook her head. 'Are you saying Harper-Bennet put the letter there deliberately, knowing I'd find it?'

'Well, he did take your knickers and he did invite you to his room. What happened after he'd cleared up the drink, by the way?'

'I made my excuses and left,' Sally told him. 'By the way, whatever record Sally Gunnell holds now, I broke sprinting back along that corridor. This time I did take your advice and I locked the door. I didn't get much sleep, Max, trying to work out that note. Oh, I feel so guilty. I should have left it there. I feel such a shit. So . . . ashamed.'

'Now, now,' he patted her hand, 'there's no need for that.'

'It was what you said clinched it. When you made me realise a few minutes ago that Harper-Bennet was trying to put the finger on Dr Moreton.'

'I'm not sure he was,' Maxwell mused.

'What?'

'Harper-Bennet came by car. He probably assumed Moreton was with the others in the bus because that was the original plan. There's no reason for Moreton to have told Harper-Bennet about his interviews, is there?'

'We've got to go back, Max.' Sally was gathering up her bag.

'Whoa,' he said. 'Sit down. Where's the fire?'

'Max, we must,' she said, but she did as she was told.

'No, we mustn't,' he said, 'the fuzz must have had their reasons for detaining Moreton.'

'But if I'd left this bloody note where it was, they'd have had reason to detain Harper-Bennet too.'

'Possibly,' Maxwell agreed, 'but we mustn't jump to conclusions.'

'Do you . . . do you recognise the writing?' Sally asked him.

Maxwell shook his head. 'Not joined up,' he thought aloud. 'Could be anybody's.'

'The police can analyse it, Max,' she said, 'make comparisons.'

'So can we,' Maxwell said.

'We?' Sally frowned at him.

'It's a common enough word, Mrs Greenhow,' the Head of Sixth Form said. 'The plural of I.'

'Oh, no,' Sally was shaking her head, 'no, no, Max. If you don't think it's right to go to the police, then I'll hold off — for now, that is. But I'm going home now.' The girl was on her feet again. 'I need a shower, a stiff drink, the arms of my loving husband and a good night's sleep. In the morning, I'll decide what to do.'

'A minute ago you were all for going back,' he reminded her.

'A minute ago,' she told him, 'I'd forgotten how much I need a shower, a stiff drink and all the rest of it.'

'You don't fancy going the pretty way, I suppose?' Maxwell asked. 'Via Luton?'

Sally's eyes widened. 'It's taken me a while,' she said, 'but I finally know why the kids call you Mad Max. It's because you're stark staring bonkers, isn't it?'

'The simplest explanation is always the best.' Maxwell winked at her. 'Can I keep this?' He held up the blackmail note.

'All right,' she said. 'But I'm trusting you, Max, not to lose it. It's got the murderer's prints all over it.'

'And yours,' Maxwell nodded, 'and mine. I hear Holloway is particularly lovely at this time of year.'

'Max,' Sally was serious, 'Max, you know I love you dearly, don't you? That you're like a sort of dad to me?'

'Now, Sally,' Maxwell sighed, 'it's not pay-day for another fortnight yet . . .'

She waved the comment aside. 'I've got to ask this, Max,' she said. 'Is that . . . Could that be . . . Rachel's writing?'

Maxwell put the note in his inside pocket without looking at it again. 'No,' he said softly, 'it isn't and it couldn't be. Harper-Bennet got it wrong twice.'

* * *

Terry Malcolm was known universally as Bum-Bum in the McBride household. It wasn't meant to be offensive — though neither was it a term of endearment. It just happened to be the closest little Sam could get to pronouncing the name when he was younger. But then, for the '90s, Sam was a surprisingly deferential little kid — it was always Mr Bum-Bum.

Mr Bum-Bum was the tallest copper John McBride knew. And one of the least pleasant. Just as Stony Warren never smiled, so Terry Bum-Bum never swore. He didn't have to. His eyes said it all. That and a curiously rich vocabulary, for a copper, that is. And if there was one thing Superintendent Bum-Bum didn't like, it was cock-ups by his team.

He got to Carnforth a little before lunchtime, just as Sally and Maxwell were roaming their way along the A259 in a homewardly direction. Malcolm called his team together in the incident room, gave them a pep talk and then got down to cases.

'John, isn't it?' The cold eyes searched the open, honest face of Inspector McBride, sitting across the table in the interview room.

'Yes, sir.'

'You can drop the sir,' the Superintendent told him. 'Mr Malcolm will be fine. Does your girl do a decent tea?'

'Er . . . WPC O'Halloran? Fair, Mr Malcolm.'

'Right. I take mine black. With one sugar.'

McBride relayed the order over the intercom, and his finger was no sooner off the button than Malcolm hit him straight between the eyes with his next question. 'What exactly was your part in the termination of Miles Warren's career?'

'Sir?'

Malcolm looked under his eyebrows at the Inspector. 'I thought we had an understanding,' he said.

'Sorry.' McBride looked uncomfortable. 'Mr Malcolm,' he corrected himself. He hadn't felt like this since the promotion board to Sergeant.

'Would you like me to repeat the question?' Malcolm asked him.

'I'd like you to rephrase it,' McBride said. 'I'm not sure what it means.'

'Very well.' Malcolm turned to the window. The blinds were up now and the midday sun was gilding the Carnforth roses. 'Forced,' he said.

'I'm sorry?' McBride wasn't with him.

'Those roses.' Malcolm pointed to them. 'Forced. What I mean is, whose idea was it to use this place as an incident room?'

'Mr Warren's.'

'Too incestuous,' Malcolm said, taking in the cedars at the end of the lawns. 'We should stay close, but not too close. Whose idea was it to keep the suspects here?'

'Mr Warren's, but—'

'That was a wrong 'un,' Malcolm said, 'and if that "but" of yours was an attempted stab at loyalty, Inspector, I'd advise you to keep schtum. I've known Miles Warren for sixteen years. And I've known him to be a good copper. But he's blown it this time, lad. He'll be on his way to the coppers' graveyard. If you don't want to see it happen, keep your nose out of tomorrow's papers.' He turned to face McBride. 'And if you don't want to join him, let's have no more "but"s.'

McBride fell silent.

'Whose idea was it to hold off the use of search warrants?'

'That was mine,' McBride said.

'Oh?' Malcolm raised his head.

'Mr Warren had gone to Bournemouth, to St Bede's School to ask around. In his absence I decided to wait. Was I wrong?'

Malcolm smiled. 'That's one of those imponderables, isn't it?' he said. 'It may have been a mistiming, perhaps. At the moment, I'm inclined to be charitable.'

There was a knock on the door. 'Oh, WPC O'Halloran, is it?' Malcolm said.

'Yes, sir. Where would you like your tea, sir?'

'Down my throat, dear, in the fullness of time,' he smiled. 'But for now, I'll settle for the table. Aren't you joining me, Inspector?'

'It's almost lunchtime, Mr Malcolm,' McBride reminded him.

'So it is.' Malcolm checked his watch. 'Do a mean buffet here, do they, at the Carnforth?'

'Antonio's pretty good,' McBride said.

'WPC, order an egg and cress sandwich, would you, from this Antonio. White bread. Diet Clover. Anything for you, Inspector?'

'Er . . . no, thanks. I'll get mine later.'

'Right you are. Have we got any "Do Not Disturb" signs, WPC?'

'I believe so, sir.'

'Then put one on the door, there's a good girl. Leave my sandwich outside on the nearest filing cabinet. Mr McBride and I are in conference.'

CHAPTER 10

Superintendent Malcolm was eating his egg and cress sandwich, slowly chewing each mouthful with the deliberation of a prize Guernsey. In his hand were the forensic photographs of Rachel King nee Cameron. She lay face down on her bed, her hair matted with blood, her shoulders and the right sleeve of her powder blue nightdress saturated. A trail of blood spots led from her body across the mat and carpet to the door, where it ended abruptly. Mrs King was still wearing her watch. The hands had stopped at nineteen fifteen.

'Right.' Malcolm finished his lunch. 'What have we?'

'If you'd come to see the scene of the crime . . .' McBride suggested.

'Who's SCO?' the Superintendent asked.

'DS Latymer.'

Malcolm nodded. 'Good man, Dave Latymer. He won't have missed much. Are there any more photographs?'

'No, that's it,' the Inspector told him. 'Shall we look at the room?'

'In the fullness of time, yes,' Malcolm said. 'Now, you've talked me through the death of Mrs Striker. Talk me through the death of Mrs King.'

'Dr Anderson's preliminary report—'

'Anderson?' Malcolm interrupted him. 'Is he that foul-mouthed geriatric?'

McBride smiled, not something he felt able to do often in Malcolm's company. 'That's the one,' he said. 'His preliminary report gives the time of death as between nineteen and twenty hundred hours.'

'Do you mean seven and eight o'clock?'

'Yes, Mr Malcolm.' McBride began wondering how old his new boss was. 'The watch narrows it down still further.'

'Probably,' Malcolm nodded, 'but I'm far from convinced about such things. I broke my watch the other day. As you see, I am still walking around. Was there a date on Mrs King's watch?'

'No.'

'Was the glass shattered, by which I mean were there pieces missing? Out of the case?'

'No.'

'Then she could have broken it that morning or the previous evening. Go on.'

'From the state of the room, there was a struggle. The door hadn't been forced, so whoever her murderer was, we assume Mrs King let him in.'

'You're presuming a male perpetrator?'

'With the sort of force involved, yes. A woman might be capable, but no one on the course here at the moment, I wouldn't think.'

'All right.' Malcolm would accept that for the moment.

'The first blow, Anderson says, was delivered at the foot of the bed. There are blood spots on the carpet at that point. This came from the front and broke the victim's nose. There would have been profuse bleeding. She fell backwards, probably rucking up the mat as she went down.'

'Damage to fingernails? Debris?'

'None. But the knuckles of her right hand were grazed.'

'Implying?'

'That she punched him.'

'You didn't see any obvious signs, I suppose, on any of the guests?' Malcolm asked. McBride shook his head.

'Well, that was a bit too much to hope for,' the Superintendent said. 'What then?'

'The second blow was delivered as she lay on the bed, face up. It shattered the front of the skull — these are the later photographs you have there. At this point she'd have been virtually unconscious. Her killer either rolled her over or she rolled by herself and two more blows were delivered, probably in quick succession, destroying the back of the skull.'

'So Anderson thinks four blows in all?'

'Yes. And of course we have the murder weapon.'

'Of course,' Malcolm smiled. 'I look forward to seeing that. Where is it now?'

'At the lab.'

'Photographs?'

'Not yet.'

'You'll have to tell me, then,' Malcolm shrugged.

'It's all in the report,' McBride told him.

'I know it is, John,' the Superintendent smiled. 'I've read it. But I'd still like to hear it from you.'

'An iron pipe, wrapped in tape.'

'Lord Lucan,' Malcolm said.

'Sorry?'

'There's no need to be sorry, lad,' the Superintendent said. 'I was just reminiscing. Before your time, that one. Lord Lucan's children's nanny, Sandra Rivett, was bludgeoned to death with a pipe wrapped in tape. Why the tape, do you suppose?'

'To give a better grip,' McBride guessed.

Malcolm nodded. 'And that's all the better for us, because it screams premeditation. We don't have the situation where our hot-tempered friend just grabs the nearest blunt instrument in the heat of an argument. You don't tend to find iron pipes lying around in conference centre rooms and even if you do, they're not usually wrapped in adhesive tape for a better grip. Do we know where he got it from?'

'It's a section of scaffolding,' McBride said. 'Conventional stuff, but I had the lads combing the site yesterday. It didn't come from here.'

'So he brought it with him. The lab is sure about the weapon, of course?'

McBride nodded. 'Eight of Mrs King's hairs found clinging to the tape. And two of Mrs Striker's. All genetically matched.'

'The labs are excelling themselves,' Malcolm nodded. 'I didn't think old Collins had it in him. Can't have much on at the moment.'

'Mr Malcolm, I'd like to get back to my interrogation of the prime suspect as soon as possible.'

'Ah, yes, Dr Moreton. Where is he now?'

'At the station.'

'Has he had his phone call?'

'He has. Solicitor was supposed to be on his way.'

'Right.' Malcolm slid back his chair. 'We'll need to move out by tomorrow.'

'Tomorrow?'

'Oh, I know it's inconvenient,' Malcolm waved his hand, 'but on my way in this morning, I had my ear bent by Mr Leonard, who in turn is being badgered by his managing director who had already put in a timely call upstairs. See it from the Carnforth Centre's point of view. One death is bad for business. Two might put them out of business.'

'Or it might increase it,' McBride was cynical enough to observe.

'It might, John, it might.' Malcolm nodded at the door. 'But that would be openly pandering to the sanguinary tastes of Joe Public, wouldn't it? It's a brave conference centre manager who'll do that. Now, we've got our marching orders. We'll set up back at the nick. Anyway, there's not much more we can learn here. The birds have flown.'

'We've got our man, Mr Malcolm,' McBride said.

'Have we, John?' Malcolm asked, allowing the Inspector to open the door for him. 'I wonder. I tell you what, you try and convince me of that on the way, will you?'

* * *

Sally and Maxwell had timed it badly. Lunch hour at Leighford High was a euphemism for hell. Upwards of seven hundred delinquents, all of them at varying stages of adolescence which involved zits, hormones, anti-establishment attitudes and fantasies about Michelle Pfeiffer — the boys were worse — milled in the three classrooms that did double duty as a dining-hall.

Peter Maxwell hadn't had a school lunch in nearly twenty years. It was to that sole fact that he attributed his longevity. Merely padding through the dropped chips in the corridor was enough — secondary eating — and it was here he found Paul Moss, the Head of History, on duty.

'Max! You're back!'

'What's the matter with it?' The Head of Sixth Form tried looking over his shoulder. With colleagues like his, he was fairly adept at that.

'I thought you were off all week. Year 13 historians will be ecstatic'

'Calm them down, Paul. I'm just passing through.'

'Ah, forgot your pen?'

'Something like that. Seen Legs?'

'It's lunchtime, Max,' Moss chided him. 'He'll be hiding in his office.'

'Of course.' Maxwell clicked his fingers. 'It's been so long.'

'Oi!' Moss bellowed at a weasel-eyed boy who had just dropped an empty Coke can at his feet.

'What?'

Now Paul Moss was fast. He was thirty-something, genial, good-natured, one of the new school, but his heart was in the right place. But Peter Maxwell was one of the old school and he was faster. His right hand snaked out and caught the litter lout by his ear.

'Ow!' he wailed. 'Get your hands off me!'

'Mr Moss, are my hands on this boy?'

'No, Mr Maxwell,' Moss beamed. 'Merely your thumb and index finger.'

'As I surmised. McDevitt, isn't it?'

'Yeah.' The kid tried to shake himself free, but the pain was too much.

'Do you know the film, *The Dirty Dozen*, McDevitt? Lee Marvin, Telly Savalas and Co, where a bunch of misfits like yourself are trained for a suicidal wartime mission?'

'Yeah.' McDevitt frowned, not quite sure where all this was leading.

'You remember that scene, McDevitt, where Lee Marvin — that's me, by the way — takes aside malignant dwarf John Cassavetes — that's you — and says, "March, you little bastard, or I'll kick your head in"?'

'Yeah.'

'Well, this is an action replay, McDevitt. Pick up that can, you little bastard, or I'll kick your head in.'

'Are you threatening me?' McDevitt asked.

'Er . . . yes,' Maxwell beamed, 'I believe I am.'

'Oh. Right,' and McDevitt bent to pick up the can, grateful the ear was still attached to his head.

'Have a nice day, Mr Moss,' Maxwell said.

'Thank you, Mr Maxwell. You too.'

Along the corridor, McDevitt was hailed by two cronies who'd witnessed his come-uppance. 'Fuckin' hell, Den, that was a close one.'

'Yeah,' said the other, 'that's Mad Max. He killed a kid last year. Just for looking at him.'

'Fuckin' hell.'

'Yeah?' McDevitt tried to swagger, which was difficult with a throbbing ear. 'Well, he don't scare me.' And he dropped his Mars Bar wrapper carefully in the next litter bin.

* * *

Maxwell never actively sought the company of Deirdre Lessing. She was the Morgana Le Fay to his Arthur, the fly in his ointment. And she was the last person he wanted to see ensconced in Legs Diamond's office that Wednesday lunchtime.

'Max,' the Headmaster said, 'you're back.'

Maxwell only did the back joke with them he reckoned. And Jim Diamond wasn't one of them, so he just said, 'Yes,' and left it at that.

'Aren't you a trifle early, Max?' Deirdre asked. As Senior Mistress, Deirdre had the broadest shoulders in the school and no one seemed to have told her that power dressing like that had gone singularly out of fashion. She also had legs which would put a gladiator to shame. Probably, under that mantle of pure bitch, there lurked a remarkable body. But Peter Maxwell would never find out.

'Ah, Deirdre, you trifle with me at your peril,' he beamed. 'Might I have a word, Headmaster? Alone?'

Diamond glanced hopefully at Deirdre, who for once did the right thing and got up. 'Ah, well,' she smiled acidly at Maxwell, 'the sixth form needs me for something again.'

Punch-bag practice, Maxwell assumed, but he was too much of a gentleman to say so. When she'd gone, in a vapour trail of Dune, Maxwell took a seat.

'I thought I caught a glimpse of Sally Greenhow a few minutes ago,' Diamond said, 'but I thought I was seeing things. What's happened, Max? GNVQ course not going well?'

'Sort of, Headmaster,' the Head of Sixth Form nodded. 'We've had an incident. Well, two, actually. Two course members have been murdered.'

'Murdered? Oh, my God, the Carnforth Centre.'

'I wondered whether you'd heard.'

'Well, I don't take a daily, but I did catch it on *South Today* a couple of days ago. Do you know, I didn't connect the two. How stupid of me.'

The grey suit, the gold-rimmed specs, the attempt to juggle all the balls that were Education Now. No wonder Jim Diamond was losing his grip.

'How awful. What happened? Two women, I think, the telly said.'

'Liz Striker and Rachel King,' Maxwell nodded. 'Battered to death by persons unknown.'

'Good God. Have there been any developments? I mean, I haven't heard for a day or so.'

'A man, I think you'll find, is helping police with their enquiries.'

'Who? Er . . . I mean, you can't tell me, of course, I understand that.'

'I don't,' Maxwell said. 'His name is Dr Andrew Moreton — no relation — and he didn't do it.'

'How do you know?'

Maxwell crossed his legs as far as his male anatomy would allow. 'Call it female intuition,' he said.

'Good God. Um . . . Sally. How's she taking it?'

'Like a man,' Maxwell nodded. 'But I'm afraid I shall need compassionate leave for a day or two.'

'Compassionate . . . ? Really? Oh.' Diamond took off his glasses and twirled them around for a while. 'Oh, really? Well, that's not like you, Max.'

'You do have supply cover for me until Friday afternoon?'

'Well, yes, we do, but—'

'Well, there you are, then.' Maxwell was on his feet. 'I just called in to apprise you of the situation. I'd hate to muck up Roger's supply arrangements. See you Monday, Headmaster.'

'Max . . .'

But Max had gone.

In the corridor, Jim Diamond bumped into Sally Greenhow, nipping back to the Learning Support Centre with a pizza and chips. 'Sally,' he hailed her, 'I've just seen Max. He's talking about taking the rest of the week off. Compassionate leave. That's not like him. Is he all right?'

'What did he tell you?' the tall kid asked her headmaster.

'Only that two people had been murdered. Of course, I knew that from the news coverage anyhow.'

'One of them Max knew personally,' Sally said.

'Really?'

'Rachel King was an old flame. Now, I don't really think the corridor is the place to discuss this, Headmaster. I do have a number of things to do.'

'Oh, quite, Sally, quite,' and Jim Diamond did what he did best in life. He beat a hasty retreat.

* * *

The interview room at Ashford nick was altogether more austere than the improvised one at the Carnforth Centre. More purpose-built. More permanent. The walls were painted brick, the solitary light bulb harsher than Carnforth's spots and strips. In the centre, in time-honoured tradition, was a table, with three chairs. Only the recording apparatus placed it squarely at the back end of the twentieth century. Otherwise, Haigh, the acid bath murderer, would have felt at home here. So might Dr Harvey Hawley Crippen.

But a different doctor sat in the limelight now. A Doctor of Biology, confused, lost, out of his depth. Behind him, in the murky half-shadows, his brief stood, looking for a fourth chair. He found one and pulled it alongside Moreton's as the investigating officers came in.

'I am Superintendent Malcolm,' the taller of the two announced. 'Dr Moreton, I believe you already know Inspector McBride.'

'Anthony Walters,' the solicitor introduced himself. 'I represent Dr Moreton.'

No one shook hands. The solicitor hadn't left his new-found seat. 'I've read your statement, Dr Moreton,' Malcolm said. 'What will happen now is that I will ask you some questions. You have been cautioned already and that caution still stands. Your solicitor will have explained to you your rights. John?'

McBride switched on a tape. 'Interview three with Dr Andrew Moreton, conducted by Superintendent Malcolm with Inspector McBride in attendance. Mr Anthony Walters representing Dr Moreton. Interview commenced at sixteen thirty, Wednesday 11th May.'

'Dr Moreton,' Malcolm looked his man in the face, 'how do you account for the fact that an iron pipe was found in your room at the Carnforth Centre?'

Moreton flashed a glance at his solicitor. Walters didn't look up, merely jotted something down in a notepad.

'I can't,' the Head of Science said.

'You've no idea how it got there?'

'None.'

Malcolm leaned back a little, watching his man, giving him space. Terry Malcolm was an expert at this game. Nearly twenty years' experience had given him the edge. He'd seen them all in his time — con-men and women, pimps, prostitutes, cat-burglars, psychopaths. And his pattern was always the same — ask them a devastating question head on and watch 'em squirm. Sit back. Give 'em time. Watch the sweat break out on their foreheads, upper lips. They never knew what to do with their hands, like amateur actors suddenly stuffed into a pair of tights and having no recourse to pockets. Watch the hands. Watch the eyes. Gauleiter Malcolm would have been perfectly at home in the SS.

'My officers tell me,' Malcolm said at last, 'that the pipe was found in a hold-all with your name on it. Is that so?'

'Yes.' Moreton didn't have to look at Walters for that one. It was already established fact.

'How many bags did you take to the conference?' Malcolm asked.

'Er . . . two. And a suitcase.'

'How well did you know Rachel King?'

'Not very,' Moreton said. 'I'd worked with her on and off during the course. Attended lectures with her and so on.'

'You worked with her on the afternoon of her death, I believe.'

That too was a verifiable statement and Moreton nodded.

'For the tape, please.' McBride tapped the table.

Moreton cleared his throat. 'Yes,' he said, 'that's right.'

'Did you find her attractive?'

Moreton saw Walters shaking his head out of the corner of his eye. 'I decline to answer that,' he said.

Malcolm smiled at McBride. 'Did you know Mrs King beforehand? Before the course, I mean?'

'No.'

'And Mrs Striker?' Malcolm leaned forward. 'No, doctor, I'm not going to ask if you found her attractive. Did you know her previously?'

'No.'

'Are you married, Dr Moreton?'

'No.'

'A bachelor gay, eh?'

Moreton saw Walters' head come up and he saw the Superintendent smile.

'How long have you taught at the John Bunyan School?'

'Er . . . eight years.'

'And before that?'

'A school in Basingstoke.'

'The Wyndham School?' Malcolm said.

'Yes.' Moreton cleared his throat again. 'Yes, that's right.'

'Would you like to tell us about the trouble you had there?'

'Er . . . just a moment, Superintendent,' Walters intervened for the first time. 'Does this have any bearing on the matter in hand?'

'Dr Moreton has a criminal record, Mr Walters,' Malcolm said. 'Surely, as his solicitor you know that.'

'I do, but—'

'A criminal record that involved common assault. He hit a woman with a squash racquet.'

'I lost my temper!' Moreton snapped. At the touch of Walters' hand on his arm, he checked himself. 'I . . . do have rather a short fuse.'

'Would you have any objection to telling us what happened?'

'Superintendent Malcolm—' The brief was getting agitated.

'It is a matter of public record, Mr Walters,' the policeman said. 'I could tell you, but I'd like to hear Dr Moreton's version. The written record is so cold, isn't it? So unreasoning, somehow.'

'It's all right, Tony,' Moreton said, 'I'm all right. I used to play squash. Quite well, in fact. One day I was playing in a league match and found myself paired against a local gymnast. It was one of those daft mixed set-ups. Anyway, she beat me. I don't like losing, Superintendent; and I like losing to a woman still less. Well, at the time I took it like a man and we shook hands. In the bar afterwards, however, well, I just couldn't take the ribbing.' He buried his face briefly in his hands. 'It was inexcusable.' He surfaced again, pale at the memory of it. 'I grabbed the nearest thing to hand — my squash racquet — and lashed out. Needless to say I was sorry afterwards, but it was too late by then.'

'A suspended sentence,' Malcolm said. 'So it all ended reasonably happily ever after.'

'Happily?' Moreton looked at him. 'Ever after?' He shook his head. 'Isn't that why I'm here now?' he asked. 'Isn't that why one of your boys planted the pipe in my room? Because you know about my conviction and saw a way to make an arrest? Isn't it all about arrests these days? Productivity? Quotas?'

Throughout, Moreton had ignored Walters' tugging on his sleeve. Now, he snarled at him, 'Fuck off,' and took his arm away.

Malcolm's eyes narrowed. 'Are you making allegations — serious allegations — against a member of my force, Dr Moreton?' he asked.

'No, he isn't,' Walters cut in. 'For Christ's sake, Andrew, try to control yourself. You're in enough trouble as it is.'

'Indeed you are, Dr Moreton,' Malcolm nodded. 'Why, for instance, did you tell colleagues that you were on interview on the day of Elizabeth Striker's death?'

'I was.' Moreton's palms felt clammy, his mouth dry. As a biologist, he knew the physiology of fear, but he couldn't control it any more than the next man.

Malcolm smiled at him. 'Don't insult my intelligence, Dr Moreton. We checked. You should have gone on interview, granted. But the fact is, you didn't go, did you? Why was that?'

Moreton's face disappeared into his hands again. 'I couldn't face it,' he said. 'At the last moment, I suppose, I chickened out. Having a PhD in a comprehensive makes me a pretty big fish, but the pond — my God — the pond is small. I've been in the classroom too long. I can't hack the real world any more. I've lost it. But I couldn't lose face. I pretended to everybody that I hadn't cared for the job when I'd been offered it. Actually, I spent the day in a pub in Lydd. The Farmers' Arms.'

Malcolm leaned towards the microphone. 'I have the right to hold you on suspicion, Dr Moreton, for a further twelve hours. That is exactly what I intend to do. Interview terminated sixteen fifty-one,' and the policemen left the room.

In the corridor outside, John McBride caught his new guv'nor's arm. 'Mr Malcolm?'

'Well, now, I really don't know,' the Superintendent said, in answer to the unspoken question. 'We've got a testy gentleman with a murder weapon and a record of potential GBH. If that squash racquet had been a bottle, he'd have done time already. As it was, he clearly had to leave Basingstoke — that, in itself, I should think, was a blessing in disguise. What sort of idiot appointed him at Luton, of course, is another issue. We also know he's a liar and a braggart whose only alibi for the Liz Striker murder is a pub-load of winos who, I am prepared to wager, won't remember him from Adam. In that sense, things look rather bad for Dr Moreton.'

'In that sense?' McBride frowned. He thought the book was open and shut. Why hadn't the Super thrown it at him? Not only was Moreton shifty and something of a surprisingly loose cannon, but he was trying the old fabricated evidence ploy. Nothing was designed to get further up a copper's nose.

'In another sense,' Malcolm leaned back against the wall to allow a uniformed cohort to pass, 'we've got no prints on the murder weapon, nothing yet from the search of his home — no more news from the Bedford boys, I assume?'

McBride shook his head.

'And no established previous links with either of the dead women. No, John, this case is closer to home than that. It lies with somebody who knew one or both of the dead women before.'

'Which means St Bede's,' McBride said, unconvinced.

'Or Whatsisname,' Malcolm nodded. 'Who is it? Peter Maxwell.'

* * *

Peter Maxwell was back in his attic study again, the place he always returned to when the world got a bit much; when the bitch that was life got up and slapped him in the face. Some men fish, others run around a football pitch, still others collapse after too many pints. Mad Max Maxwell? He painted model soldiers.

His brush deftly etched in the gold braid on the hussar jacket of Lieutenant Fitzgibbon. Then Maxwell took a deep breath and started on the double gold stripes on the overalls. That was the only way to do it, really, in one. Start at the waist and don't slacken up on the pressure until you've reached the ankle.

'How's this for size, then, Count?' He talked to the cat who shared his inner sanctum because sometimes silence was just too painful. 'The filth have picked up Dr Andrew Moreton — no, he didn't write the book, I've already done that one — on the grounds, I would think, of what they found in his room.'

The cat known as Metternich yawned ostentatiously, stretching out on the dormer windowsill as only cats can.

'Now . . .' Maxwell started work on Fitzgibbon's second leg. 'We don't as yet of course know what that was. Sally is convinced they've got the wrong man.' He reached the right ankle and breathed a sigh of relief. 'Well, I'm about to tell you,' he said. 'Don't be so impatient.'

Metternich licked his back with boredom.

'Sally rifled the drawers of one Alan Harper-Bennet. No, I don't think you'd like him, Count — not a cat person. She found — and I have it downstairs; I'll show you later — what does appear to be a blackmail letter. No, it's printed. Almost as corny as cut from bits of newspaper, isn't it? But actually, quite clever, because you know how difficult it is to identify block capitals. Well, what do you mean, what's wrong with that?'

Count Metternich paused in his ablutions to tweak his left ear.

'I'll tell you what's wrong with that. Let's surmise for a moment . . .' Maxwell squinted in the harsh lamplight to apply his brush to Fitzgibbon's sabretache. 'Bugger me, Count, Irish harps are a bitch to paint, aren't they? Yes, I suppose he would have carried a plain patent leather one really, but allow me some artistic licence, please! Let's surmise that I . . . no, let's make it more interesting — you. You are being blackmailed. Well, I don't know why. What about your nocturnal habits involving getting your legs over feline fatales of the neighbourhood? Someone is blackmailing you and you're tired of shelling out. So what do you do? Yes, all right, you claw them to death and toss them about the garden with a curious disembowelling motion, but I'm being metaphysical here, Count. We humans aren't quite that nasty. No, you've bashed the blackmailer over the head. Only it wasn't the blackmailer.'

Metternich looked at Maxwell suspiciously.

'You've got the wrong — put your tongue away. Your tongue.' Maxwell tapped his own, careful not to do it with the loaded brush. 'Put it . . . that's it. You've got the wrong person, and the right person — the real blackmailer — sends you a note to that effect. What's the first thing you do?'

Metternich rolled over and splaying his hind legs began to apply his tongue to his bottom.

'Well, yes, probably,' Maxwell agreed. 'Gives you time to think, I suppose. But then you kill the right one, don't you . . .' He paused in his brushwork, putting the half-painted soldier down for a moment. 'Was that it, Count?' He was asking himself. 'Was Sally right after all? Was Rachel really blackmailing him?'

Metternich's cleaning noises stopped abruptly and the animal straightened and looked at his master.

'Well,' Maxwell said, 'we'll see. But my point is, you'd destroy the note, wouldn't you? You wouldn't leave it around where the most obvious and cursory search would find it? No,' Maxwell shook his head, 'it's too damned pat. So,' he took up the officer of the 8th again, 'Luton tomorrow, Count. Ever been to Luton?'

Metternich flopped down on to the floor and padded his way down the loft ladder rungs.

'I only asked, Count,' he heard Maxwell say.

CHAPTER 11

'"God, I will pack,"' said Maxwell, quoting Rupert Brooke, '"and take a train" and get me to Luton once again, for Luton's the one place I know where men with shady pasts do go.' He looked down from his shaving mirror to the black and white thing that slunk round his ankles. 'All right, purist,' he said to the cat, 'I'm paraphrasing rather extravagantly. What's for breakfast? Oh, yes, it is your turn.'

There was a sharp ring at the door bell. Maxwell checked his watch. Too early for the postman. He'd cancelled the milk last week. He hauled on his dressing-gown and made for the stairs. In the knobbly glass at the end of the hall, he saw the distorted outline of a figure he thought he knew.

'Sally?' he said, peering round the door. 'I thought you were going home for a bath, a drink and the loving arms of your husband.'

'That was yesterday,' she said. 'Been there. Done that. And anyway, you relic, it was a shower. Have you ridden British Rail recently? Tried to carry a coffee back from the buffet car? I thought I'd save you the hell of all that. It was Luton, wasn't it?'

* * *

It had to be said that Alan Greenhow hadn't been too keen. Sally had been through enough in his opinion. And he knew what an old bastard Maxwell was. They'd talked about it in the wee small hours and eventually, he'd said yes. With the proviso of course that Maxwell was to look after Sally. And if he didn't, he (Alan) would break both his arms. Fair enough.

'Well?' Sally shouted over the 2CV's rattle as they neared their destination.

'Well, what?' Maxwell couldn't see where he was going in the driving rain and the mist of deceptive early summer.

'Aren't you going to fill me in on Luton?' she asked.

'What, you mean the church of St Mary's, with its black flint and white limestone chequered tower? The Butes' house at Luton Hoo built by Robert Adam in 1767 and rebuilt after the fire of 1843? The local industries of hat and lace making? Nah, I don't know anything at all about Luton — oh, except that they've got a girls' choir, of course.'

'As Dagenham has its girl pipers,' Sally added.

'Ah,' Maxwell closed his eyes and did his utmost to get comfortable in the cramped passenger seat, 'the skirl of the pipes.'

'Tell me,' she said. 'Arsehole!' she suddenly yelled at a passing motor cyclist.

'No, I am awake,' Maxwell assured her. 'You don't have to shout.'

'Do you think we're going to learn anything about Harper-Bennet — at his school, I mean? If it was . . . I don't know, Paul Moss or Roger Garrett at Leighford and two total strangers came nosing about, would you be inclined to talk?'

'About Paul Moss, no,' Maxwell told her. 'No, I don't think I would. But Roger Rabbit, now, that's an entirely different matter. A talentless no-hoper like him should have been pegged out over an anthill years ago. I'd shop him to anybody.'

Sally raised an eyebrow. 'Come on, now, Max, off the fence. What do you really think of Roger?'

'You take my point, though, Sal. It all depends on politics. How the weirdo is regarded by his colleagues. Gregory

Trant's going to be there, though. We'll have to come clean as to who we are. No chance of posing as publishers' reps or anything. It's the next exit.'

'What is?'

'The Luton road. Anything to get off the vicious circle that the Ministry of Transport laughingly calls the M25.'

Out of Luton — which is really the best place to be — they took the A6129 to sleepy Wheathampstead. The John Bunyan School stood to the left of the road, screened on one side by the forest that once marked the boundary of the Danelaw and on the other by the vast sprawling housing estate whose kids fed the school and whose adults still worked in Luton's dwindling motor trade. It was a dull building, made even duller by the grey drizzle that had replaced the torrents of the morning.

Sally Greenhow parked in the space reserved for School Nurse, as there was nowhere else to do it, and they made their way to Reception.

A rather spotty girl with adenoids grinned up at them.

'Good morning.' Maxwell raised the panama he habitually wore in summer, the one which gave him the air of an unemployed — and probably unemployable — cricket umpire. 'May we see Mr Harper-Bennet, please?' He dripped his brim over her.

'Mr Who?'

Maxwell threw a glance at Sally Greenhow. It had definitely said 'John Bunyan' on the gate. 'Mr Harper-Bennet. Big bloke. Teaches games and sociology, a bizarre combination I think you'll agree.'

'Don't know him,' the girl said.

In previous years, Maxwell would have grabbed the stupid little secretarial shit by the collar and hauled her across the counter. But that was then. Now it was political correctness and children's rights and the International Court at The Hague. Anyway, Maxwell had been to a good school himself. He was too much of a gentleman.

'Is there a real person around?' he asked.

The girl was still gaping at him when an older one popped her head around the corner. 'I'm sorry,' she beamed, 'Sharon is on work experience.'

'That must be a first,' Maxwell smiled. 'We're looking for Mr Harper-Bennet.'

The older girl looked at Maxwell, then at Sally. 'Ah, no. You'll want our Mr Watkin.'

'Will I?' Maxwell asked, wondering who this man was and how he could possibly fulfil his requirements.

'Yes. He's our Head of Sixth Form. He deals with new entrants.'

'New entrants?' Maxwell was lost.

'Your daughter.' The secretary nodded in Sally's direction.

'Look, dear,' it was Sally's turn to weigh in, 'I'm twenty-nine years old with a higher degree in Education, so could you possibly do as you're told and get Mr Harper-Bennet for us?'

'That's it, Sal,' Maxwell muttered. 'Really get 'em on our side.'

'Oh.' The secretary bridled and Maxwell saw the shutters come down. 'It's a free period for him. I don't know where he is.'

'Thank you so much.' Maxwell tipped his hat and pushed Sally ahead of him out of the office.

'Max,' she protested, 'we haven't found out anything.'

'Precisely,' Maxwell sighed. 'Never mind. And Sally, leave it to me, there's a good girl. Ah,' he caught sight of a figure in the corridor ahead, 'a human being. Excuse me.' The figure half turned. 'Have you seen Alan in your travels?'

'Alan Harper-B?' The figure was a rather homely woman with short-cropped hair and a bum that ought never to have been squeezed into a pair of electric blue cycling shorts. 'He's on the multi-gym, I think. Straight on, turn left. There's the gym. Can't miss it.'

'Thank you.' Maxwell tipped his hat again and waited for the homely woman to waddle away. 'Sit this one out, Sal,' he murmured to his colleague.

'Look, Max,' she frowned, 'I'm not just a bloody taxi service. I'm involved in this too, you know.'

'Up to a point, yes,' he nodded, 'but I don't want you to get involved any further. I owe it to Alan.'

'Sod Alan!' Sally shouted, only then remembering to check the length of the corridor. 'I don't need my husband's permission to talk to people and I don't need yours.'

'All right.' Maxwell laid his hands gently on the girl's shoulders. 'I knew it was a mistake to give you people the vote, but there it is. You find Trant. He knows Harper-Bennet and Moreton and I didn't get much of a crack at him at Carnforth.'

'What about Harper-Bennet?' she asked.

'He's mine,' Maxwell said. 'See you back at the car in . . . what? Half an hour?'

Funny how all '60s schools are the same. Peter Maxwell had never been to the John Bunyan in his life, but he found the gym as simply as his own navel — in fact with a lot less hassle. The familiar smell hit him squarely in the nostrils, that indefinable combination of jock straps, liniment and sweaty humanities. There was a soft drinks machine to his left, boys' changing-rooms beyond that. Through the double doors of the gym, he saw half a dozen nubile lovelies draped around a trampoline while a seventh, no doubt the Olga Korbut of Luton, was gyrating in the air above the canvas like a thing possessed. Maxwell shuddered. Turning over sharply in bed often had his stomach leaping.

He took the twisting stairs to the gallery that ran the length of the gym. A deserted table tennis table stood at one end. And at the other, the object of his search. Alan Harper-Bennet sat with his back to a contraption, his legs straight out in front of him, his fists clenched on a bar above his head. He wore a track suit and trainers and he'd left his glasses in the changing-room.

'Hello, Alan,' Maxwell hailed him.

'Who is it?' Harper-Bennet paused in mid-pull, his biceps flexed.

'Peter Maxwell. From the Carnforth Centre. Remember?'

Slowly, Harper-Bennet let the weights bar down. 'What are you doing here?' he asked.

'Oh, Alan,' Maxwell perched on the other seat of the multi-gym, tinkering with the weights, 'what a cliché. I happened to be in the area, and I thought I'd catch up on all the gossip. Dr Moreton, for instance.'

'"Happened to be in the area"?' Harper-Bennet smirked. 'Pull the other one, Maxwell. You're snooping.'

Maxwell clicked his fingers. 'Rumbled,' he said. 'Shucks!'

'Look.' Harper-Bennet climbed off the contraption and reached for a nearby towel to wipe the sweat from his neck. 'I'm not sure I care for this.'

'What?' Maxwell beamed up at him.

'You, coming here like this.'

'Well, actually . . .' Maxwell rummaged in his pocket. 'I can't con you, can I? I've got a little present for you,' and he handed Harper-Bennet a pair of lacy panties.

'What . . . ?'

'They're another pair of Sally's. She thought you might like them for your collection.'

Harper-Bennet blinked. 'What the fuck is all this about?' he asked, eyes blazing.

'Oh, come on, now,' Maxwell chuckled, 'we're men of the world, Alan. Mind you,' he jerked a thumb over the wall behind him, the one that led into the gym, 'you're in your element here, aren't you? Furtive little fetishist like you. Blue serge, eh?' He winked at Harper-Bennet. 'Very nice.'

The games master stood there, mouth open, staring at Maxwell rather stupidly. 'I can't decide whether to punch you on the nose or call the police,' he said.

'Well,' Maxwell rested his elbow on the wall, 'you could try the former, but then the spectacle of you committing GBH on an old man would be witnessed by your gels down there, not to mention your colleagues.' He beamed and waved to the homely woman who was yomping her way across the gym floor. 'On the other hand, if you call the police, they're going to want to see the blackmail note, aren't they?'

'Blackmail note?' Harper-Bennet was having one of those days. Maxwell was holding a piece of paper under his nose. His glasses were elsewhere so Harper-Bennet had to take it over to the window to read it properly. 'What is all this?'

'Well, Alan,' Maxwell had not moved from his conspicuous position in full view of the trampoline team, 'I've come rather a long way in the hope that you would tell me.'

'This is some kind of sick joke, isn't it?' Harper-Bennet said. 'Was it that King woman? Someone said you knew her way back. It's got to you, hasn't it? Knocked your oars out of the water.'

For the first time, Maxwell crossed to his man, his smile gone, his eyes hard. 'Rachel's death has got to me, yes. When some bastard beats to death the woman you once loved, well, you do get just a threat unreasonable.'

'You think I did it.' Harper-Bennet looked horrified. 'You've come here to accuse me.'

'Got it in one, Alan, baby,' Maxwell growled.

'You're mad!' and Harper-Bennet moved for the door. Maxwell was faster though and hauled him back. 'Take your fucking hands off me, you maniac,' the games master snarled.

Maxwell stepped back, his hands in the air. 'Who wrote the note?' he asked. 'Or who do you think wrote it?'

'This?' Harper-Bennet still had it in his hand. 'This is crap!' and he tore it in half and scattered the pieces in a flutter over the floor.

'That was a photocopy, in fact,' Maxwell said, smiling again. 'It's hard to tell from the original these days, isn't it? The original, of course, has your fingerprints on it.'

'How do you know?'

'Because it was found in your room at the Carnforth Centre.'

'Where?'

'Top drawer. Sideboard facing the bed.'

Harper-Bennet licked his lips. 'Who?' he asked. 'Who found it?'

'That doesn't really matter, does it, Alan?' Maxwell said. 'The point is that in you we have a man with a secret. And that means a man with a motive.'

'What?' Harper-Bennet did his best to laugh. 'What secret? What motive?'

'Your vast and comprehensive knicker collection, perhaps. Oh, harmless in itself of course, but the great British public — the parental generation — wouldn't understand, would they? Phrases like "What's a bloke like that doing in charge of young girls?" would start to be heard. Someone knew, didn't they? Knew about your little proclivities. And you had to pay up. That must have been hard, on a teacher's salary, I mean. Cheaper to kill, wasn't it? But then, of course, you got the wrong one. You killed Liz Striker by mistake. Tell me, did you work with her before? Or was it Rachel who knew you? One or both of them must have known you before last week or—'

'Or your theory of blackmail is a load of bollocks!' Harper-Bennet snapped. 'Look. OK, I knew about the note. Some silly sod slipped it under my door late one night—'

'Which night?'

'I don't know. Tuesday, was it? Wednesday? I can't remember. I assumed it was some sort of practical joke. I had Greg Trant down for it.'

'Trant?'

'Yes. Look, he was off form last week. Had a 'flu bug or something. Normally, he's a sod for practical joking. As a matter of fact . . . well, it sounds a bit sick now, but when the police called us together to tell us about the first murder, I naturally assumed it was Greg up to his usual tricks. No, you mark my words, he's behind that note.'

'And the knickers?'

'For Christ's sake, Maxwell,' Harper-Bennet spread his hands, 'you're holding those, I'm not. All right, so I admit I rather fancied Sally Greenhow. That's what conferences are all about, isn't it? Who gets off with who?'

'You were watching her in the pool,' Maxwell said. 'In the shower.'

'I bloody well was not!' Harper-Bennet was adamant. 'I sensed she wasn't too keen, so I let it go.'

'And that's it?'

'Well, of course that's it.'

'Why didn't you go to the police, when the blackmail note appeared, I mean?'

'I told you. I assumed it was Greg. I didn't want to get him into trouble. I intended to tackle him about it the next morning. Only the next morning Rachel King was found dead and I forgot all about it.'

'So what did you do with the note itself?'

'Put it in the top drawer . . . where you found it. Now, you answer my questions, Maxwell.' Harper-Bennet jabbed the Head of Sixth Form in the waistcoat. 'How did you come by that note?' And he didn't give Maxwell time to answer before he'd answered for him. 'You stole it, that's how. You broke into my room, stole the note and now you come here accusing me of God-knows-what kind of perversion and murder. Well, you can go to hell, Peter Maxwell.' Harper-Bennet jabbed his man again. 'And on your way there, expect a letter from my solicitor.'

And he was gone. Maxwell tucked the lacy panties into his pocket and waved at the trampoline team on the floor below.

* * *

A tall kid sat in the steamed-up 2CV in the car-park. 'Did you find Trant?' Maxwell jerked open the door.

'Teaching all day,' she said.

'Ah,' Maxwell nodded, shaking the surplus water off his panama and closing the door, 'one of Those Days. Thursday's mine. Duty day and not a free period in sight. I teach all day and then have my weekly session with the First Deputy — six hours at the chalk face followed by two at the shit face. Oh,' he glanced in the mirror, 'and talking of face . . .'

'What?'

'There appears to be egg all over mine.'

'Why?' She turned the ignition.

'Because Alan Harper-Bennet isn't our man.'

'Not?' She frowned at him.

'Not,' he smoothed down the more unruly elements in his hair, 'unless my thirty-one years of psychiatry has let me down.'

'Shouldn't that be psychology, Max?' Sally peered behind to reverse out of the Nurse's space.

'Psychiatry is the study of the disordered, isn't it?' he asked.

'I suppose, yes,' she said.

'Thirty-one years of psychiatry, then,' he said. 'No, I just got the impression that Mr Harper-B. is not the weirdo we surmised.'

'But the pool . . . ?'

'Well, that was somebody,' Maxwell said. 'I agree that panties don't walk away by themselves. It may even now have been Harper-Bennet, but the note . . . I don't think he was the original recipient of it.'

'Why?'

'As I told you back at the Carnforth, a murderer wouldn't leave evidence like that lying around. He'd destroy it. Distance himself from motive. Harper-Bennet said he thought Trant wrote it.'

'Trant?' Sally crashed her gears with the ease that years of experience had given her.

'According to Harper-Bennet, the man's a practical joker — a sort of Laurel, Hardy, the Marx Brothers and the Keystone Kops all rolled into one.'

'Struck me as rather a boring old fart,' Sally said.

'Me too,' Maxwell agreed. 'Where are we going, by the way, Sal?'

'Well, there's quite a decent pub in Wheathampstead, if I remember rightly. You're paying.'

'Oh, goodie!' Maxwell clapped his hands together.

'Then we can wander around the countryside for a bit, if the rain lets up, before looking for Verender House.'

'Verender House?'

'The home of one Andrew Moreton, PhD,' Sally beamed triumphantly.

'How did you . . . ?'

She tapped the side of her nose and the 2CV swerved alarmingly to the right. 'I went back to make my peace with the ladies of the office,' she said, 'and I used my Learning Support skills to read staff addresses upside down on the desk.'

'Brilliant. Sal,' Maxwell was suddenly serious, 'you're not going to break in, are you? To Moreton's place, I mean? With your flexible friend? Or the crowbar you habitually carry in that carpet bag of yours?'

'No need,' she said, 'he's out on bail. We're all going to have a nice little chat. Now, far more importantly, I think I'll have the lasagne for lunch.'

* * *

Verender House stood well back from the road. It was a rather grand baroque sort of place with the multiplicity of styles the Edwardians loved. There were the spiralling chimneys of Compton Whinyates, the brave arches of George Nash and over it all the measure and reason of Edward Lutyens.

'You won't get in,' a gentleman of the press had assured them, pulling his yellow hood closer around his head. 'We've all tried. Who're you with?'

'*Horse and Hound*.' Maxwell tipped his hat and ran the gamut of puddles in the wobbling wake of Sally Greenhow, for all the world like something out of Challenge Anneka. She pulled the bell-pull, once Maxwell had explained to her what it was. No reply.

'He's in there, all right,' Maxwell said. 'There wouldn't be the entire contents of Fleet Street or wherever they make newspapers nowadays ranged around his grounds if the bugger was out. Dr Moreton!' he bellowed through the letter box. 'It's Peter Maxwell. And Sally Greenhow. Might we have a word?'

The two shivered in Moreton's portico. The weather had turned with a vengeance now and the rain was clearly in for the day. The view wasn't brilliant. A fishing rod lay discarded against the wall and a pair of green wellies. Beyond the gravel of the drive, the lawns stretched away to a line of oaks and the ring of paparazzi on the ridge, like some hostile army deploying for the fray.

'Maxwell?' a muffled voice called from beyond the door. 'What do you want?'

'A word,' Maxwell repeated.

'I've been told to speak to no one,' the disembodied voice responded.

'We aren't anybody,' Maxwell wheedled, 'and anyway, we might be your only lifeline.'

There was a pause. Then a bang. And the rattle of bolts. The door swung back and a haggard Head of Science stood there. He didn't appear to have slept for the last decade.

'I can't give you long,' Moreton told them, scanning the photographers and reporters at the gate. 'I've got my solicitor coming.' And they ducked inside.

'Fuck me,' whistled the gentleman of the press. 'He's talking to *Horse and Hound*!'

'Yeah,' his nearest colleague spat out his fag. 'Which of them was the hound, would you say?'

Verender House from the inside was a huge, leaking barn of a place. Moreton, even under suspicion of murder, retained the banalities of all humans, whatever their predicament. He apologised for the mess. His charlady had gone and he wasn't finding it easy. There was family money but it hadn't come his way. He'd just been about to put the place on the market when all this had happened. It was far too big for one man, anyway. Mowing the lawn was a major project.

He led them into a dining-room where ancient furniture lay at odd angles. One corner of the settee was supported by a pile of Moreton's remainders. Though Maxwell didn't think it the moment to tax him on the subject, Moreton would have been forced to admit that his *The Krebs Cycle and its Place in the Environment* was not exactly a runaway bestseller. But it propped up furniture beautifully.

'Coffee?' he offered, rather half-heartedly.

'Charmed,' Maxwell beamed. 'You regretted, Dr Moreton, that you and I hadn't had the chance to get better acquainted at the Carnforth Centre. I thought I'd offer you that chance now.'

'I'm not sure now is a good time, Mr Maxwell,' the Head of Science muttered. Mechanically, in the cold kitchen, he sprinkled Maxwell House into three cups and switched on the kettle. 'Have seats, won't you? You said something about a lifeline?' Moreton was looking at Sally as he said this and she felt suddenly lost, out of her depth. She didn't know this man; had barely spoken to him, yet she could read all the pain etched on his face like an open book. For a moment, her nerve failed her. And she was a kid again.

'He did,' she said, pointing at Maxwell. 'He said it.'

CHAPTER 12

'So,' Peter Maxwell lolled back in the exquisitely uncomfortable chair at the Hurlington Motel, 'it's about now,' he checked out of the rain-dashed window, 'that Norman Bates comes to offer you a sandwich and a glass of milk. And you say, "No thanks, I'd rather be knifed to death in the shower and so star in one of the great cult scenes of all time."'

'If that was Janet Leigh,' Sally said, unwrapping a new twenty-pack, 'I have to say, Max, it wasn't very good.'

'If it had been, you'd have been right. As it happens, it was a perfectly masterly Alfred Hitchcock.'

'You haven't given me your verdict on Dr Moreton,' she reminded him, mechanically flicking through the channels with her black plastic remote. Peter Sissons was being particularly patronising while reading the news and *Only When I Laugh* hadn't been particularly side-splitting the first time round, let alone the third. When Clive Anderson grinned broadly at her as a third option she crossed herself and switched off.

'All right,' Maxwell crossed his legs on Sally's bed, 'what do we know? First of all, he was surprisingly forthcoming, for a man who'd been told to talk to nobody, I mean.'

'He's scared, Max.' Sally flicked into the ashtray. 'You could see it in his face.'

'You're a softie, Sally Greenhow,' Maxwell chuckled. 'A big girl's blouse.'

'Well, he's on his own, Max. You must know how that feels. His family were obviously something once, great big house and so on. Suddenly, it's all collapsing around his ears and he's Head of Science in a fourteenth-rate comprehensive.'

'But he's an arrogant sonofabitch with it,' Maxwell observed. 'A straight old-fashioned BSc would have done for the job he's doing. But no, he has to get a PhD.'

'Jealous?' Sally twitted him.

'I turned mine down,' Maxwell told her. 'Just like I sent my OBE back. Bad enough for anyone to buy Jeffrey Archer's books, but when they made him a lord, well, that was the last straw. What did surprise me, though, about old Jelly Roll was the way he coughed about clocking that woman — oh, sorry, I've been watching re-runs of Minder recently; I mean, the way he admitted to hitting the lady who beat him at squash.'

'Yes,' Sally mused, 'that was a little odd, wasn't it? Even odder for him to leave Basingstoke because of it.'

'Small-town morality,' Maxwell said. 'Whiff of scandal like that. Some people can't take it.'

'Nowhere to hide in Basingstoke, eh?' Sally smiled.

'Know what I think?' Maxwell rubbed his chin between the whiskers. 'I think our Dr Moreton has a yellow streak a mile wide.'

'Why?'

'He's afraid of responsibility. A Doctor of Biology shouldn't be working at the John Bunyan.'

'He did go for an interview on the day Liz Striker was murdered. That must say something for the man.'

'Perhaps,' Maxwell nodded, 'though we've only got his word for that. But you've got the leaving of Basingstoke thing. Couldn't cope with that situation at all. There's nowt so queer as folk.'

'What about that, Max?' she asked. 'It gives Moreton a perfect alibi for Liz. He told us he wasn't there.'

'Where was he on interview for this World Health job, did he say?'

Sally shook her head. 'We didn't think to ask,' she said.

'No,' Maxwell sighed. 'Well, we're absolute beginners in some respects. A bloody pipe, complete with human hair, is found in Moreton's bag. He doesn't know how it got there.'

'He blamed the police,' Sally said, 'for framing him.'

'Well,' Maxwell's eyes narrowed, 'it's true every other time.'

'No, no,' Sally shook her head, 'that's not what you're thinking. I've got used to your devious little face, Max. Where's your mind going now?'

'Out of the window,' Maxwell nodded, curling his lip. 'Alan Harper-Bennet said the blackmail note was slipped under his door.'

'Right.' Sally was with him so far.

'Andrew Moreton didn't explain how the murder weapon got into his bag.'

'Well, presumably,' Sally reasoned, 'you can't slip an iron pipe under a door.'

'No,' Maxwell agreed, 'you break in. Or you put it there while the room's occupant's back is turned.'

'Which brings us back to the bent policeman.'

'Or the practical joker.'

'Trant!'

'Who was teaching all day.'

'Whose address is 63, Morningside Crescent, Luton.'

'Sally Greenhow,' Maxwell said, 'remind me to put you forward for the New Year's Honours List. Whoever wrote the blackmail note gave it to Trant. Trant already had the murder weapon stashed in his room somewhere. What a crafty move, what a whizzo wheeze. He passes one to Alan Harper-Bennet, the other to Andrew Moreton. Two birds with two stones. And while the police are questioning them and chasing their own tails, he's away and laughing.'

'Except that I intercepted the note, by accident.'

'Well, if you call rifling Alan Harper-Bennet's private property an accident, yes, I suppose so. By the way, when his solicitor's letter arrives, I'm passing it to you, OK?'

'Not until he's passed my knickers to me,' she said.

'You still think it's him?' Maxwell asked.

'I don't know,' Sally said. 'I only know I felt a real presence in that pool, Max. Evil. Sheer evil. There's no other word for it.'

'Trant,' Maxwell said softly, 'Trant is another word for it. Goodnight, Sal. I'll be next door if you need me. Oh,' he paused in the doorway, 'and if a rather wizened old girl in a rocking chair appears, hot foot from the fruit cellar, and calls you Norman, run like hell!'

* * *

They divided in order to conquer the next morning, Friday. Liz Striker had been dead for eight days, Rachel King for four. For Malcolm and McBride, established in their new incident room at Ashford, it was early days. They had not yet reached the first plateau that inevitably marked any murder enquiry. But mistakes had been made. Bum-Bum Malcolm was hastening very slowly. He didn't want any more.

For Sally and Maxwell, there was an aching sense of working in a void. In Maxwell's case, it was like trying to teach Napoleon without knowing the first thing about the man — rather as Paul Moss must feel most days, Maxwell mused. He didn't know what the police knew. He was looking for a needle in a haystack. And he was looking in the dark.

And over it all he kept seeing the smiling face of Rachel King. In his mind, she was walking with him on the shingle along the Dungeness coast, the wind in her hair. Or lying in the cool grass of a Cambridge summer, listening to the whisper of the water. Only once did he see her that last day, the day he'd lost her for the first time, the day he told her it was over. It had been raining, it seemed, for ever, but that night of their last May Ball was the loveliest he'd seen and the glittering glass ball flashed firefly light along the Backs. And when he told her it was over she was holding his hand and running his finger around her lips and she bit down hard so that her teeth were bloody. And she'd said in a voice he'd never forget, 'I hate you, Peter Maxwell.' And he shook himself free of the memory and went in search of Gregory Trant.

Maxwell and Sally had had words that morning. She wanted to tackle Trant. What possible use could Phyllida Bowles be? Maxwell agreed, probably not a lot, but if Trant was their man, he'd killed two women already. It just wasn't safe. And Maxwell had made a promise, albeit by proxy, to Alan Greenhow. Gregory Trant was a Second Deputy, a sort of Dan Quayle of the British education system. In some schools, they oversee the pastoral work of the Year or House teams, liaising with outside agencies like welfare and social services. In others, they do the timetable. In others — and the John Bunyan turned out to be one of these — no one knows what the bloody hell they do.

The man's office was quite difficult to find, up stairs and along corridors, but at least the sun was shining again today and Maxwell was shown up by a monosyllabic youth with a prefect's badge pinned to his scrawny chest.

'Gregory!' Maxwell hailed the man like a long-lost brother. The swivel-eyed git had a swivel chair too and he swung it round to greet the Head of Sixth Form.

'Max!' Trant extended a hand. 'Thank you, George,' he called after the already retreating prefect. 'Oh, George?' The boy turned. 'Flies,' and he pointed a finger at the lad's nether regions. The lad looked down, only to hear Trant chuckle as he closed the door.

'Gets him every time,' the Deputy said. 'Have a seat, Max. Can I offer you an indescribable cup of coffee?'

'No, thanks.'

'Now, I know why you're here.' Trant switched off the computer he was working on. 'Oh, bugger, just wiped the entire Year 10 records there. Never mind. Those women in the office don't have enough to do, anyway.'

'Do you?' Maxwell asked.

'Do I what? Have enough to do? God, yes.'

'No,' Maxwell smiled. 'I mean, do you know why I've come?'

'Yes. Or at least the gist of it. I had Alan Harper-Bennet bleeding his heart all over my carpet yesterday. Seems you accused him of being a knicker-sniffer, murderer and so on. I haven't seen him so annoyed since I locked him in the shower last term.'

'Oh, I think Alan's over-reacting,' Maxwell smiled, trying to decide which one of Trant's roving eyes was actually doing the seeing.

'I must admit, I do find it a little bizarre,' Trant said.

'What?'

'You asking all these questions.'

'Why?'

'Well, it's the job of the police, isn't it? You don't actually have any right.'

'No,' Maxwell agreed, 'no more than somebody had the right to cave in the skulls of Liz Striker and Rachel King.'

'Oh, quite, but—'

'You'll forgive me for saying this,' Maxwell leaned forward so that the sun was out of his eyes, 'but you appear to be more . . . how can I put it? Extrovert than you were at Carnforth.'

'Really?' Trant chuckled. 'Well, I wasn't well last week. Had a bug or something. It's doing the rounds here. When I wasn't actually at lectures or sessions at Carnforth, I was getting my head down. And I don't mind confessing the sight of poor old Liz Striker in the stock cupboard wasn't exactly a bundle of laughs.'

'You were there on the Thursday, when Liz Striker died?'

'Yes.'

'What did you do?'

'Look, Max—'

'Humour me, Gregory,' Maxwell cut in, sensing the man's reluctance. 'I hear you have something of a reputation as a humorist.'

'Well, you know how it is,' Trant said. '"You don't have to be mad to work here . . ."'

Maxwell nodded. He was mad and he didn't work there. 'So,' he said quietly, 'Thursday.'

'Thursday.' Trant shut his eyes to remember. 'We got there in the minibus about eleven. Phyllida was keen to get her photocopying done—'

'Photocopying?' Maxwell asked.

'Yes. We had a presentation to give. As a school with some GNVQ experience. Phyllida's a nice woman, Max, but she has the organizational abilities of a gerbil. She hadn't had time to photocopy bits and pieces, so she used Carnforth's.'

'What time was that?'

'I don't know. Lunchtime? Yes, it must have been, because she was late in to lunch and said that's where she'd been.'

'Did you go down to the basement?'

'No. My end of the presentation was the display boards. We had all those in the bus so I spent the day unloading and setting up. Alan Harper-B. was with me. By about three I'd had enough. I was feeling deathly, so I went to have a lie-down.'

'In Room number . . . ?'

'Er . . . 218, I think. Yes, it was.'

'Did you know Liz Striker beforehand?'

'No. In fact, I didn't ever meet her. Looking back, she must have been the woman I saw talking to Michael Wynn and that vicar bloke — Whatsisface? Gracebrothers?'

'Gracewell.'

'That's right,' Trant clicked his fingers. 'That was when we arrived.'

'Does this look familiar?' Maxwell rummaged in his jacket pocket and handed Trant a letter, the second of his photocopies. The Second Deputy read it. 'No,' he frowned. 'Should it?'

'That's a copy, of course.'

'Of course.'

'The original was found in Alan Harper-Bennet's room on the night after Rachel King died.'

'Really? Well, well, well. What is it?'

'Quite obviously a blackmail note, wouldn't you say?'

'Ho, ho, ho. Well, I don't want to be a bitch, Max, but I can quite see why Alan was so miffed. You thought he was being blackmailed.'

'It did occur,' Maxwell nodded. 'So you locked Alan in the shower last term?'

'Eh? Oh, yes, yes.' Trant was still looking at the letter.

'Make a habit of this sort of thing, do you?'

'Well, it passes the time.'

'Like embarrassing boy George there a minute ago?'

'Oh, he's used to it. No harm meant.'

'Bit different with murder though, isn't it?' Maxwell asked.

'I'm sorry,' Trant said, 'I don't follow.'

'Alan says that someone slipped it under his door.'

'Well,' Trant giggled, 'he would, wouldn't he?'

Maxwell had heard better Mandy Rice-Davieses.

'I also talked to Dr Moreton yesterday.'

'Andrew? How is the poor old bastard? I heard he was out. Why did the police hold him?'

'Oh, come now, Greg, me ol' mucker, you and I both know you know the answer to that one.'

'Come again?' Trant frowned.

'The iron pipe with the bloody tape wrapped round it. A conventional piece of scaffolding, such as you have on your science block out there, for instance,' Maxwell pointed to the building work in progress through Trant's window, 'adorned, for a better grip, no doubt, by the sort of gaffer tape you doubtless use in your school shows' electrical set-up. What did you do this year?'

'Er . . . Oliver.'

'Yes' Maxwell nodded, 'I somehow knew it would be.'

'What are you saying, exactly?'

'My, my,' Maxwell beamed, 'we are obtuse today. Must be why you're only a Second Deputy, Greg.'

'Now, look—' The renowned humorist appeared to have lost his sense of humour.

'The bottom line, Greg,' Maxwell wasn't smiling either, 'is that someone caved in the head of Liz Striker because he thought she was blackmailing him. Why, I don't know. When he realised his mistake, he demolished Rachel King's skull likewise—'

'Because she was the blackmailer?'

'I don't know,' Maxwell said, 'I really don't know. But however that turns out, our friend had a blackmail note and a murder weapon on his hands. He also had policemen swarming all over the Carnforth Centre. If he ran, they'd have him. My guess is that if he so much as left the building, he'd be followed — I was. So he couldn't bury the bits of pipe anywhere. Then an idea occurred to him. Why not muddy the waters a bit? Why not slip the blackmail note into somebody else's room — say Alan Harper-Bennet's — and hide the pipe? The police would be bound to carry out a search sooner or later. And bingo! Two prime suspects.'

'Are you saying I did that?' Trant was astonished. 'I framed Alan and Andrew? There are laws of slander in this country, Maxwell.'

'Sod the laws of slander,' Maxwell growled. 'A woman I once loved is lying on a slab somewhere because of this, Trant. And I'm going to get to the bottom of it.'

'That's ridiculous.' Trant was on his feet, the muscles in his jaw rigid. 'I barely knew Rachel King . . .'

Maxwell sat back in the chair. From his left the morning sun flickered across his view of Gregory Trant. Then the Second Deputy slumped into his own chair and sat staring at the floor — and the wall.

'That's one little gem I bet you didn't tell the police,' Maxwell said.

'It's not important,' Trant said.

'You'll forgive me if I decide that.' Maxwell clasped his fingers across his chest.

'You're enjoying this, aren't you?' Trant snapped, blinking.

'You know how it is,' Maxwell said. 'No one expects the Spanish Inquisition.'

I don't have to talk to you at all,' Trant bellowed.

'It's me or the police,' Maxwell told him. He reached for the phone. 'Press 9, do I, for an outside line?'

'All right,' Trant took the receiver from him, 'all right, you've made your point. What do you want to know?'

'Your relationship with Rachel,' Maxwell said.

'Relationship is hardly the word for it,' Trant said. 'I worked with her husband, Jeremy.'

'In teaching?'

'No. I came late to the profession.'

Maxwell raised an eyebrow of derision. He at least had the excuse that he was young and naive when he started teaching. Going into the profession when you're mature and with both eyes open — well, that was inexcusable.

'Before that I was in insurance. No money in it, but somebody said the hours were good. Jeremy was my boss.'

'And you met Rachel socially?'

'Yes. We — my wife Gail and I — had the Kings round for dinner. We were still in Bournemouth then. I don't want to talk ill of the dead, Maxwell, especially of someone you say you were fond of, but . . . well, not to put too fine a point on it, Rachel King was a bitch.'

'Really?' Maxwell could feel his knuckles whiten.

'She was a first-class flirt. Gave me the come-on from that evening.'

'The come-on?'

'Do I have to spell this out?' Trant grunted. 'She got me into bed with her. Oh, it took a while. What was it? Two weeks? Three? Gail knew nothing, of course. I felt rotten about it.'

'How very *Brief Encounter* of you.'

'Look, Maxwell,' Trant snarled, 'I am, in my own warped and rather belated way, trying to help you. Now, this may not be what you wanted to hear—'

'I want to hear the truth, for Christ's sake,' Maxwell shouted.

A bell punctuated the silence that fell between them and they heard that familiar sound that haunts all schools — the rumble of an army on the move, of hell on the march as children went from one lesson to the next.

'All right,' Trant said, 'the truth is what you'll get. I fancied her. Of course I did. I was twenty-three then. Gail was pregnant with Harry. The bedroom was a tad boring. Well, if you loved her, you must remember what she was like. The older woman, but a body like . . . Well, anyway, we'd meet whenever we could. Jeremy was often away on various financial conferences and so on. I could come and go without Gail suspecting. It worked, in a cheap sort of way. I even — and this is the daft bit — I even found myself falling in love with Rachel. One day — I seem to remember it was a Friday, like today — I went to see her, unannounced. I knew Jeremy wouldn't be there. What I didn't know was that Phil was.'

'Phil?' Maxwell frowned.

'I think that was his name. He was wearing one of Jeremy's bathrobes and she was in the shower. There was the most almighty scene. I managed to get her on her own and told her how I felt. Do you know what she did, Maxwell? She laughed at me. Like I was a little boy. I could have killed her.'

'Could you?' Maxwell asked.

Trant caught the look on his interrogator's face. 'That was then,' he said quietly. 'What? Ten, eleven years ago. I'm not talking about last week.'

'What did you think?' Maxwell asked after a while. 'What did you think when you saw her again, at the Carnforth Centre?'

'I couldn't believe it. I hadn't seen her from that day, when we had our row. For months I kept expecting her to drop me in it, to tell Gail. In the end I left the job.'

'Because of Rachel?' Maxwell frowned.

'Oh, not totally,' Trant sighed. 'Insurance wasn't for me, anyway, I'd realised. Rachel King was just the icing on the cake. What did I think? I thought, "You bitch." She was making eyes at Moreton, Harper-Bennet, had that snivelling snotnose chaplain dribbling over her. You were joined to her by the hip. When we came face to face she looked right through me. It was as if I didn't exist. OK, so I didn't feel on top form anyway; the flu, Liz Striker. But seeing her again, that was why I was so low last week.'

'And now she doesn't exist,' Maxwell said softly.

'You knew her before, obviously,' Trant said.

'Oh, yes. She was Rachel Cameron then. We were students together at Cambridge. It's as if . . . as if she were a different person.'

'Perhaps she was,' Trant said. 'Perhaps something made her change.'

'Yes.' Peter Maxwell stood up. 'And I think that something was me.'

* * *

It was one of those sunsets that evening. One of those moments of pure magic when everything is gilded and you want it to last for ever.

'Thank God it's Friday,' Sally said, watching the rooks flap homewards against the purple lines of cloud. 'Here's looking at you, Max.'

He raised his glass automatically and for a second it flashed in the dying sun. 'Home tomorrow, Max?' she asked.

He looked at her, this girl who hadn't wanted to come. She'd phoned in sick to Leighford High the day before. All she'd wanted was her home, her husband, the comfortable routines of whining, whinging kids with attitude problems. She hadn't wanted lies and tears and blood. But that's what she'd got. That's what they'd both got.

'Home tonight if you like,' he said.

'No,' she shook her head, 'it's getting on. And I don't actually like driving in the dark. Look . . .' She moved closer to him, shuffling forward and nudging his knuckles with hers. 'You mustn't read anything into what Gregory Trant said. About Rachel changing, I mean. If she sent that note to whoever she sent it to, that was her business. She had her reasons. And she'd have done it anyway, whether she'd ever met you or not.'

'Would she, Sal?' He looked at her. The Great Cynic was suddenly small, vulnerable. Sally Greenhow wanted to put her arms round him, hold him, tell him it was all right. 'Would she? We'll never know now, will we?'

And he swigged back the last of his travelling bottle of Southern Comfort.

'You didn't tell me,' he said, feeling the amber nectar sting his tastebuds. 'Phyllida Bowles. What did the fair Phyllida confide?'

'The fair Phyllida's taken it rather badly. Apparently she'd given up smoking,' Sally flicked her ash vaguely in the direction of the litter bin and missed, 'before all this. What happened at the Carnforth Centre tipped her over the edge and she's back on thirty a day.'

'So, between puffs and coughs, you didn't learn very much.'

'Well, I strolled in the grounds with her, you know, away from the kids.'

'Always therapeutic,' Maxwell nodded.

'I got her talking about our colleagues on the course.'

'Ah.'

'I'm paraphrasing here, of course . . .'

'Safer than paragliding, I've always found,' Maxwell said.

'Well, she's always thought Andrew Moreton was unstable. You only have to hear him bawling out kids apparently — makes Attila the Hun look like the Dalai Lama.'

As an historian, Maxwell had often noted the physical similarity, but it would have spoiled Sally's analogy had he pointed it out, so he shut up instead.

'She'd got Trant pegged for an idiot. False fire drills and false noses aren't her idea of professionalism apparently. Infantile was her final verdict. She felt uncomfortable in the presence of Valerie Marks for some daft reason, but then I happen to know Valerie's happily ensconced with some frilly type; has been for years.'

'Sort of Nanette Newman in *The Stepford Wives*? Baking, preening and robotic?'

'If you say so,' Sally nodded, not always sure what Mad Max was on about.

'How does Phyllie rate Alan Harper-Bennet?'

'Impotent,' Sally beamed.

'She's good at the one-word put-downs, isn't she? Perhaps I can get her a job at Leighford High,' and he rubbed his chin thoughtfully.

'I think . . .' It was Sally Greenhow's turn to get a funny look in her eye.

'Yes?' Maxwell put on his best Frazier Crane.

'I think Phyllida developed a bit of a crush for Michael Wynn.'

'Really?' Maxwell was all ears.

'She mentioned him a lot. "Michael said this" or "Michael did that".'

'Did he reciprocate?'

'If you're going to talk dirty, Max,' Sally winked, 'I'm leaving.'

'Fine,' the Head of Sixth Form said, 'but this is your room and you haven't answered the question.'

'Apparently not. He just showed her photographs of his wife and the boys.'

'That's what Rachel said,' Maxwell suddenly remembered.

'What is?'

'That Michael was very much the family man.'

'Except that he was sweetly shy about it.'

'Sweetly shy?' Maxwell frowned.

'Her words. He'd only show her the photos when they were alone.'

'They were alone?' Maxwell mouthed.

'Apparently,' Sally grinned. 'I didn't like to pry too deeply.'

'Phyllida is a Miss, isn't she?'

'By a mile,' Sally said. 'Oops, there's another sexist gaffe. Shot myself in the foot again.'

'Did she say any of them could, in her opinion, be guilty of murder?' Maxwell asked.

'She's afraid, Max,' Sally told him. 'Even here, back on the old treadmill, she can't get it out of her mind. She told me she can't sleep and when she does, she has dreams of those corridors at Carnforth. She's done no photocopying since she's been back.'

'I wonder,' Maxwell said softly, turning to the red-gold of the sky, 'I wonder if any of us can forget it. Ever. Anyway, she needn't have worried about Michael Wynn. He was making eyes at Tracey the receptionist.'

'Was he now?'

'So Margot Jenkinson told me. But then, we must assume that Margot's vision is a threat impaired by the little pink elephants. You know what I found odd about Phyllida Bowles?'

Sally shook her head. It was late and she felt desperately tired.

'What she said when we got back from the beach on the problem-solving day. She saw the cop cars and said, "They must have found Liz Striker." Prophetic soul, isn't she, our Phyllie?'

CHAPTER 13

That Saturday, Inspector John McBride went to Luton. And the first person he went to see was Phyllida Bowles. WPC O'Halloran was with him and a motley crew of kids were playing unseasonal football in the park, spurred on by the forthcoming World Cup in America.

Phyllida Bowles was a wall-coloured woman, with straight, shoulder-length blonde hair and glasses frames that matched her pallid skin. It wasn't impossible for Mr Right to have come along, but the fact was that he hadn't in all her thirty-nine years and in that time she'd become over-fussy, pedantic to the point of neurosis. And on Saturday morning, she walked in the park, come hell or high water, with the repulsive little Chihuahua which minced at her ankles.

McBride hadn't objected to the stroll. It was pleasant wandering under the acacias and the silver birch and he found himself wondering, as he often did in those situations, what passers-by thought of the threesome and if they knew what he and O'Halloran did for a living and that the woman who walked between them was a suspect in a murder enquiry.

'What sort of opinion did you form of Rachel King?' he asked Phyllida.

'Opinion?' She tugged the scampering Chihuahua to heel. 'Well, actually, I didn't like her.'

'Really?' McBride said. 'Why was that?'

'I don't know.' Phyllida pushed the glasses back up the bridge of her nose, another of the little habits she'd acquired in twenty years of solitude. 'It's difficult to quantify it.' Phyllida was a Maths teacher at heart. 'Something to do with men, I suppose.'

'Men?' Being allowed to wear plain clothes had clearly given Mavis O'Halloran ideas above her station. She was asking the questions now. 'In what way?'

Phyllida didn't like having to twist her neck in two directions. Still, the walk had been at her insistence, so she could hardly complain. She hadn't liked the idea of the police in her house, invading her privacy. 'She was a man's woman,' she said, frowning as if to concentrate on Rachel and her memories of her. 'A flirt, if you like. She was one of those annoying people who don't seem to be paying attention all that much. Oh, they say "yes" and "no" in the right places, but their eyes are always wandering. Always looking over your shoulder. It's very disconcerting.'

'And who was Rachel looking at during these conversations?' McBride asked.

'Oh, I don't know. Just men in general, I think. I can't recall anyone in particular, except . . .'

'Yes?' the police persons chorused.

'Peter Maxwell was here yesterday. At school, I mean.'

McBride had stopped walking. So had O'Halloran. 'Was he?' the Inspector asked.

'And Sally Greenhow. I didn't actually speak to Mr Maxwell, but Sally and I went for a walk.'

'What did you talk about?' McBride resumed the two and a half miles an hour stroll he'd learned at Bramshill.

'Oh, people on the course mostly. At Carnforth. What I thought of them. Pretty well what you're asking now.'

'I see. While you were talking to Mrs Greenhow, where was Mr Maxwell?'

'I don't know,' Phyllida shrugged, reaching in her handbag for her cigarettes. 'But I know he talked to Gregory.'

'Gregory Trant?'

'Yes. And to Dr Moreton too, I understand.'

'Well, well,' McBride threw a glance at the WPC, 'he has been a busy little bee, hasn't he?' And all three of them knew that 'bee' stood for bastard.

* * *

'Pull him in,' was Superintendent Malcolm's order over the car phone. 'Pull both of them in. If they're going to play Nick and Nora Charles all over the place, they must expect to have their collars felt. You've got their addresses?'

McBride had their addresses. He and O'Halloran left Phyllida Bowles by the tennis courts and drove south. The M25 was the sluggish bitch it always was and, infuriating though it was, this was not an enquiry that merited blue flashing lights and screaming sirens, so the unmarked police car idled along with all the other Saturday strollers, belching fumes into the ozone over Surrey.

It was nearly three before they reached Leighford and neither of them had eaten. At a service station they grabbed a Ginsters and a packet of Salt 'n' Shake each and washed it all down with something diet in a can. Then they drove for Maxwell's home in Columbine Avenue.

Like all the houses in Columbine, number 38 was a town house, built in the heady '80s before the recession bit hard and builders went out of business, leaving scaffolding and rain-filled holes in the ground where dreams and profits lay together in the mud. McBride had driven all the way from Luton. O'Halloran could have the honour of ringing Maxwell's chimes.

'He's not in, you know.' The rather plummy elderly voice came from nowhere. McBride peered through the privet bush to his left. A rather plummy elderly lady stood there, in gardening gloves, inspecting her roses.

'We're looking for Mr Maxwell,' the Inspector said, walking round the bush to look the old bat full in the face.

'Yes, I know you are,' she said, looking at the callers over her pince-nez. 'I've told you. He's not in.'

'Do you know where he's gone, Miss . . . ?'

'Mrs,' the elderly lady insisted quietly. McBride narrowed his eyes at her. It could be possible. 'I'm afraid before I can tell you that, I shall need to know who you are and what your business is with Mr Maxwell. I am a member of the Neighbourhood Watch Committee, you know.'

'Of course you are,' McBride smiled, and he flashed his warrant card. 'I am Detective Inspector McBride of the Kent CID and this is WPC O'Halloran.'

'Hello, my dear,' the old girl smiled. 'My name is Jessica Troubridge. I'm Mr Maxwell's next-door neighbour.'

'Hello,' WPC O'Halloran smiled back.

'WPC,' Mrs Troubridge tutted, 'that's about as unattractive as those awful hats they make you wear. What's your real name, dear?'

'Er . . . Mavis,' the WPC confessed.

'Oh dear.' The old lady's face fell. 'Still, there it is. Damage's been done now, I suppose.'

'You were about to tell us where Mr Maxwell is.' McBride thought it time to intervene.

'Was I?' Mrs Troubridge frowned. 'Oh no, I don't think so.'

'You don't?' It was McBride's turn to frown. Any minute now the old girl would probably start painting the roses red.

'Well, how can I?' She spread her scrawny arms. 'You see, I don't know where he is.'

'Has he just popped out for a minute, Mrs Troubridge?' O'Halloran asked. She had a granny about the old girl's age. You had to give them a bit of help. 'Gone down Tesco's?'

'Please don't patronise me, Policewoman O'Halloran. With a first name like yours, you can't afford to. Mr Maxwell wouldn't be seen dead "down Tesco's", as you put it. He has an account at Rohan's, a delicatessen and vintners in the High Street. And if he's popped anywhere, it's a long pop.'

'Er . . . in what sense, Mrs Troubridge?' McBride knew a venomous old besom when he saw one.

'Why do you people, out of your jurisdiction, I may add, want to talk to him? That business at Leighford High was cleared up.'

'We aren't concerned with anything at Leighford High, madam,' McBride said, 'and neither are we out of our jurisdiction. This isn't America, you know.'

'You haven't answered my question.' She stood her ground.

'We are pursuing a murder enquiry,' McBride told her.

'Good heavens.' Jessica Troubridge gripped her pruning shears. 'Perhaps this is America. I'm sure Mr Maxwell is in the clear. He has a degree, you know.'

'Where has he gone, madam?' McBride could sense his hackles rising uncontrollably.

'I've told you. I don't know.' She stood nose to chest with him. 'All I know is that he has gone for the weekend. I have instructions to feed his cat.'

'And he didn't say where he was going?'

'He did not.' Mrs Troubridge was adamant. 'Am I my neighbour's keeper?'

'No, madam.' McBride turned to the road. 'And I bet you're glad about that.' He glanced at Mavis O'Halloran. 'I know I would be.'

* * *

There weren't many state boarding schools in the '90s. Most of them began life as institutions for forces kids, in the days when Britain still had a Commonwealth of sorts and the Army of the Rhine was there in case the Germans misbehaved themselves for a third time in the century. St Bede's School, Bournemouth was doubly unusual to the point of being unique. It was a Catholic state boarding school.

Maxwell knew this already of course — that St Bede's was Catholic, that is. What he wasn't prepared for was the boarding bit. He'd taken the train that Saturday morning and rattled west. There were rumours of an impending rail strike, but Jimmy Knapp couldn't be that much of a dinosaur, could he? To take his union into a running fight with Mr Major and the forces of progress? Maxwell had staggered back to his seat from buying his tea and his limp bacon and egg roll, fully aware as he caught his groin for the umpteenth time on a seat corner why it was called the buffet car.

The Head of Sixth Form knew Bournemouth tolerably well. In keeping with Sally Greenhow's view that he could town-bore for England, Maxwell was aware that Squire Lewis Tregonwell had transformed the bare Dorset heathland as far back as 1811 when he'd built a summer house where now stands the Royal Exeter Hotel. He was also aware that Sir George Taps-Gervis built on the site twenty-six years later. A jetty, a pier and an arcade followed as inevitably as trouble followed Peter Maxwell.

He followed the Bourne as it wound down to the sea through the pine-scented Upper Gardens. It was an oddly geometric town, Bournemouth, with the Square, which he crossed, and the Triangle off to the west. He took the Old Christchurch Road past the Railway Museum and on to Madeira Road and the police station. The traffic was heavy. It was the hard court tennis championships that week and the hotels were bustling as the town enjoyed an early boost to the season. It all made Leighford look like a graveyard.

Off Holdenhurst Road, he reached it, a cluster of '30s buildings surrounded by '60s high-rise, already swathed in scaffolding. The only thing that made the school look different from any other was the wrought-iron monstrosity welded to the wall; the Venereal Bede, monk and scholar, fifteen foot high in gilded metal.

Peter Maxwell didn't really know why he'd come. He only knew he wasn't happy with the answers he'd got from the Luton lot. And that he didn't want Sally with him. He knew that if he'd breathed a word to her yesterday, about his intention to make this journey too, she'd have been there, outside number 38, Columbine, engine ticking over, tapping ash into her ashtray and listening to something indescribable on FM. And that wouldn't have been fair. Sally had been through enough.

* * *

Sally sat with her back to the wall watching Superintendent Terry Malcolm. She'd wanted Alan to be with her, but Superintendent Malcolm had pointed out that he wasn't a solicitor and that his presence would only complicate things. Did she have a solicitor? Only some office junior who'd stung the Greenhows pretty sharply when they'd bought their house. And the little shit had had trouble conveyancing. She knew he'd be totally out of his depth with this. So Sally was alone. And Alan sat in a bleak waiting-room where posters pointed out the fairly obvious fact that there was a thief about. Others urged him to lock his car. An earnest-looking desk man had offered him a cup of tea, but Alan didn't drink tea and they didn't do coffee. So he sat and he looked at his watch and he waited.

Sally watched Malcolm and she watched the tape recorder spool turning.

'Tell me again,' the Superintendent said, 'just for the record.'

Sally hadn't caught the name of the Sergeant from West Sussex CID sitting next to the great man; but she didn't like him. The WPC over by the cold radiator had an irritating sniff and, for a moment, Sally wondered if this was part of the routine — a sort of nasal Chinese torture designed to make her crack. If that was so, it was damn close to working.

'We went to investigate,' she told the Superintendent, 'Mr Maxwell and I. We knew the police . . . you . . . had detained Dr Moreton. We wanted to know why.'

Malcolm smiled. 'Tell me, Mrs Greenhow,' he said, 'if you had a toothache, would you do your own root canal work?'

'No.' She blinked at the stupidity of the question.

'Or deliver your own baby?'

'Probably not.' Sally felt her throat mottling. Who did this objectionable bastard think he was, probing in this highly personal way?

'Then why do you presume to carry out enquiries which are properly the business of the police?'

'I felt . . . I just felt . . .' Sally had been too long in Special Needs. The cut and thrust of intellectual debate was not her daily fare. When you're dealing, day in, day out, with kids with room temperature IQs, you don't have to be Einstein.

'You just felt you had to support Peter Maxwell,' Malcolm finished the sentence for her.

'No. I . . . Well . . .'

'Sally,' Malcolm said softly, 'we know. We know he knew Rachel King before. We know he was personally involved.'

'You can't possibly think he killed her,' she said, staring the man in the face. She took a deep breath. She wouldn't let him rattle her. She wouldn't let him rattle her and she wouldn't shop Max. She owed him more than that.

'I don't know who killed Rachel King,' Malcolm said, 'but it's only a matter of time until I do. Or it would be if we didn't have amateurs tripping over each other in the middle of it.'

'It was Maxwell's idea, though, wasn't it?' the dislikeable Sergeant asked.

Sally's eyes flickered across to him. His face was flat, cold, expressionless. Alongside the elegant Malcolm, he looked like a squashed bug. 'I drove him,' she said. 'Max doesn't drive.'

'That's odd,' the Sergeant said. 'In a bloke, I mean.'

Sally just scowled at him. The remark was so predictable, so sexist, she wouldn't give it the satisfaction of a reply.

'All right,' Malcolm said. 'So you spoke to whom?'

'Er . . . Phyllida Bowles, Gregory Trant, Alan Harper-Bennet, Andrew Moreton.'

'The whole gamut,' Malcolm nodded.

'We wanted some answers,' Sally told him. 'Look, can I have a cigarette?' She fumbled in her bag.

'They're bad for you,' the Sergeant said with a smirk.

'Of course,' Malcolm interrupted and flicked out a lighter. Smooth bastard, thought Sally, but she let him light the ciggie for her. Her own hand was shaking and she couldn't trust herself. The Superintendent put the lighter away and leaned back. 'Inspector McBride had paid a visit to Mr Maxwell before he called on you,' he said. 'Unfortunately, Mr Maxwell wasn't in. A couple of boys from the Sussex force have kindly consented to sit all night in a cold, cramped car, just in case he returns. You wouldn't care to save them the trouble, would you? By telling us where he is, I mean?'

'I don't know where he is. The last I saw of him was early this morning. I dropped him at home and that was it.'

'You'd driven straight from Luton?'

'That's right.'

'What time did you get to Leighford?'

'I don't know. Nine thirty? Ten? We left early from the motel.'

'Share a room, did you?' The Sergeant still had the same smirk on his face.

Sally leaned to the microphone. 'No, you smutty little bastard, I did not share a room with Peter Maxwell. The man is a colleague of mine. Nothing more. I don't have to be here at all, still less listening to your infantile innuendo.'

The WPC against the radiator felt like clapping, but she was not a brave soul and her whole upbringing had conspired to persuade her it was a man's world. In the event, she simply sat.

'I'm afraid you do have to be here,' Malcolm said, his smile gone. 'Interfering in a police enquiry is a criminal offence.'

'I wouldn't call asking some questions interfering,' Sally said, trying to keep her voice in check. She got a bit shrill when she was annoyed and she felt her larynx tightening for the big one.

Malcolm jerked his head at the Sergeant who glared at Sally, then scraped back his chair and made for the door. The Superintendent quickly adjusted the volume control as the slam shook the room.

'You know, Sally,' he said quietly, 'you've made life a bit difficult for us.'

'Have I?' She fidgeted with her cigarette, then sat back and crossed her knees. 'How?'

'We've had rather a bad press recently,' he told her. 'Miscarriages of justice, calls to arm us, longer night sticks and so on. It all smacks to people of a police state.'

'Is this relevant?' She was summoning up her reserves of defiance and he knew it.

'Bear with me,' he smiled. 'We are surrounded by the yob culture, Sally. Depending on whose figures you believe, we're either drowning or we've been at the bottom for years and fishes gnaw our bones. Our job is not made any easier by the cognoscenti like you, the great middle class we were created to protect. You're intelligent enough to realise that we're actually on the same side, you and I.'

Sally knew that Mad Max would have had an answer to that, but Mad Max wasn't there. And she was. She felt like a little girl again, that time her kid brother had smashed a window and she was left to take the rap.

'I found the note,' she said and even then she couldn't believe she was saying it.

'Did you?' Malcolm said, his face expressionless, his eyes cold. He hadn't the first idea what Sally Greenhow was talking about, but he'd thrown her a lifeline in that cruel sea of the yob culture and she'd caught at it.

'I didn't realise what it was. Not at first.' She was feeling better already. 'Then I knew it was blackmail.'

The WPC in the corner stiffened, but she was young. Naive. Had a long way to go. Malcolm hadn't moved.

'Where was the note?' he asked.

'Top drawer. Left-hand side,' Sally remembered. 'Alan Harper-Bennet's room at the Carnforth Centre.'

'And what did it say?'

'Er . . .' She shut her eyes tight. 'I can't remember exactly. The gist of it was that whoever it was had got the wrong person. The blackmailer was still alive and wanted paying.'

'So you assumed, you and Maxwell, that Mr Harper-Bennet was the murderer?'

'That's what I thought,' she nodded. 'He'd been chatting me up, making a play in a rather schoolboyish way. I . . .' She noticed her cigarette had gone out, but the Superintendent didn't offer to relight it. 'I think he was watching me in the swimming pool.'

He nodded.

'I also think he stole my underwear.' He nodded again.

'Well, I know it sounds ridiculous, but I wanted them back, Superintendent. I felt . . . dirty, somehow. The fact that he was watching me. By getting my underwear back . . . well, I'd have burned them, of course, but I'd feel . . . complete again. It's difficult to explain.'

'So you broke into his room?'

'No. He invited me there. While he was in the other room, I had a look in the drawer. There was the note.'

'On top?'

'Yes,' she smiled quickly. 'That's what Max thought as well.'

'Really?' Malcolm was bemused. 'What did Mr Maxwell think?'

'That it was peculiar to find such a damning piece of evidence so relatively easily. The first place I looked I found that.'

'That was peculiar as far as Mr Maxwell was concerned, was it?'

'Of course. He said it was planted. We now think it was Gregory Trant.'

'Mr Trant?'

'One thing we learned at Luton,' she said, getting into her stride now, on a high of confession, 'is that Trant is a notorious practical joker. Either he is the murderer and implicated Harper-Bennet with the blackmail note and Moreton with the iron pipe, or at least he knows who the murderer is.'

'And, having talked to Mr Trant, to which conclusion did you and Mr Maxwell come?'

'Neither,' Sally said. 'I think that by the end of yesterday, all this had finally got to Max. You see, he once loved Rachel King. He can't bring himself to believe that she was the murderer's real target; that she was a blackmailer. They could have married. You don't want to believe that about your other half.'

'No, indeed,' Malcolm nodded. 'And tell me, where is the note now?'

'Max has got it. He's . . . Oh, God.' And only then did Sally Greenhow realise what she'd done. She'd sold Mad Max down the river. She leaned her head to one side, looking straight at Terry Malcolm. As though she were listening. As though she'd heard, in Pontius Pilate's presence, the cock crow thrice.

CHAPTER 14

Now Peter Maxwell had heard of POOO — Parents Opposed to Opting Out. He'd even been pressured into joining TOOO — Teachers Opposed to Opting Out — though he'd never paid his sub. Yet, here he sat in the Principal's study, trying to come to terms with the excruciating chesterfield and the fact that St Bede's had opted out last year. He'd had to walk past two hideous photographs, first of the Pope, then of a benign old boy beaming at and shaking hands with John Patten.

The benign old boy shuffled noiselessly into the room as Maxwell sat, watching the gulls wheel in the May sunshine over St Bede's extensive playing fields.

'Mr Maxwell?'

The Head of Sixth Form rose to grip the benign old hand. 'Father Brendan?'

'Do sit down. Can I get you a coffee? Something stronger?'

For a moment, Maxwell was tempted to order a Southern Comfort, but the ancient Father might have been referring to tea, so he declined. Father Brendan sat back in his opulent chair, the other side of his opulent desk. This could have been a little ante-room in the Vatican. It bore no relationship to the graffiti-strewn corridors and scruffy staff-room offices of Maxwell's own dear high school. The old man bore a passing resemblance to Wilfrid Hyde White and Maxwell had seen many a film where he'd found the old actor to be rather sinister and anything but what he seemed.

'It's good of you to give me your time on a Saturday, Father,' Maxwell said, trying to arrange his buttocks differently this time.

'It's my pleasure, Mr Maxwell.' Brendan leaned forward so that his white collar disappeared behind his pointed chin. 'My secretary tells me you have a personal matter to discuss.'

'It's about Rachel King,' Maxwell explained.

'Ah,' and the old boy crossed himself. Maxwell wasn't too surprised at that. He'd often seen Father Dowling do it on the telly, always in the winter streets of downtown Chicago. He was a little surprised by what followed though. 'A victim if ever I met one.'

'I'm sorry?' Maxwell frowned.

'No, no,' Brendan leaned back, fluttering his fingers, 'it is I who should apologise. Many people take my view to be unchristian, though I assure you it isn't. You see, I believe there are victims in the world, Mr Maxwell. People whose outlooks, walks of life, even their names, lead them into murky byways. Wrong people. Wrong places. It's sad. Very sad.'

'I would have said Rachel King was anything but a victim,' Maxwell said. 'Outgoing, vivacious, charming.'

'You knew her well?'

'Not, apparently, as well as I thought.'

'We closed the school,' Brendan said, 'on the day we heard the news. Some of the children were inconsolable. And with Michael and Jordan away . . .'

'Did that leave something of a gap at St Bede's?' Maxwell asked.

'Mr Maxwell,' Brendan smiled, 'I have to ask you on what authority . . .'

'None,' Maxwell smiled back. 'I have no right to be here at all. Except that . . . except that Rachel King was once a dear friend of mine and I think I owe it to her to find out what really happened.'

'The police have been here already,' the Principal told him.

'I'm sure they have.'

'But they weren't once dear friends of Rachel?' Brendan twinkled.

Maxwell chuckled. Why wasn't his headmaster like this one? Why was everybody else's headmaster a human being? 'Exactly,' he said.

'Did Michael's and Jordan's absence leave a gap?' Brendan took up the threads of the conversation. 'Yes, it did. I'm proud to say I'm seventy-six, Mr Maxwell. No, don't bother to mouth the platitudes. I look every week of that. The point is that I can still follow a dialogue, but running a school is more complex than that, isn't it? Michael Wynn is our St Peter, Mr Maxwell. The rock of St Bede's. Our anchor in a sea of change. He handled all the opting-out business, runs the curriculum like a well-oiled machine. I'll go next year, I expect, and I'll be happy to hand over to Michael. A worthy successor in every sense.'

'And Father Gracewell?'

'Ah, yes,' Brendan smiled. 'A very earnest young man.'

'Is that it?'

'Mr Maxwell,' Brendan said, 'I understand that Rachel King meant something to you and that is why I am talking to you now. But I cannot discuss the personalities of my staff with you. As a teacher and as a Catholic, that would be totally wrong. I'm sure you understand.'

'Of course,' Maxwell smiled, 'but I'd like to talk to them both if I may.'

* * *

But it was Saturday and the Deputy Principal and the Chaplain weren't there. Father Brendan was very obliging however and he made sure that Maxwell had their addresses before he left. The Head of Sixth Form grabbed a sandwich and a swift half at the local and made his first visit.

There was no doubt about it. Deputy Heads in opted-out schools seemed to have a bigger slice of the action than Heads of Sixth Form under the yoke of the good old local authorities. Michael Wynn's pied-a-terre must have set him back all of £200,000. It was Thirties Cute in style, owing a little to Edwin Lutyens, a little to Rennie Mackintosh and a little to Toby Twirl. There was even a Range Rover parked nonchalantly on the gravel sweep before which ghost koi slid effortlessly through the clear, dark waters of the lily pond.

Maxwell felt a little uncomfortable, a little out of his depth. His own modest 38 Columbine could have fitted neatly in the lobby of the house that stood before him. But he was in blood steeped in so far, there was no going back now. He rang the bell. A crop-headed kid put his face around the door and there was a dog barking somewhere in an outhouse.

'Is your dad in?' Maxwell asked.

'Mum,' the boy called back into the darkened hall, 'it's for dad.'

The tiny woman who stood in the doorway peered out at the visitor through cautious eyes. 'Yes?' Her voice was thin, as though her throat wouldn't last the afternoon.

'Mrs Wynn?'

'Yes.'

Maxwell swept off his panama. 'My name is Peter Maxwell. I wonder if I might have a word with your husband?'

'What's it about?' He noticed her eyes flicker. Strangely cold, they were, and empty.

'I was on the GNVQ course at Carnforth last week, Mrs Wynn. One of the women who died was a friend of mine. I'm trying to find out what happened to her.'

'She died, Mr . . . er . . . Maxwell. Isn't that what you said?'

'Yes,' Maxwell nodded, wondering quite what he'd stumbled on here. 'But I need to know why.'

Mrs Wynn hesitated, then let the door swing back. 'You'd better come in,' she said and led him through the hall into the kitchen and out on to a sunlit patio. 'Can I get you some home-made lemonade?' she asked and offered him a garden seat.

'That would be lovely,' he said and watched her wander away. For all the world Mrs Wynn looked like an older woman. She couldn't be more than forty, yet her movements, her vagueness gave her the air of an old biddy. Perhaps she'd had a hard life. The boy who'd opened the door to Maxwell was tinkering with an upturned mountain bike, clattering spanners and spinning wheels.

'Bit of chain trouble?' Maxwell asked him.

'No, it's the pedal,' the boy said. 'Keeps coming off.'

'Perhaps your dad can fix it?' Maxwell suggested.

'My dad's never here,' the boy said and hauled the machine upright.

There was a movement out of the corner of Maxwell's eye and he saw a little girl, younger than the boy, dart across the gap between two apple trees. Then she peered around the trunk at him and grinned a gappy grin.

'Hello,' Maxwell said. 'What's your name?'

'Belinda,' she said.

'That's a lovely name,' Maxwell smiled. He never quite knew how to handle kids under eleven. Always felt he was over-compensating, condescending.

'My mummy's name is Gwendoline Josephine,' the little girl volunteered.

'Belinda was my mother's name.' Mrs Wynn had returned, carrying a tray. 'I'm afraid Michael's not here at the moment. He's gone fishing. He always goes fishing on a Saturday.'

'Doesn't your boy enjoy that?' Maxwell asked.

'Charlie?' It was almost as if Mrs Wynn had to remind herself of the boy's name. 'Yes, he doesn't mind it. But Michael deserves his quiet. He works so hard at the school. He needs his peace. He's rather a solitary man in many ways.'

'You know, it's funny, but I could have sworn that Michael had two boys.'

'No,' she looked at him oddly, 'only Charlie.' She smiled at the boy, but there was no warmth there. 'Sometimes he seems like two. I wonder why you'd think that?'

Maxwell sipped the lemonade. It lacked the bite of Southern Comfort, but it would pass muster on a hot, dry early summer's day. 'Delicious,' he said. 'You have a lovely house, Mrs Wynn.'

She sat down at the green enamel table and for the first time he saw how scrawny her hands were, how thin her neck. Anorexia clearly ruled OK. 'Thank you,' she said. 'It's been in my family for three generations.'

'Oh, it's your house,' Maxwell chuckled. 'I was wondering how Michael had done so well for himself.'

'My family were in shipping for years. Grandfather was very careful with his money. Of course, it's all Michael's now.'

'Is it?'

'Well, it will be. I don't really understand money, Mr Maxwell. I leave all that sort of thing to Michael. Is that how it is in your house?'

'Ah, well, I'm a bachelor, Mrs Wynn,' Maxwell smiled. 'I'm Chief Accountant, Gardener, Head Cook and Bottle Washer all rolled into one.'

'That must be very difficult.'

'Well,' Maxwell shrugged, 'it can lead to acute schizophrenia, but I usually win the arguments with myself. Er . . . any idea when Michael will be back?'

'It's usually late,' she said. 'Dawn sometimes.'

'He fishes overnight?'

'Oh, yes,' Mrs Wynn said, 'frequently. He says there's nothing like standing in the roaring surf in the dark with the wind on your face and the line straining.'

'That's almost poetic,' Maxwell said softly. 'I don't suppose you know exactly which stretch of coast he uses?'

Mrs Wynn shrugged. 'It could be anywhere. I suppose you could look for him, if it was that urgent.'

'I'm on foot,' Maxwell told her. 'That might take a little time. Never mind, I'll catch him at school on Monday,' and he downed his lemonade.

'Which of them was your friend?' she suddenly asked him.

Maxwell blinked. 'Rachel King,' he said. 'Did you know her?'

Mrs Wynn nodded. 'Not all that well. I knew Liz Striker better. Rachel came here once or twice. I think Michael even took her fishing once.'

'Really?'

'Does that surprise you?'

'Well,' Maxwell laughed, 'I knew Rachel a long time ago, Mrs Wynn. She didn't know one end of a fish from another in those days. But I am going back a few years. People change.'

'Yes.' She looked steadily into his eyes. 'Yes, they do.'

'You don't go fishing then?' he asked her.

'Oh, no,' she said. 'When Michael and I were first married, I went with him a few times. I'm afraid I don't share his poetry. I find it cold and . . . well, boring.'

'I couldn't agree more.' Maxwell winked at her. 'Tell me, Mrs Wynn, how well do you know Father Gracewell?'

'Jordan? Better than I knew Rachel King, I suppose. Michael took him rather under his wing, especially when he first joined St Bede's. He had nowhere to live, so he spent a few weeks with us. Belinda was still a baby. I felt very sorry for him.'

'Why?'

'Some people are born to teach, Mr Maxwell. Michael was. He has a natural, wonderful gift with children. I'm sure you're the same.'

'I'm sure there are four hundred or so children at Leighford High who would take issue with you on that point,' Maxwell said.

'Well,' Mrs Wynn said, 'Jordan was not a natural. He was diffident to the point of embarrassment. I am not a particularly maternal type, Mr Maxwell, but even I wanted to mother him. Or I did until . . .'

'Until?'

Mrs Wynn stood up abruptly. For a moment, she swayed, steadying herself with her knuckles on the garden table. 'I'm afraid I have an appointment, Mr Maxwell, the children and I. I'm sorry your journey has been wasted.'

'Not at all, Mrs Wynn, the lemonade was delicious. I'll see myself out. Goodbye, children,' and Maxwell retrieved his hat and left, aware of three pairs of eyes burning into his back.

* * *

He'd seen dead houses before. Places where the windows watch you like sad eyes. Where the halls ring hollow and no one answers the bell. Rachel King's house was like that, on the edge of a small estate with cedars behind it and sprinkled lawns at the front.

Maxwell stood there for a few minutes until he realised that someone was looking at him, watching from a picket fence to his left.

'Can I help you?'

'I hope so,' Maxwell scowled. 'CID.' And he remembered not to tip his hat.

The old boy in the neighbouring garden peered at the policeman on the pavement. What sort of rozzer wore a bow-tie and waistcoat and a hat out of a television ad for Yellow Pages? Still, the old boy had caught a nasty one at Arromanches and he'd never been quite the same since. The Normandy landings had left their mark on all of them. The shrapnel he carried made him blurred, uncertain. And the years hadn't helped.

'Can I see your identification?' he said.

Maxwell fumbled in his inside pocket and flashed his Countdown card, the one that membership of the National Union of Teachers gave him access to. He flicked it away again before the old boy could focus his bifocals.

'Your blokes have been here already,' the old boy said.

'I know,' Maxwell said. 'Just a follow-up visit. Routine. They said you had a key.' Maxwell was fishing. For all he'd told Gwendoline Josephine Wynn that he found it boring, every now and then it paid dividends.

'That's right,' the old boy nodded. 'Who? Who said?'

'The lads at the station.'

'Are you the bloke what's in charge?'

'Nah,' Maxwell breathed in. 'Dogsbody, that's me. Mind if I have a look around? I'll lock up again afterwards.'

'Well . . . I s'pose it's all right. I'll just get the key, shall I?'

'That's the ticket.' Maxwell winked at him. He shuddered inwardly. He'd been patronising to a small kid and a wrinkly and it wasn't even supper time yet. Even so, he'd stay close to this old boy. Just in case he wasn't the giddy old gander he appeared. Just in case he took it into his head to ring the station, just to check.

'Well, well,' Maxwell said, 'I've seen some roses in my time.'

'Do you grow 'em?' The old boy turned to him. Since his Ethel had gone he'd had nobody to talk to about his roses. Nobody seemed to have the time to listen any more.

'Nah,' Maxwell shrugged. 'Couldn't grow a bunion by myself. But my neighbour at home, she's got some first-class blooms. Is the key this way?' And he elbowed past the old boy into a dilapidated kitchen.

'Here it is.' The old boy reached the key down from a shelf. ''Ere, where's your squad car?'

'Cutbacks,' Maxwell scowled. 'I've got to sign a chit to take a bike out.'

'Get away! I tell yer, it's the bloody government.'

'Well, there it is,' Maxwell nodded grimly.

'Do you know what I get for my disability?'

'Yes, it's a bloody shame, isn't it, Mr . . . er . . . ?'

'Jackson. D'you know I was a colour sergeant in the war?'

Maxwell paused and took a good look at the man. 'I knew it,' he said.

'What?' The old boy squinted at him through misty lenses.

'By your bearing. I knew you'd seen service.'

'Normandy, mate, me. I'd be off next month, you know, for the fiftieth. Only I can't afford it. The bloody froggies 'ave pinched all the 'otel rooms, y'know. Christ, if it wasn't for us, they wouldn't 'ave 'otels.'

'You never said a truer word.' Maxwell had lured the old boy as far as Rachel King's front door. Now it was time for fond farewells. 'Er . . . I'm sorry, Mr Jackson,' he said, 'I'm afraid I can't let you in.'

'What? Oh, no, right. 'Course not. No. Well, I'll just wait outside, then, shall I?'

'No, no. You just carry on with your roses. It's a grand evening for it. I'll pop the key back when I've finished.'

'Oh, right. I can tell you all about 'er, y'know. That Mrs King.'

'Can you?' Maxwell clicked the key in the Yale and the door swung inwards. 'Perhaps you'd do that, then. I don't suppose it'll hurt if you come in for a minute.'

'Well, I told your mates, of course.'

'Of course. Who was it you spoke to? Do you remember?' He led the man into Rachel's hall. There was a scattering of post on the mat. Somebody had piled other mail on the hall stand.

'Nah. Some kid who hadn't finished shitting yellow. Curly hair.'

'Inspector McBride.'

'Yeah, that'd be it. Shifty bastard. Course, I never 'ad any time for coppers. Not since them MPs in the war . . .'

'Have you lived here long, Mr Jackson?' Maxwell was reading the addresses on the envelopes. Apparently, Mrs Rachel King, along with half the inhabitants of the county, was already eligible for a substantial cash prize and her six lucky numbers would go forward into the Grand Prize Draw to be held in August. But only of course if she returned them within seven days. Well, mused Maxwell, she wouldn't be doing that now.

'Eight years come July,' the old boy said. 'I 'ad a bit of a windfall, see. Bloody great door fell on me in the factory and

I got compensation. Did all right too. Ethel and me could buy this place with a real garden and everything. And then, guess what? She ups and dies, don't she?' He shook his head. 'Now what did you want to go and do that for, Ethel?'

Maxwell looked at the decaying wreck of a man before him. It was like looking into a mirror. There but for the grace of God and twenty years went Peter Maxwell. 'You were going to tell me about Mrs King?' he said.

'Oh, yes.' Jackson tried to edge his way into the lounge, but Maxwell blocked him with his bulk. 'Well, she was a nice woman. Proper lady. Always well turned out. Got a good job, of course.'

'Really?' Maxwell raised an eyebrow. 'I understood she was a teacher.'

'Well, that's it, yes,' Jackson nodded. 'That's a good job in my book, mate. All that money and all them holidays. Last year she went to Bermuda.'

'Did she now?'

'For all six bleedin' weeks in the summer.'

'Very nice.'

'Nah. She was loaded.'

'She was?'

'Oh, yeah. Got a house in the Algarve, wherever the bloody 'ell that is. Bit of all right, though, weren't she?'

'Er . . . I don't know.' If Maxwell was going to impersonate a police officer, he had to go all the way. 'I never really met her, I don't think.'

'Yeah, bit of a one for the men.'

'She had men friends?'

'Yeah, lots of blokes used to come 'ere. No sign of an 'usband, though.'

'You told my colleagues all this, of course. Inspector McBride?'

'Yeah. Didn't they tell you?' The old man frowned.

'I haven't had a chance to read the full report, yet,' Maxwell hedged. 'Tell me, Mr Jackson, was there anyone in particular? Anyone who visited a lot?'

'There was this one bloke, yeah. Younger than the rest. What do they call them? Toyboys?'

'Could you describe him to me?'

'Nah. Your Inspector blokie asked me that. He had brown hair and he was young. That's all I know.'

'Did he stay the night, this young bloke?' Maxwell asked, leaning against Rachel's door that led into Rachel's lounge.

'Dunno,' Jackson shrugged. 'Contrary to what you might think, I am not a naturally nosy person. My Ethel used to say . . .' and the old boy paused. 'Well, what does it matter now, eh? Terrible thing, ain't it, mate? Old age? Y'know, it's only yesterday, it seems to me, I was up to my neck in water wading ashore on the Normandy beaches. Where've they gone, eh? All them bloody years?'

'Where indeed?' Maxwell asked.

'Anyhow,' Jackson shrugged off the mantle of gloom he found himself wearing more and more often these days and wobbled towards the door, 'you've got some murdering bastard to catch,' he said. 'You ain't gonna do that with me rabbiting on, are yer? 'Ere, do you like cocoa?'

Maxwell smiled. 'I love cocoa,' he said.

'Right.' The old boy hovered in the doorway. 'You give me a shout when yer ready and you and me'll have a cup, shall we? I've got some shortbread somewhere.'

'That'll be great,' said Maxwell, and he watched the man go, whistling through his roses.

Maxwell had never impersonated a police officer before. He'd never consciously lied to anyone, except habitually at parents' evenings, when he told Mr and Mrs So-and-so that he was sure little Johnnie/Ermintrude/Ali would be a credit to them come exam time. Now, he had committed a felony. Well, in for a penny. He closed the door on Mr Jackson and the all-seeing, unseeing world of Glenalmond Close and checked the kitchen. The drawers were full of cutlery or clothes pegs or instructions for electrical gadgets. Nothing different. Nothing unusual. But then, the police had been here already. They'd have found anything, wouldn't they?

Taken it away with them in anonymous black plastic bags. But then, the police didn't know the whole story, did they? They hadn't got the blackmail note, the one Sally Greenhow had half-inched from Harper-Bennet's room.

And as the thought crossed his mind, he saw it. A memo written on the wipeable wall board. In block capitals. Reminding Rachel to cancel the milk. With trembling fingers, Maxwell fumbled in his inside pocket and held the note at arm's length alongside the board.

He was no graphologist. But the tall uprights of the Ns gave it away. If there'd been any doubt in his mind, it had gone now. Rachel King was a blackmailer.

Maxwell drifted from the kitchen, back through the hall with its unopened mail, and made for the stairs. He'd just reached the landing when he heard the door bell ring. He froze, half turning. He checked his situation. It wasn't likely he could be seen from the glass-panelled door, but he could make out a figure, distorted by the bubbles. A man certainly. Had the fuzz come back? He could hear their enquiries now. 'And what exactly were you doing in the dead woman's house, sir? With a blackmail note in your possession, in her handwriting, which we know nothing about?' McBride would throw away the key.

Then he heard voices, saw the figure at the door move away. Maxwell braced himself on the banister rail and leapt the stairs two at a time, trying to land as he'd seen Metternich the cat land, and doing it rather badly. He ducked through into the lounge looking for the back door. Then the voices stopped him. Rachel's secondary glazing was not of the best and although he couldn't make out words, he recognised the sounds. Mr Jackson was talking to Rachel's visitor. And Rachel's visitor was Father Jordan Gracewell.

He heard the volume increase, heard Jackson say as he fiddled with the lock, 'He's in here now. I've told him all about you. He'll want to have a word.'

Then he heard the bell ringing again and Jackson hammering on the glass. 'Officer. Officer. Are you there?' And he saw Jordan Gracewell making a run for it, sprinting down the path and along the pavement until the privet hid him from view.

'Are you there?' Jackson was shouting through the letterbox now. 'He's come back. That young bloke I was telling you about. Only . . . he's gone again. ''Ere! I say! What the bloody 'ell's going on?'

What was going on was that Peter Maxwell had found the dining-room and with it, the french window to the garden at the back. He flicked the key and saw himself out, cutting through the public footpath that dissected the little estate and out on to the roads and the world beyond.

* * *

Mad Max Maxwell spent that Sunday morning wandering the beaches of Bournemouth, watching the demented English paddling and building sandcastles and throwing frisbees and hitting their children. And all the time, he was wrestling with the problem of who killed two women. By evening, he thought he knew. By supper time — fish and chips in vinegar and grease — he was certain. And he made his phone call.

'Sally?' Maxwell leaned into the plastic-domed booth in the bed and breakfast lobby where the hideous red and cream carpet swirled its way on and up the stairs.

'Max?' the startled girl answered. 'Where are you? No, don't tell me!'

'Sally, are you all right?'

'Is the Pope a Seventh Day Adventist?'

'Well,' Maxwell beamed as an old guest zimmered her way past him, 'I have to confess I've occasionally had my doubts. What's the matter?'

'Max . . . oh, Max . . .' and her voice trailed away.

'Max?' A male voice had taken over.

'Alan?'

'Look, I don't dislike you, Max. On the contrary, I've often spoken up for you when you've behaved like a prize prat in the past, but this has got to stop. Where the fuck are you?'

'Bournemouth,' Maxwell told him. 'Alan, what's going on? What's wrong with Sally?'

'Well, the bottom line, I suppose, is that she had the misfortune to go on that bloody silly course with you.'

'I see.' Maxwell was still beaming at the old lady, bearing in mind the speed of her movements through the lobby. 'And the top line?'

'The top line is that the police have been questioning her. No, Sal,' he heard Alan back away from the receiver, 'I'm handling this now. Enough is enough.' Alan was back with Maxwell. 'She's been through hell in the last twenty-four hours. And all because of your bloody ego. You're like some goddam knight errant, aren't you? Thundering around the country tilting at windmills. Well, Don Quixote, you can do it by yourself from now on. Sancho Panza here isn't coming out to play any more. The filth know about the blackmail note.'

'Ah.'

'Sally doesn't know where you are. And doesn't want to know. But I do. Could you be a little more precise? Then I'll get on to Malcolm and McBride and drop that little gem into their earholes. I think we'd all feel a little safer with you behind bars.'

'Thanks for your support, Alan,' Maxwell said, 'and tell Sal I'm sorry. She's the last person in the world I'd want to land in it.'

'Well, how touching,' Alan sneered. 'You're all heart, Max.'

'Tell her something else, Alan, will you?' Maxwell said. 'Tell her I know who killed Liz and Rachel.'

CHAPTER 15

That night something happened. Sally Greenhow tossed and turned until the early hours. Then she got up, disentangling herself from the cradling arms of her husband, and left. By the time she'd had a chance to clear her head and reflect on the brief note she'd left him on the kitchen table, she was rattling towards the west and the dawn was coming up like thunder out of Sussex to her back.

She felt so stupid. So furious with herself, sniffing back the tears as she drove. All she could think of was Alan and the row they'd had after the police had let her go. He hadn't meant to shout, of course. And nor had she. It was just the tension of the day, the hour. They'd kissed and made up afterwards and made love in the king-size bed he'd had imported from Sweden, the one less than a foot off the floor. But then, in the quiet of the night-time, after she'd had a ciggie and dipped into the latest Rendell and he had drifted into sleep, draped over her shoulder, an apparition came to Sally Greenhow. A man, in battered armour, riding a clapped-out bike wobbled into view. He was balancing a lance across his handlebars and beneath the uptilted visor of his helmet were the steady eyes of Mad Max. The image was so real she'd heard the whirring of his chain and the creak of his saddlebags as he passed. She couldn't, in the darkness, make out what he was tilting at, the lance level now under his armpit, the pedals flashing in the fleeting vision. All she knew was that it was huge and black. And she'd had this sudden sense of dread. It hit her like a wave and she'd sat bolt upright. Maxwell was riding into the dark. Alone. And suddenly she knew she had to be with him.

* * *

A similar thought had occurred to Superintendent Malcolm.

'If there's one thing Stony Warren got right,' he told John McBride that Sunday night, 'it was to wind up Peter Maxwell and see which way he goes.'

'The trouble is,' McBride said, 'he's gone too far, hasn't he? I'm going to throw the book at him for withholding that blackmail note.'

'Technically,' Malcolm reminded him, 'it was Sally Greenhow who withheld the note.'

'Complicity, then,' McBride said. 'We'll get him on that.'

'Very likely, John,' the Superintendent nodded, 'but let's see exactly where he is first.'

'St Bede's,' McBride said, passing a sheaf of papers to a passing DC. 'That's where we'll find Mr Maxwell.'

* * *

Mr Maxwell took his time over the full English breakfast. Mrs Elderflower's mixed grill had more grease than the West End show, but when you had arteries the hardness of which would put a diamond to shame, it really didn't matter very much. And anyway, Mrs Elderflower's tea was out of this world.

What made it all particularly glorious was not just the sunshine streaming in on to the slabs of cold toast waiting in their elegant chrome rack, but the fact that this was a Monday morning. Sixth Form Assembly followed by an hour of Key Stage 3 with 9S4, attempting to explain Neville

Chamberlain's policy of appeasement — largely akin to wading through treacle in snorkel and flippers.

'Everythin' all right, ducks?' Mrs Elderflower had had a rough night. One of her curlers was still in and her upper lip, or at least the line of scarlet lipstick that traced it, was making a determined bid to reach her nostrils.

'Fine, thanks.' Maxwell waved a limp sausage at her and beamed broadly.

He collected his overnight bag, his Italian ice-cream salesman's jacket and his panama, paid his dues and left. But he didn't take the bus to St Bede's. He took the bus to Higham Corner and padded on down the road to number 12, Elphinstone Gardens.

Briefly, Maxwell was buggered. The obliging Father Brendan had given him Jordan Gracewell's address, but had neglected to tell him the place was subdivided into flats. There was a barrage of six bells by the door frame and none of them carried the name Gracewell. So Maxwell rang Flat 1 and assumed the bonhomie of a travelling salesman. He was assuming more personas than Kirk Douglas in *The List of Adrian Messenger*.

An elderly lady peered around the door. Maxwell beamed and doffed his panama. Luck was a lady this morning. Maxwell was particularly good with elderly ladies.

'Good morning, my dear. My name is Peter Mawhinny. Of Mawhinny and Murdoch, Ecclesiastical Suppliers. I'm looking for Father Jordan Gracewell.'

'Pardon?' The old girl was still in her nightie and hideous quilted housecoat.

Pump up the volume, thought Maxwell and launched himself again. 'Peter Mawhinny of Mawhinny and Merton, Ecclesiastical Suppliers. Er . . . Father Gracewell. I have some merchandise to offer him. For his church.'

'Oh, the Father doesn't have a church, Mr Maw . . . He's a school chaplain, you know.'

'Indeed?' Maxwell did his best to look interested. 'Well, anyway, could you tell me which is his flat?'

'Oh, he's not there.'

'Not?'

'Pardon?'

'I said, "Is he not?" '

'No.' The old girl did her best to focus on her visitor. 'I just told you that.'

'Can you tell me where he is?' Maxwell was shouting now.

'St Bede's,' the old resident told him. 'And there's no need to shout, you know, young man. I have twenty-twenty hearing.'

'Yes, of course. In case I miss the Father at St Bede's though and have to call again later, could you tell me which is his flat?'

'Well, I don't know if I should. He's a very private person, you see. Keeps himself to himself.'

'Of course, of course.' Maxwell was still doing his best to smile. 'Tell me, Miss . . . er . . . ?'

'Mrs,' she corrected him, 'Mrs Verlander.'

'Mrs Verlander. Does the Father have many visitors?'

'What a funny question.' Mrs Verlander frowned, still ready to slam the door in a second should Mr Maw . . . prove to be a pervert.

'Oh, I like to do a bit of research into my clients,' Maxwell explained, 'and what with you in the ground-floor flat, I thought perhaps you'd notice people coming and going.'

'Just a moment,' she said. 'How do I know you're who you say you are?'

'I'm sorry?' Maxwell toyed for a second with doing a runner, but he checked himself and held his ground.

'Well, nothing personal, you understand, but I watched that *Boston Strangler* last night. The way that man could get into those women's flats. It's quite scary.'

'Ah,' Maxwell flattered, 'but that was Tony Curtis. You'd let Tony Curtis into your flat, wouldn't you?'

'Forty years ago, possibly,' Mrs Verlander told him. 'Now, I'm not so sure. Have you seen him lately?'

'No,' Maxwell assured her, 'I can't say that I have. Now, about Father Gracewell . . .'

'You have to show me some identification.'

'I have?' Maxwell loomed over the frail old bat.

'That nice Mr Ross on *Crimewatch* advises it.'

'Ah, but he also tells you not to have nightmares, doesn't he, Mrs Verlander? And do you?'

'Do I what?'

'Have nightmares.'

'Oh, yes. From time to time.'

'Well, there you are.' Maxwell spread his arms as though he'd just explained with dazzling clarity the mechanism of the Corn Laws to a bewildered Year Niner. 'Now, Father Gracewell's flat?'

'Number Three,' she told him without hesitation. 'Two floors up.'

'Thank you, dear lady,' Maxwell sighed and replaced his hat.

'By the way,' she called as he turned his back.

'Yes?'

'You're not unlike Albert de Salvo yourself, you know. The lift's not working. You'll have to use the stairs when you come back.'

Maxwell did. He waited until the old girl had gone in, then took them two at a time. Jordan Gracewell's door was just like Mrs Verlander's, except that it was locked and the ringing of the bell elicited no response. Clearly, the Chaplain had gone to school like all good padres, which was precisely why Maxwell had taken his time over breakfast. The last thing he wanted to do at the moment was to come face to face with the man he was after. He'd have given his eye teeth at that moment to have had Sally Greenhow's skill with a credit card. As it was, he'd have to try rougher methods. Mentally he threw back his poncho from his right hip, unlooped the leather thong that tied his gun hammer and bit down on the soggy cigar. In his head the wail of Ennio Morricone's Fistful of Dollars filled the silent corridor. Then Maxwell's right boot came up and crunched against the woodwork. The door swung wide.

Still reeling from the effort and the surprise that it had worked, Maxwell hobbled inside and secured the door behind him, using the bolt as the lock was smashed. He'd now added breaking and entering to his crimes of withholding evidence and impersonating a police officer. Perhaps Mrs Verlander was right. He wasn't unlike Albert de Salvo.

There was much in Gracewell's pad that Maxwell recognised in his own. Slippers discarded at rakish angles. The breakfast dishes unwashed. The light still on on the coffee machine; all the hallmarks of bachelorhood. And there were bits he didn't recognise: the portrait of the Pope on the lounge wall, the untidy pile of back numbers of the *Catholic Herald* and the all-pervading smell of incense. It was a smell he'd smelt before. At Carnforth. He checked under the cushions of Gracewell's settee, rummaged in the drawers of Gracewell's computer desk, ferreted around in Gracewell's CD collection. Nothing.

Right. Try the bedroom. There was a brass crucifix on the wall, a rowing machine on the floor next to the bed. Clearly the good padre believed in muscular Christianity. Maxwell looked in the wardrobe, the bookcase, the dressing-table. Nothing. Nothing you wouldn't expect to find in the house of an earnest young priest on the threshold of his ministry.

Maxwell sat down on the settee. He was back in the lounge and back to square one. Yet Rachel King's visitor had been Jordan Gracewell or Maxwell was a one-legged Negro transvestite. Nothing odd about that, though, was there? One colleague going to visit another? After all, everybody had said that Jordan Gracewell wasn't much of a teacher. Lacked what it took in the balls department. Rachel King had helped him. Liz Striker had helped him. Michael Wynn had helped him. But that only made sense while Rachel King was still alive. Jordan Gracewell knew perfectly well yesterday that Rachel King was dead. So why had he gone to her house? Did he expect old Mr Jackson to let him in? Perhaps so that he could retrieve something he'd left behind? And was it only the presence of what he took to be a policeman that made him run? If that was so, then Jordan Gracewell's teaching would be all to hell today. He'd be rattled. Wouldn't have slept. The police were on to him. And Father Brendan, no doubt as honest as the day was long, would have told him that a Mr Maxwell had come calling and that he'd given Mr Maxwell Gracewell's address.

But there was nothing here. Nothing at all. 'What did you expect, Maxie?' the Head of Sixth Form mused to himself. 'Four or five victims under the floorboards? Another six in the roof space?'

The roof space. Maxwell dashed to the window, then ducked back in case he could be seen from the road. Gracewell's flat was on the top floor of the block. That meant he had an attic of sorts. And Maxwell knew what treasures were hidden in his attic — an army in being, nearly four hundred plastic souls, saddled and waiting to ride down the Valley of Death. But more importantly, those toy soldiers were Maxwell's heart; his life. It was what he'd spend his retirement completing. They and Metternich the cat were all he had in the world. And chosen and few were those who knew about them.

So, he reasoned to himself as he hauled down Gracewell's loft ladder, what secrets lay beyond the trap door? What little mementoes were locked away from the gaze of the heartless, cynical world? He lowered the door back carefully, so that it didn't crash against the wall that supported it. There was nothing like the space up here that Maxwell had at home. He fumbled in the darkness and found a light switch. Then he rested on his elbows and shook his head, whistling softly.

Jordan Gracewell had a video collection to rival Paul Getty's — almost as impressive as Maxwell's own. But there was no sign of the *Road* films or *The Name of the Rose* or *Les Parapluies de Cherbourg*. Instead, they were in plain wrappers with typed titles like *College Girls, Fun in the Dorm* and *The Milkman Cometh*. Most of the stuff seemed to be Dutch and promised, in slightly fractured English, to show young girls as never before, wild, wet and wolling. But it wasn't the porn shows that interested Maxwell particularly. It was the dressing-up box alongside them. He raised himself up and peered inside the battered cardboard that once, apparently, held Spanish tomatoes. Now it held knickers by the dozen. Skimpy lace ones, blue gym ones, black thonged ones. Father Gracewell had enough lingerie here to open a branch of Woman at C&A. And among them, Maxwell knew, was a pair that once belonged to Sally Greenhow. And God knew who else besides.

* * *

Jordan Gracewell had not had a good day. First, on his way to Evensong on the Sunday, he'd called at Rachel's house. But the police had been there. And that was the last thing he'd wanted; to have to explain his presence there to the police. Making a bolt for it was hardly conducive to cool, but he'd panicked and probably made matters worse. He hadn't slept, expecting a ring at his door bell at any moment. He'd cooked himself some breakfast, but couldn't manage more than a mouthful and to cap it all, he had a sneaky suspicion that he'd left the coffee machine on.

And then Father Brendan had told him that Peter Maxwell had been there, snooping. Not Father Brendan's word, of course, but accurate nonetheless.

It was worse than he'd thought as he reached his landing. In his anxiety of the morning, he'd even forgotten to close his door and he saw the daylight shining through. Thank God this was still a quiet neighbourhood, where no one was likely to just walk in.

It was the screen he saw first — the video on pause. A naked girl was kneeling up, a line of static across her blurred breasts. Her head was thrown back, her mouth open in a silent orgasmic scream. Behind her, a black-haired stud was thrusting away, or he would have been if someone hadn't pressed the pause button. A hand extended from the armchair, the one with its back to the door. Dangling from the fingers was a pair of black lacy panties, swinging gently to and fro. They were joined almost immediately by the genial, smiling face of Peter Maxwell.

'I estimate,' he said, 'bearing in mind the position of the girl and her gentleman caller, vis-a-vis each other, that his membrum virile is at least sixteen inches long. No wonder her eyes are watering,' and he pressed the play button, so that the line vanished and the couple continued to gyrate to raucous dubbed music.

Gracewell had crossed the room in a couple of strides and switched off the set. Maxwell did the same with the video.

'Actually,' the Head of Sixth Form said, 'I'm glad you did that. I'd dismissed the low budget, the total absence of production values, and was actually getting round to admiring the girl's bum. Tell me, Jordan, are you a leg or a tit man?'

The padre was paler than an altar cloth and visibly shaking, the dark eyes bulging in his head. 'Get out! Just get out!'

Maxwell just sat there. Then he threw the black knickers to Gracewell who signally failed to catch them by not even trying. They fell silently to the floor.

'Forgive me, Father,' Maxwell said, 'for you have sinned.'

For a moment, Jordan Gracewell stood in front of the telly, for all the world like a schoolboy caught scrumping apples. Except, as Maxwell knew, schoolboys didn't scrump apples any more; they sniffed glue instead. Then the Chaplain of St Bede's crumpled like burning paper and dropped to his knees, his head in his hands, crying softly.

Everything in Maxwell made him want to grab the man's hair, jerk back his head and kick the shit out of him. Instead he reached forward and gently pulled the hands away. 'You confessed something to me once,' he said, 'that you thought Rachel King was a murderess. Would you like to tell me anything now? Before I call the police.'

'The police?' Gracewell looked up suddenly in a blur of tears. 'Surely, we don't need the police?'

Maxwell shook his head. 'They don't have ecclesiastical courts any more, Jordan. Criminous clerks like you have to take pot luck with the rest of us. I've got a nasty surprise for you — they abolished benefit of clergy too; 1831, I think it was.'

'But this . . .' He waved the arm he'd got free of Maxwell's hand, at the television. 'Oh, God, it's horrible, I know, but loneliness . . . you'd know.'

'I stick model soldiers together,' Maxwell told him. 'That's how I cope with loneliness. Don't — please, Jordan — tar me with your brush.'

'It's not illegal.' Gracewell was sitting back on his haunches, defiant now. Maxwell had seen it all before, when he'd caught kids bang to rights. Especially girls. First the tears. Then, when that didn't work, the excuses. And finally, the outrage.

'The videos perhaps not,' Maxwell said, 'although I think I read something somewhere about pornographic material in the post. I wouldn't like to hazard a guess how old some of these girls are. But you and I know we're not talking about the videos, don't we, Jordan?'

'Well,' Maxwell watched the Chaplain's eyes flicker, 'yes, I suppose . . . I suppose you're talking about the underwear.'

'The . . . ?' Maxwell's face betrayed for a moment his utter astonishment. Was it possible that Gracewell had blinded himself to all reality? That he'd blocked out the image of Liz Striker's skull disintegrating under his blows with the iron pipe? The woman he'd told Maxwell he loved? That his tortured mind had cancelled out those frenzied seconds when he'd demolished the head of Rachel King? Maxwell sat back, remembering to close his mouth as he did so. Softly, softly. That had to be the approach now. 'Yes,' he said, 'tell me about the underwear.'

Gracewell was still kneeling on his hearthrug, the tears drying now on his pale cheeks. 'I don't really remember how it all started,' he said, the warm glow of confession sweeping over him. 'Ever since I can remember — long before my teens and long, long before the Church, I had this . . . thing for women's underwear. Oh, I expect a psychiatrist would have the answers. It's a common enough fetish, isn't it? I remember once, my sister . . . well, that was rather a long time ago.'

'You stole them,' Maxwell said flatly, 'from clothes lines, gym lockers, launderettes. I assume it was the used ones you went for.'

Gracewell nodded, unable to look the man in the eye.

'And while you were a kid — or even a theology student — all this was fine and dandy, wasn't it? The frisson of sneaking into people's houses and snatching things from laundry baskets or back gardens — all very exciting.'

'Yes, yes.' Gracewell's eyes were glittering. 'You understand — Mr Maxwell, you understand.'

The Head of Sixth Form nodded. 'Yes,' he said, 'I understand. But understand something yourself, Jordan,' and now he was shaking his head, 'I don't condone.'

'No,' Gracewell's optimism sank, 'no, of course not. How could you? You aren't a priest.'

'Exactly,' Maxwell said. 'And that was the problem, wasn't it? Once you were ordained — and once you got a job as a Chaplain — that put the squeeze on you. Suddenly, you were somebody in the community. It wasn't only God watching your nasty little habits, but potentially any one of a thousand people or more — kids, colleagues, parents, the Bishop, the whole bloody College of Cardinals for all I know.'

'How . . . did you know?' Gracewell had to ask.

'I didn't,' Maxwell said. 'Not at first. But the parameters were there from day one. Contrary to popular belief, the murder of a stranger by a stranger is quite a rarity. Most murderers kill people they know. I went for that assumption at Carnforth. There were only two groups of visitors at the centre on the day Liz Striker died — the staff of John Bunyan, Luton and you lot from St Bede's.'

'Er . . . I don't follow,' Gracewell frowned.

'All right. It could have been a member of the Carnforth staff. And yes, all right, they presumably had access to lists of conference members. So if someone there knew Liz or Rachel, then they'd have their victims under one roof. But the coincidence of that is pretty remote, isn't it?'

'What are you talking about?' Gracewell asked.

'In my long experience,' Maxwell looked at the man steadily, 'people don't shit on their own doorsteps unless there's absolutely no choice. Where, for example, does most of your little collection come from?'

'Here and there,' Gracewell said.

'More there than here, I'll wager,' Maxwell persisted. 'Hence the knicking of Sally Greenhow's knickers at Carnforth. I knew I'd smelt the smell in this flat before. It's incense, isn't it? I was aware of it in the Carnforth pool, too. Must be something about the mix with chlorine that brings it out from your clothes.'

'Yes,' Gracewell muttered, 'yes, I took them.'

'So, I wrote off the Carnforth staff too. Now, I must admit, I had Alan Harper-Bennet in the frame for a while. Sally still thinks he's got her knickers. But really, it had to be someone from St Bede's, didn't it?'

'Why?'

'Because you'd known both Liz and Rachel. And with your little secret . . . well, it was only a matter of time before someone found out.' Maxwell leaned forward. 'You know what gets further up my nose about all this mess than anything else?'

'No.' Gracewell shook his head.

'The unpalatable truth that Rachel was blackmailing you.'

'Are you mad?' Gracewell blinked.

'It took me a long time to come to terms with that.' Maxwell shook his head. 'She wasn't the same girl I once knew. That I once loved.'

'Mr Maxwell—'

'That's not important now, though, is it?' Maxwell said. 'The point was that Rachel discovered your secret somehow and decided to cash in on it. You had too much to lose — your reputation, your job, your frock. So you looked big and paid up whatever it was she was milking you of and you bided your time. You waited until there was a chance. And all of you going off to the Carnforth Centre must have seemed a little miracle. A chance to get her on her own well away from St Bede's, away from Bournemouth. What did you do? Ask Rachel to meet you in the basement? Or was it something more innocent, like could she do some photocopying for you? Oh, I can see how it happened. You were tense, keyed up. It was dark. You saw a figure in the corridor. A female figure. And you lashed out. Only then did you realise, when you turned her over, that you'd killed the wrong one. You'd killed Liz Striker by mistake.'

Gracewell was on his feet now, pale again and quivering all the more. 'No,' he whispered. 'No. For God's sake.'

Maxwell was standing with him, shaking him by the shoulders. 'Face it, man,' he growled. 'Rachel sent you a note, didn't she? This note.' He wrenched it out of his pocket and held it against Gracewell's nose. 'You probably panicked for a moment. All right, you knew who it was from. You knew you were back to square one. Except that now it was worse, wasn't it? Now, Rachel knew you weren't just a pervert, you were a murderer too.'

Gracewell's hand snaked out and caught Maxwell a stinging slap across the face. For a second Maxwell's vision spun. Then he brought his right hand back and sent the younger man crashing into the television and sprawling backwards. The priest curled up, covering his head with his hands and whimpering in the corner. Maxwell winced as he nursed his fist and stood looking down at the wreck by his feet.

'You're not so handy face to face, are you?' he asked softly, his heart thumping. 'Not without a bloody iron pipe, that is.'

Gracewell was muttering something under his hands.

‘What?’ Maxwell hissed.

Gracewell muttered again.

This time Maxwell crouched in front of him, wrenching the hands from the Chaplain’s face. ‘What?’ he bellowed.

‘I don’t know what you’re talking about!’ Gracewell shouted back. ‘No one knew about me. No one. Not until you. Now. Today. The police came here. To ask me more questions. But they didn’t have a warrant. They didn’t even look round. No one was blackmailing me, Mr Maxwell. I swear to God.’

Maxwell blinked, his face and eyes stinging. ‘It’s a bit late to invoke the Almighty, isn’t it, Gracewell?’ he snarled. ‘You’ve got the blood of two women on your conscience. Not to mention your rather feeble attempt to frame two men.’

‘No.’ Gracewell was whimpering, shaking his head slowly, backwards and forwards. ‘No, I haven’t. I couldn’t kill anybody.’

Maxwell stood up sharply. He suddenly remembered a ’60s film noir. Crusty old policeman Sean Connery is interrogating slimy shit Ian Bannen whom he suspects of child murder. Crusty old Sean beats slimy Ian to death because he can’t crack him and because he’s frustrated and, well, just because. And that’s how Maxwell felt. He wanted to demolish Gracewell’s skull just as Gracewell had demolished Rachel’s and Liz’s. But that wasn’t how civilised men did things. And in this world gone mad, where people kill people for their trainers, or a packet of white powder or a cause, Maxwell liked to think that he at least was still civilised. Perhaps, indeed, the last bastion of civilisation.

He took a deep breath and turned his back. ‘Don’t make any plans to leave the country,’ he told Gracewell. Shit! In the tussle, Gracewell’s phone had gone down with him and was making a duff noise. Maxwell had seen a call box on the corner. He’d phone from there.

He took the stairs again, two at a time, past the door of Mrs Verlander who thought he looked like the Boston Strangler, Albert de Salvo. ‘Wrong again, lady,’ Maxwell mumbled his best Bronx as he reached the front path. 'Albert de Salvo's upstairs.'

He glanced up at Gracewell's window, glanced down at the call box. He was fumbling in his pockets for change, deliberating whether he should be really gung-ho and ring 999. Then he remembered something. That film noir, the one where Sean Connery kills suspect Ian Bannen. Ian didn't do it, did he? Sean had got it wrong, just like Mrs Verlander. Just like Peter Maxwell.

And he was still working all this out in his head when the sky came down to hit him and the grass rolled away at his feet and his life came to a full stop.

CHAPTER 16

'Would you like a corned beef sandwich, lover?'

That was the first sensible thing anyone had said to Peter Maxwell in a long time. Try as he might, he couldn't actually remember the nonsensical things they'd said in his vivid, turning dreams, but he knew they were nonsense.

'No thanks.' He shook his head and his vision reeled for a moment, like the depths of flu when your eyes and brain can't quite catch up with reality or a slow motion death in a Sam Peckinpah film.

'What about a cuppa, then?'

Maxwell focused as well as he could. His quiz inquisitor was a middle-aged black woman, in the starched greenness of a nursing auxiliary. She was leaning on a trolley of fairly unappetising goodies and Maxwell knew he was in an NHS ward of a Trust hospital. That or hell.

'That would be nice,' he said. He could actually move his head freely and there was no box over his bed, so unlike Kenneth More in *Reach for the Sky* he hadn't lost his legs. Both arms seemed to be attached, and he had to assume his body still held all the offending limbs together.

'There,' the nursing auxiliary propped him up a bit, 'that's nice. You look like a two-sugar man to me, lover,' she said, 'so that's what I've given you.'

'Spot on, Nurse . . . ?'

'Janice,' she said, smoothing down his pillow, 'just Janice.'

'Thank you, just Janice,' Maxwell croaked. His mouth felt full of tongue, but his teeth seemed to be OK.

'You stopped worrying about that phone call yet?' she asked him.

'Phone call?' he frowned.

'Yeah. When they brought you in last night you were rambling on about making a phone call and did I have any change. You wanna get one of them phonecards, lover. Useful, they are.'

There was a commotion from somewhere behind Janice and she turned to bellow something that sounded like pure Barbados by way of Brixton at an old fogey in the next bed. Then she tutted as she turned back to Maxwell. 'Geriatric ward, eh? Never quiet a bloody moment. Still, you either love 'em or hate 'em. Most of the time I hate 'em.'

'Geriatric ward?' Maxwell was confused.

'Yeah.' She ticked something off on a clipboard. 'Wrinklies, lover, you know. Senior bleeding citizens. I don't know why they don't call it Paediatrics Part Two and have done.'

'Why am I in a geriatric ward?' Maxwell wanted to know. He may have been unconscious for a time, but he had his pride. 'How many years have I been out for?'

Janice trilled her ululating laugh. 'Nah, lover. It's just overcrowding, that's all. You've only got bruising and suspected concussion, so they put you in here. Quite convenient really. Just as they brought you in, old Mr Binks died, so there was a bed. Well, he'd had a good life, so he couldn't really complain. Anyway, talking of complaining, I'd better get the tea round or there might be a lynching. See ya later. All right, Albert,' and she wheeled off down the ward, 'keep yer bleeding wig on. Corned beef sandwich, lover?'

Maxwell was just sampling his hot, sweet tea and taking in the bunches of flowers on the tables ahead of him when he was aware of two nurses, younger and whiter than Janice, whisking screens around him. Oh God, his brain screamed, not a blanket bath! Worse. The next face he saw was that of Inspector John McBride.

'How are you feeling?' The Inspector pulled up one of those steel-framed plastic seats they keep under the beds.

'I've been better,' Maxwell said, watching WPC O'Halloran and a man perch themselves on his other side. 'What, no grapes?'

'This is DS Jervis,' McBride introduced the man, 'West Sussex CID.'

Jervis nodded.

'You know WPC O'Halloran, I believe, from the Carnforth Centre.'

Maxwell nodded too. Mavis O'Halloran flashed him the briefest of smiles.

'Well, Mr Maxwell,' McBride said, 'we nearly didn't get to you at all.'

'I think,' Maxwell said, after a pause, 'it's about now I'm supposed to say, "What am I doing here?" Or even, on a more B feature level, "Where am I?"'

'You're in Bournemouth General.' DS Jervis had his notebook poised, like a rather unlikely-looking personal secretary. He even had one knee cocked coyly over the other. The short-thighed Peter Maxwell was always quietly jealous of people who could do that.

'As to what you're doing here,' McBride took up the tale, 'you're recovering from what might have been a fatal accident. We think you were hit by a car.'

'Oh no,' Maxwell groaned, trying to put his cup and saucer on the bedside thingy. 'From where I'm lying, I can assure you it was at the very least a twenty-ton truck.'

'You walked away from whatever it was with a slight concussion and severe bruising,' McBride told him. 'We're actually more interested, not in where you are now, but where you were when the accident happened. Or rather, where you'd been.'

'I don't remember,' Maxwell said.

McBride leaned back, smiling at his colleagues. 'Selective amnesia,' he said. 'Very common among those with something to hide.'

Maxwell took in the pale green screens that shielded him from the outside world of the geriatric ward. On McBride's instructions, no doubt, they'd turned Maxwell's bed and its environs into an instant incident room. But there was no solicitor, no tape recorder, no single phone call. And that could work in his favour.

'And isn't it about now,' he asked them, 'that I yell very loudly,' and he raised his voice, the one that had sent generations of schoolkids — not to mention colleagues — scurrying for cover. 'What are you doing with that rubber truncheon? No, please, no! Don't hit me again!'

As if on cue, a white-capped nurse poked her head around the screen. 'What's going on here?' she wanted to know. The police persons hadn't left their seats, but Maxwell was cowering under the covers.

'Just testing, nurse,' the impatient patient beamed. 'Reaction time — six seconds. Well done. I shall never believe them again when they say the NHS is on its last legs. And by the way, I've always thought our nurses are wonderful.'

Her face said it all. 'Any more nonsense and I'll have to fetch Sister,' and she snapped the curtains closed again.

'There you are,' Maxwell said, widening his eyes. 'Sister,' and he mouthed the words almost noiselessly.

'This whole thing is a game to you, Mr Maxwell, isn't it?' McBride sneered.

Mad Max sat upright as well as the dizziness would allow and looked the blue-eyed Inspector full in the face. 'Don't let this *bon viveur* exterior fool you, Inspector,' he said. 'A woman I once loved had her head caved in last week. I'm trying to do something about that.'

'I know you are,' McBride said, 'and I tried to warn you off it, didn't I? It's not your job, Mr Maxwell. People get hurt. You've been hurt. You should have left it to us.'

'Perhaps you're right,' Maxwell nodded. 'Maybe it's just the vigilante in all of us. Charles Bronson hasn't got a monopoly on that, you know.'

'We'll sort it out,' McBride assured him.

'No doubt you will,' Maxwell said. 'But the difference between you and me, Mr McBride, is that to you, it's just a job. Oh, I have no doubt you're a thorough-going professional, what in Jack Warner's day was called a good copper. And no doubt, you're under pressure from on high to get a result and close the book. But I knew Rachel King. I once loved Rachel King. If . . . if things had turned out differently, I'd have spent two-thirds of my life with Rachel King. And when she died, well, it became personal.'

'All right,' McBride said quietly, 'let's start with this, shall we?' and he produced a piece of paper from his inside pocket. 'The blackmail note.'

'Where did you get that?' he asked.

'From your jacket pocket,' the Inspector told him, 'along with a wallet, a few credit cards, a house key and fourteen pounds thirty-eight pence in change. That's how we knew you were here.'

'Inter-force co-operation,' Jervis said. 'We got a wire through the telex that the Kent boys were looking for you. When you turned up on a stretcher here at the General, their search was over.'

'Does that mean I'm under arrest?' Maxwell asked.

'That all depends,' McBride said, 'on your answers to my questions. Now, once again — the blackmail note.'

'You might as well tell us,' Mavis O'Halloran said. 'Mrs Greenhow has talked to us already.'

Now Maxwell knew the ploy. Divide and conquer. Nice policeman. Nasty policeman. One offers tea and ciggies, the other electrodes on the testicles. But they both imply they know more than they do, that another villain has already coughed. That's how they got the Krays. In this case, however, Maxwell knew it was true. Alan Greenhow had told him so over the phone.

'Sally found it in Alan Harper-Bennet's room at the Carnforth Centre,' Maxwell said.

'And what did she do with it?'

'Took it,' Maxwell said. 'I took it from her.'

'With or without her knowledge?'

'With,' Maxwell came clean. 'I had copies made.'

'Why?'

'I wanted to confront certain people with it. I didn't want the original destroyed.'

'Very enterprising,' McBride nodded. 'Who did you want to confront?'

'Alan Harper-Bennet, since it was his room the note was found in.'

Jervis and O'Halloran were scribbling away as though Peter Maxwell were some latter-day Sam Johnson and they a couple of Boswells.

'And what did he say?' McBride asked.

'Denied it was his,' Maxwell shrugged.

'Did you believe him?'

'Yes,' Maxwell said, as though the realisation had just come to him. 'Yes, I did. He said it was slipped under his door. He thought by Gregory Trant.'

'Trant?'

'Yes. Contrary to his behaviour at Carnforth, Trant has a reputation as a joker. It was the sort of thing he'd do, apparently.'

'So you talked to Trant?'

'That's right. He denied it too. But you know this already. You've talked to Sally.'

McBride smiled. 'We like to have things verified,' he said. 'Things in duplicate appeal to the police mentality, I suppose. Do you know who wrote the note?'

Maxwell paused and despite himself, sighed. 'Yes,' he said. 'It was Rachel King.'

McBride looked at his colleagues. This was something Sally Greenhow hadn't told them. She'd spilt a few theories, but they were about as useful as her views on the disappearance of the dinosaurs would have been. 'You seem pretty sure,' the Inspector said.

'You haven't been to her house recently, then?' Maxwell asked.

'No,' McBride said. 'Have you?'

Maxwell nodded. 'I posed as a policeman,' he volunteered, 'and that nice old boy next door let me in. Pop round there yourself. Compare that note with the one Rachel wrote on the memo board in her kitchen. The block capitals are identical.'

'So that let Trant off the hook, did it?' McBride asked.

'No, it didn't,' Maxwell said. 'Did you know he'd once had an affair with Rachel?'

Maxwell knew the answer to that one by the look on the face of his interrogator. He smiled. 'Well, he did,' he said. 'And you're seriously asking me why I didn't leave all this to you?' Maxwell would have laughed out loud, but the prospect of the pain was too much.

'Doesn't that put Gregory Trant in the frame?' McBride asked.

'That's what I thought,' Maxwell said. 'But I didn't, in the end, buy that bit about Liz Striker being killed by accident.'

'No?'

'No. It wasn't that dark in the basement at Carnforth. Even at night-time with the light off. Whoever the murderer was, he'd be able to distinguish Liz Striker from Rachel King. Physically, they weren't alike at all.'

'From which you conclude?' McBride asked.

'That whoever the murderer was made a mistake with Liz Striker, yes. But it wasn't a case of mistaken identity. Whoever killed Liz Striker believed that she was the blackmailer. That note convinced him otherwise.'

'I still don't see why Trant is off the hook.'

'To be blackmailed by someone, you have to know them,' Maxwell reasoned, 'or at very least, they have to know you. Now Trant was perfectly willing to admit his affair with Rachel — and the potentially damning fact that he didn't like her. But he didn't admit to knowing Liz Striker at all. Whoever killed those women had to know them both.'

'And that meant St Bede's?' McBride asked.

Maxwell nodded. 'More particularly, it meant Father Jordan Gracewell.'

'It was Gracewell who telephoned us,' DS Jervis said, 'from a call box on the corner. Apparently, his own phone was busted.'

'Really?' Maxwell frowned. 'Did he see what happened?'

'No. But he heard the thud.'

'Yes,' Maxwell tried to remember. 'I think I did, too.'

'I think you ought to know,' Inspector McBride said, 'that Jordan Gracewell has confessed.'

'Ah.' Maxwell let his head fall back on the pillow for the first time since the law had arrived. 'So there is a God.'

'He's confessed to obtaining pornographic material through the post and the theft of a large quantity of ladies' underwear. He hasn't said anything about any murders.'

Maxwell's head came up again. 'It's not for me to tell you your job, Inspector,' he said, 'but can I suggest you talk to him again? It may be he's a tougher nut than I thought. Probably used to the ways of the Spanish Inquisition. You'll have to go some if that's the case.'

Jervis and O'Halloran closed their notebooks at a nod from McBride.

'Mr Maxwell,' the Inspector said, 'I'm delighted that you're looking so chipper after your experiences. I always like to see a man standing alone and unaided at the magistrates' court when we charge him with withholding evidence, impersonating a police officer — oh, and I understand from Father Gracewell, breaking and entering.' McBride smiled. 'Don't get up. We'll be in touch.'

* * *

All day, Peter Maxwell lay in his bed and contemplated his navel. The NHS pyjamas they'd given him were comfy wincey and the shepherds' pie was almost as good as a school meal back in the Olden Times, when they were meat and veg and cost a bob. The conversation however was something else. Old Mr Merriweather on one side of him had a hiatus hernia that had come to dominate his life and even older Mr Howard was determined to prove he'd arrived in Shakespeare's seventh age of man by being sans everything except a really boring string of reminiscences about his years with the Southern Water Authority.

The sight of a girder quietly rusting therefore at visiting time would have been an exquisite relief for Peter Maxwell. But even the dark glasses couldn't disguise the fact that the rusting girder was in reality Sally Greenhow. She swept to the seat by Maxwell's bed and crouched there, fiddling with her shades.

'Subtle as always, Sal,' he whispered out of the corner of his mouth.

Mr Howard was nattering to the newly arrived Mrs Howard about his years with the Southern Water Authority.

'Max, you shit. Are you all right?' And Sally was glad he couldn't see her eyes full of tears behind the tinted glasses.

'I was about to ask you the same thing.'

'It's taken me two days to find you. I went to St Bede's. I tried hotels, bed and breakfast places. I even toyed with going to the police station.'

'Ooh,' Maxwell sucked his teeth, 'dangerous. What brought you here?'

'The local news. I stayed at a hotel last night and caught South Today. There you were. Mr Peter Maxwell, victim of a hit and run. Some thick CID bloke was appealing for witnesses. I didn't find him very appealing.'

'Sally,' Maxwell's hand was suddenly stroking her cheek, 'I've got you into a lot of bother, one way or another. And I'm sorry.'

She bit her lip to stop the tears and gripped his hand. 'It's not your fault, Max,' she told him. 'I walked into this with my eyes open.'

'Does Alan know where you are?' he asked.

'He knows I'm following you,' she said. 'That's all.'

Maxwell raised himself up on his good elbow. 'Go back home, Sal,' he said. 'You've been through enough.'

She shook her head quickly, unable, with the iron-hard lump in her throat, to answer him.

'Think of me,' Maxwell smiled. 'If you stay any longer, your husband will come and punch my lights out.'

She flung her arms around him, burying her face in the rick of his neck. He held her close for a moment, stroking the frizzy blonde hair, nuzzling her cheek. Then he uncoiled her arms and held her away from him.

'Does this mean you're not going home?' he asked her in his best transatlantic.

'That's right,' she sniffed. 'Whaddya goin' to do about it?'

'Well,' he passed her, slowly and painfully, a box of tissues from the top of his bedside thingy, 'the moment you've blown your nose and turned your back for decency's sake, I'm going to hop sprightly out of bed, nip into my outdoor togs and you and I are going to catch a murderer.'

'Who is it?' Sally asked, the tissue poised in her right hand. 'You absolute bastard. You told Alan on the phone that you knew, but you didn't say who. That's one major reason why I've put my marriage on the line to be here.'

'Your marriage?' Maxwell frowned. 'Are you serious?'

Sally shrugged and blew her nose. 'I don't know,' she said. 'All I know is that I've never seen Alan so angry.'

'Well,' Maxwell said, 'if you get any acid from Alan, you tell me and I'll go round there and punch his lights out.' But the left hook he gave the air wasn't particularly impressive. 'Though perhaps not today, if you don't mind.'

'You're changing the subject,' Sally scolded. 'Who is it, Max? For Christ's sake, tell me!'

She heard her own voice rise above the hubbub of conversation in the ward. For a moment, Mr Howard's water torture stopped and Mr Merriweather's hernia descended. Sally ducked her head and whispered again. 'I've got to know,' she said.

'Well,' Maxwell checked that the coast was relatively clear, 'if you'd asked me that question yesterday — or even early this morning — I'd have said, without much hesitation, Jordan Gracewell.'

'Gracewell?'

'He's got your knickers. Not to mention everybody else's. The sickest thing is that he was even trying to get a few of Rachel's.'

'What?'

'I went to Rachel's the day before yesterday. The neighbour let me in. And while I was looking for . . . God knows what, who should come a-calling but Jordan Gracewell.'

'Why?'

'He didn't tell me that. Perhaps that's because I didn't ask. I went to see him yesterday. Or rather I broke into his flat.'

'Max . . .' Sally's eyes widened behind the shades.

'I know,' he waved a hand in slow motion, 'I know. Breaking and entering. Anyway, I found a collection of video nasties that would make your hair curl and enough lingerie to open a shop.'

'My God!'

'That's more or less what Jordan said when he came back from a hard day at the chalk face. I was too busy accusing him of murder to ask him specifically why he'd returned to Rachel's. He was a frequent visitor, apparently, while she was alive.'

'Wait a minute, wait a minute.' Sally was confused and waggled her fingers in the air trying to rationalise it all. 'You said, if I'd asked you that question — i.e. who killed Liz and Rachel — yesterday or even this morning . . . Does that mean you've changed your mind?'

'That's the wonderful thing about our hospitals,' Maxwell beamed, 'they wake you up so bloody early, you have time to think. No, Jordan Gracewell's a wanker, knicker-nicker and voyeur, but I know now he's not a murderer too.'

'How?'

'That depends on one answer to a very simple question I must put to an old lady. Did you see any fuzz around? Outside the ward or downstairs?'

'Nobody in uniform,' Sally said. 'I must admit, ever since I talked to Malcolm, I've been watching out for them. Talk about Big Brother . . .'

'Malcolm who?' Maxwell was lost.

'Oh, of course,' Sally realised, 'you don't know. Not Malcolm Who, Who Malcolm. Superintendent Malcolm is now in charge of the Carnforth case.'

'Where's Warren?'

'Gone to ground. I don't understand how police hierarchy works, Max. All I know is Malcolm puts the wind up me something chronic. If I'd spent much longer with him, I'd have confessed to being Jack the Ripper.'

'All right, Jack,' Maxwell winked at her, 'say your goodbyes like a dutiful visitor — in fact by usual standards, you've already been here ten minutes longer than anybody else — and I'll see you by the lift.' A ghastly thought suddenly struck Peter Maxwell. 'There is a lift, isn't there, please God?'

'Yes,' Sally nodded. 'I came up in it. But Max, you can't just walk out of here. You've been hit by a car, for God's sake. You need rest.'

'No,' he told her, his face serious, 'what I need is answers. Off you toddle.'

* * *

Severe bruising was a euphemism for sheer bloody agony. They made a lot of cars from glass fibre these days, didn't they, Maxwell asked himself as he struggled into his day clothes and tottered down the ward in earnest conversation with Mrs Howard, who had had more than enough of her old man's reminiscences and was beating a hasty retreat. If that was so, he continued his inner conversation as he joined the waiting Sally by the lift doors, why did they bloody well hurt so much?

She linked arms with him carefully and steadied him as the machine jolted and clicked its way to the ground floor.

'Max,' she hissed, 'you've still got your jimmies on under your trousers.'

‘Of course I have,’ he said. ‘I couldn’t draw the screens without drawing attention to myself and I certainly had no intention of dropping my breeks in a public ward. Mrs Howard was giving me some pretty lascivious looks as it was.’

Mrs Howard had taken the stairs. Not because she didn’t trust herself to keep her hands off Maxwell’s body, but because she didn’t trust lifts.

Somehow Sally got Maxwell past the posters that asked people if they’d like to save the NHS and out into the evening air. She parked him against a bollard while she found her car and drove round to pick him up.

‘Where are we going?’ she asked, once she’d winched him in. ‘To the scene of the crime,’ he told her. ‘Chocks away, Biffo. I’ll navigate.’

CHAPTER 17

Peter Maxwell cricked his neck even further that evening, as the rain drifted in from the west, trying to keep a look-out for tailing policemen. The point was, of course, that he hadn't a clue what he was looking for. They weren't likely to follow Sally Greenhow's 2CV bumper to bumper with lights flashing and sirens screaming. So he looked for the unmarked car, three or four cars back, preferably with two grim-looking blokes in it. And he'd expect there to be more than one such vehicle, as the first realised he'd sussed them, to be replaced by a second.

He even tried tuning his way through the wavelengths on Sally's car radio to try and pick up police messages. The most outlandish he got was a very fragmented jingle from the Isle of Wight.

'Left here,' he told Sally and she screeched into the close. Maxwell recognised the telephone kiosk, the block of flats. He looked up at the top floor as Sally coasted to a halt at the kerb. Gracewell's lounge was in darkness. The perverted padre was elsewhere; out visiting launderettes perhaps or still helping police with their enquiries.

'I shan't be long,' he told the girl and eased himself out of the car. He listed a little to starboard as he crossed the grass. He saw the tyre tracks still rutted diagonally and the black rubber stains on the roadway. He couldn't bend down to see if the tread was clear enough for the police to have been able to identify the vehicle.

He pressed his finger against the bell of Flat 1. Why did his finger ache, for God's sake? An old lady poked her head around the door.

'Mrs Verlander.' Maxwell had no panama to tip. It hadn't been in his bedside thingy at the General, along with the rest of his clothes.

'Mr Mawhinney!' The old girl's eyes and her door opened simultaneously. 'Oh, I'm so glad to see you're walking about. I telephoned an ambulance as soon as I saw what had happened. Are you all right? You must have been thrown several feet in the air.'

'Yes,' Maxwell tried to smile, 'I must have.'

'I must say, I admire your persistence.'

'You do?'

'Oh, yes. Coming back after the tumble you took, to see Mr Gracewell. Your firm must be very proud. You don't get that kind of loyalty these days.'

'Indeed not,' Maxwell nodded earnestly, 'but . . . well, that's just the kind of bloke I am. Tell me, did I hear you correctly a moment ago when you said you saw what happened?'

'That's right,' the old girl told him.

'And you told the police, presumably?'

'Oh no,' Mrs Verlander frowned, 'I haven't spoken to a policeman since they hanged poor Derek Bentley. When was that now? 1953, wasn't it?'

'I believe so,' Maxwell nodded. 'But presumably, you don't mind telling me?'

'No, of course not. In fact, I'd say, of all people, you have the biggest right to know. It was odd, really, because I hadn't expected to see you going that way. I mean, I'm rather a nosy old trout, I suppose, and I hadn't seen you on your way up to Father Gracewell's — only on the way down. You seemed in such a tearing hurry and rummaging in your pockets. Then I saw a vehicle start up from down that way, towards the end of the road. It didn't have its lights on and that struck me as odd because it was getting quite dark by then. Suddenly, it veered to the left. There was a screech of tyres, or whatever screeches on a car, and it mounted the pavement. Then the grass. I think I banged on the window and shouted out, but of course you couldn't hear. That's the pity of double glazing, isn't it? Everything happened in slow motion, then. They say these things happen in an instant, but they don't. It seemed ages before you somersaulted over the bonnet.'

'I don't suppose you remember what sort of car it was?' Maxwell hoped vaguely. 'The colour or anything?'

'Oh dear,' Mrs Verlander said, 'now I'm not very good on these things. And my eyes aren't what they were. I couldn't see very much. It was dark, you see. I couldn't see a number plate or anything like that.'

'I see,' Maxwell said. 'Well, thank you, Mrs Verlander. I'm grateful for your help,' and he turned to go. He'd pinned his hopes on this, naively, stupidly. What kind of idiot was he to rely on the chance that an old lady had even been standing at her window at the crucial time, let alone that she'd be compos enough to remember what she'd seen.

'But . . .' her voice stopped him at the end of the path, 'I'm pretty sure the driver was a man and the car was one of those Range Rover things. Bottle green.'

* * *

The bottle green Range Rover stood on the gravel in front of the Thirties Cute house, the one with the hint of Toby Twirl.

'Where are we now?' Sally Greenhow had turned off her engine and her lights and was wiping the condensation off the windscreen.

'Journey's end,' Maxwell muttered. 'Really depressing play, that. Did they ever film it? I must consult my Arthur Halliwell. He'd know.'

'Whose house is this, Max?' Sally looked at her ancient colleague in the darkness.

'Down!' Maxwell bit his lip to avoid screaming as he ducked below the dashboard. Sally did likewise and caught her forehead a nasty one on the steering wheel.

'Oh, shit!' she hissed. For a second, the interior of the 2CV was awash with light, then it was dark again.

'He's going out. Follow him, Sal.'

She kicked the ignition into action. 'For Christ's sake, Max, who am I following?'

'"Behold,"' Maxwell was belting himself in again, '"a pale horse; and his name that sat on him was Death." Only in this case, for pale horse, read dark Range Rover.'

Sally curled her lip and crashed her gears, snarling for the road. 'OK,' she shouted, 'I should have realised it. We're following Clint Eastwood. He killed Liz Striker and Rachel King. What a dolt I've been all along not to have guessed it.'

'Bear with me, Sal,' Maxwell asked. 'I've been all kinds of arsehole in my time, but I can't afford to be wrong about this. Keep back. I don't want him to know he's being followed.'

'Are you serious?' she asked him. 'It's all I can do to keep his tail lights in sight. All right, if you're not going to tell me who it is, at least tell me where he's going.'

'Parkhurst?' Maxwell guessed. 'The Scrubs? Long Lartin? I don't know, but I hope it's for bloody ever.'

* * *

They drove through the night, the wipers of the 2CV desperately trying to cope with the lashing rain. At Ringwood, the Range Rover swung north on the A338 to Fordingbridge and on to the Salisbury road, before turning due west to Combe Bissett and the little lanes that twisted like molten silver through the sleeping Wiltshire countryside to Fifield Bavant. Here, at last, the Range Rover turned sharp right and jolted to a halt under the spreading branches of a horse chestnut.

Sally Greenhow pulled up a little way down the road. She heard the car door slam, then the house door; and lights appeared, first in the hallway and then in the lounge.

'Max?' She gripped the man's sleeve as he prepared to bundle himself out of the door.

'We've got to get into that house, Sal,' he said. 'I've got a feeling what happened at Carnforth has its roots there.'

'Whoa!' she shouted, snatching her keys from the ignition. 'You're not going in there alone.'

'Why not?'

'For a start,' she locked the car, 'it's half-past twelve at night, or in the morning, I should say. And secondly, you discharged yourself from hospital earlier this evening. There's probably whatever our police call an APB out on you already.'

'"Just the facts, ma'am,"' Maxwell drawled in his best Dragnet. 'All right — but, Sally . . .' He stopped her with a gentle hand on her left breast. 'Oops, sorry.' He dropped his hand. 'Sally, I want you to promise me something.'

'What?' she asked.

'If the going gets rough in there, I want you to promise me you'll get out. Call the police. Drive for help. Anything. But just get out. It might be dangerous.'

'Max,' she leaned her forehead against his, 'so is standing in the middle of the road. Shall we?' And she led him up the garden path.

The rain had stopped now, but everywhere the darling buds of May were drooping heavy with water, dripping on to the drive and the crazy paving. On a night as dark as this one, Maxwell couldn't make out the architecture of the house. Around its glowing windows, it just looked black and detached. There was a garage to the left, a greenhouse to the right and a high larch-lap fence beyond that.

'What do we do?' Sally hissed.

'Pray,' Maxwell said and rang the door bell.

For a moment, there was nothing. Maxwell rang again.

'Who is it?' a female voice called. 'Who's there?'

Maxwell nudged Sally in the ribs. More chance of a positive response to a female voice, at this hour, in the darkness.

'Er . . . we . . . I've broken down. My car's overheated. Can I scrounge a jug of water?' It didn't sound very plausible to Sally, let alone to whoever was beyond the door. But the bolts slid back and the door creaked open.

'Mrs Wynn?' Maxwell peered into the light.

'Yes, but . . .'

Maxwell didn't give the woman any more time to ponder the matter. He pushed the door open as far as his aching body would allow and stood damply in the hall, Sally at his elbow.

'Who is it, Jane?' A large, bearded man with the merest hint of a Geordie accent bustled out of the lounge and stopped dead. 'Well, well,' said Michael Wynn.

'Mike?' The woman crossed to him and stared up into his face. 'Mike? Who are these people?'

'My name is Peter Maxwell,' Maxwell said. 'This is Sally Greenhow.'

'Well, what do you want?' the woman asked. 'What is going on here?'

'You tell us,' Maxwell said. 'I did hear you right a moment ago? You are Mrs Wynn?'

'Yes, of course I . . . Oh, God,' and Mrs Wynn seemed to shrink back into the corner.

'It's all right, Janie,' Wynn said. 'Max, the boys are asleep upstairs. We don't need to wake them, do we? Come into the lounge, both of you.'

The odd couples sat down on the settees that faced each other across a coffee table. Maxwell was staring at Michael Wynn. Sally felt as she imagined people must feel when they've arranged a bit of wife-swapping in a contact mag, wondering who would be first to break the ice. Except she didn't fancy Max. And Michael Wynn suddenly frightened her.

'When did you find out?' Wynn hadn't taken his eyes off Maxwell for a moment.

Maxwell looked at his watch. 'About two minutes ago,' he said.

'Shit!' Wynn hissed. Jane gripped his arm. He patted her hand. 'In other words,' he said, 'you actually know fuck all.'

'I know about Edouard Locard,' Maxwell told him.

'Who?'

'Edouard Locard, the great French criminologist. One of the great guys of all time. He established the contact trace theory — "every contact leaves a trace" — I won't confuse you by giving you the original French.'

'You've lost me,' Wynn confessed.

'No, I haven't,' Maxwell said. 'You're just practising the butter-wouldn't-melt-in-my-mouth routine for a little later on tonight when Messrs McBride and Malcolm have a little chat with you in their incident room. "Guilty? Moi?" This,' he pointed to his arm, 'may seem like an ordinary jacket sleeve. And so it is. But I'd be prepared to guess that there's a forensic scientist tucked up somewhere in his little truckle bed now in the next county who, at sparrow-fart tomorrow, will be able to match microscopic bits of green paint buried in these jacket fibres with that dent I noticed on the offside corner of your bottle green Range Rover. You had a damn good go at killing me the other evening, Michael George Wynn. Now, I don't know the exact form of words, but I'm effecting a citizen's arrest on you for that. I suppose "You're nicked" has assumed a certain cache these days, hasn't it?'

'You're mad!' Wynn sneered. He crossed to the sideboard and poured himself a large Scotch. 'Anybody else?' He raised the decanter.

Sally shook her head quickly. She hated this. And was about to hate it more. Jane Wynn hadn't moved at all.

'I'd rather drink prussic acid.' Maxwell smiled at his host.

'Oh, come, now, Max,' Wynn said, 'that's a little Victorian of you, isn't it? You'll be calling me a cad, next.'

'Not Victorian,' Maxwell argued. 'I'm a Southern Comfort man myself. Not all that fond of Scotch. But, talking of cads,

Mrs Wynn, I assume you know about the other Mrs Wynn, do you? The second Mrs Tanqueray?'

'I—'

'Of course she does.' Michael Wynn had returned to her side, resting a timely hand on her shoulder. 'Now look, Max, I'll have to come clean about the other night. I'd had a few, I'm afraid, and lost control of the Range Rover. Next thing I knew it was up the kerb and I'd hit something. Christ, man, I didn't even realise it was a person, still less that it was you. All right, I should have stopped. I should have got out. I didn't and I daresay I'll be done for dangerous driving.'

'Oh no,' Maxwell chuckled, though the bravado cost him dearly, 'you'll be done for murder, Michael me boy.'

'Murder?'

'For God's sake, Mike, give it up!' Jane wailed, her eyes filled with tears. 'Can't you see it's over?'

For a moment, Michael Wynn stayed perched on the arm of the settee, grinning down at his wife and his accusers who sat opposite. He took a slow, deliberate swig from his glass, then threw the rest into Peter Maxwell's face. He followed this up with an open-handed slap round the head, then a knee in the groin as Maxwell tried to stand. The big man brought both hands down on the back of Maxwell's neck, poleaxing him to the ground. Sally launched herself at Wynn, but the Deputy Principal of St Bede's merely batted her aside.

'I'll be in touch,' he shouted to Jane. 'Keep your bloody mouth shut!' and he was gone, leaving Maxwell groaning on the floor and Sally cradling his whisky-soaked head.

'Another minute there,' Maxwell mumbled, 'and I'd have had him.'

They were suddenly aware that Jane Wynn had gone. They heard the scream of the Range Rover's tyres on the gravel and saw the flash of headlights as Michael Wynn roared away into the fugitive night.

Then they heard the calm voice of Jane Wynn in the hall. 'Hello, police? Yes. I'd like to report a murder please. No, not here. At the Carnforth Centre, Kent. Last week. You'll find the man you're looking for at Greenbank, Hawthorn Road, Bournemouth. His name is Michael George Wynn. My name? Oh yes, my name is Jane Wynn.' And they heard the click as the receiver went down.

She looked up to see Sally and Maxwell in the lounge doorway. They parted as she walked between them. 'I don't think I was on long enough for them to have traced that call, do you? I must admit I don't really understand about these things. Still, Mike's name is in the phone book. It won't take them long.'

'Mrs Wynn,' Sally said, 'did you . . . did you know about all this?'

'Oh, yes.' The woman looked at them both as though they'd asked her the time. 'Do sit down. It'll be a few minutes, I expect, before the police arrive. I might as well tell you what I know.'

As though in a dream, Sally and Maxwell returned to their settee. Maxwell's head throbbed with the pummelling Wynn had given it, but that didn't matter now. He was on the edge of his seat and nothing mattered now. Nothing except Jane Wynn sitting across the coffee table from him.

'Mike and I met sixteen years ago. We married a year later. He was Head of Geography at a local comprehensive in Salisbury. I'd never worked, not really, so money was tight. It was hard, but we managed. We have two lovely boys.' She smiled, reaching across for their photos. Two grinning kids with duck-like hair. 'Stephen's twelve and William's eight.'

'Lovely,' Sally said, at a loss to know what to say.

'They're good boys,' Jane assured her. 'But Mike . . . well, he was restless, ambitious, greedy even. He tried one or two business ventures, bought shares and so on, but it didn't really work out. Then came the day.'

'The day?' Maxwell asked.

'March 18th, 1984. Michael's interview at St Bede's. He got the job. Imagine! Deputy Principal. It wasn't a vast salary increase, but it was enough. That night we talked about it

— the move and so on. And Mike said we weren't coming with him, me and Stephen. Will wasn't born then, of course.'

'He was . . . leaving you?' Sally asked. She worked in Special Needs. She saw this kind of heartbreak every day. It invariably resulted in kids on the skids.

'Oh, no,' Jane said. 'At least, only temporarily. It was the most extraordinary thing, Mike said. The interview was held over two days and he was put up at a hotel overnight. He was having dinner at a restaurant when he met someone. A woman.'

A light of realisation dawned in Maxwell's eyes. 'Gwendoline Josephine,' he said. 'Little Jo.'

'That's right,' Jane nodded. 'Mike said she was a very strange woman. She'd just shared his table because the place was full, but the wine or her loneliness made her blurt out her life story. She'd had a kid — a boy — by a previous marriage and she was dying. She had motor neurone disease. It wouldn't kill her today. Or tomorrow. But she knew she didn't have long. And she was a very, very wealthy woman. Family money. Mike had a plan. He'd pretend he was single. If he got the job, of course.' She chuckled. Neither Peter Maxwell nor Sally Greenhow shared the joke, Jane Wynn saw that. 'Well, if he hadn't got the job, the whole thing was impractical,' she said, 'but he did get the job. Oh, we argued about it, but he's a forceful man, Mr Maxwell, is my Mike. In the end, I agreed. You read about it all the time, don't you? A man with two families. He gave Jo a daughter — Belinda. She's a pretty girl; I've seen the pictures. But he did it for us, you know,' she sounded for all the world like a woman trying to convince herself, 'because he loved us, me and the boys. So I said yes. I told Stephen — that daddy had a job that took him away on business for a long time. That's what I'll have to say now, isn't it?' A faraway look came into the eyes of Jane Wynn. 'Now that Mike's going to prison, I mean.'

Sally had to look away. For a moment she hated Michael and Jane Wynn. And she hated Peter Maxwell. But most of all she hated herself.

'Mike told Jo that he liked sea fishing, especially at night. He actually does. He even took her once or twice to prove his point. He knew it bored her rigid, so she wouldn't pester him to come along. Anyway, what with the children and her worsening illness, there wasn't much of a chance of that. He'd spend the night or the weekend or bits of the holidays here with us and buy some fish in Bournemouth on his way home, so that the catch looked convincing. Recently, though, Mike thought that Jo was getting suspicious. She seemed to be watching him, asking him questions. One day he caught her checking his fishing tackle, to see if it had been used.'

'And somebody else was suspicious too, weren't they?' Maxwell asked her.

Jane nodded. 'Mike thought it was Liz Striker. I've never met my husband's colleagues, Mr Maxwell. I didn't know any of them. All I had was Mike's version. Somehow, he thought she'd found out about me and the boys. And he had too much to lose. Not only the job — a Catholic girls' school can be very particular about bigamy — but the money too. The inheritance he intended to get from Jo. Once it was public knowledge that I was Mrs Wynn, then Mike's marriage to Jo was obviously illegal. He'd lose everything.'

'So he paid the blackmail?' Maxwell asked.

'He paid five thousand pounds in six months,' Jane said. 'All of it came from Jo, of course. He told her it was for a business venture. She has no head for figures, the other Mrs Wynn, so she believed everything he told her — at least as far as money was concerned. He put the cash into an envelope and hid it behind some lockers at St Bede's. He saw Liz Striker hovering around there an hour or so later and put two and two together. Unfortunately for her, his Maths wasn't so hot that day.'

'But he couldn't kill her at St Bede's, could he?' Maxwell reasoned.

'No,' Jane shook her head, 'but he had to do something. We talked about it. We always talked about problems like that. He was in charge of INSET at St Bede's, of arranging courses. He persuaded Liz to go to the Carnforth Centre. It was perfect. Except that Rachel King volunteered.'

'So,' Sally was confused, 'Mike just got blackmail notes from someone. Someone he presumed was Liz?'

'Yes. Always typed or word-processed or something. On St Bede's letterheads. He showed me the first one. It was horrible. All about letting "Little Jo" know, if they couldn't come to some arrangement. He took some scaffolding from St Bede's and killed Liz Striker on the first day they were there, at the Carnforth Centre. He'd checked the basement beforehand. It was little used, dark and quiet. He hoped it would be assumed that she'd gone home ill or something and that by the time she was found, the conference would be over. He put her body in a store cupboard.'

'What did he do with his clothes?' Maxwell asked.

'His clothes?' Jane repeated.

'They must have been bloodstained.'

'No, not really,' Jane said. 'There was quite a bit on the floor apparently, but he wiped that up. I believe he had some on his shirt cuff, but he washed that in the centre launderette and it came out.'

'Then he got the note from Rachel King?'

'Yes,' Jane said. 'He couldn't believe it. When he told me afterwards, he was still quite gobsmacked by it, totally incredulous. Of course, the problem was still there. But it was so much riskier now. They'd found Liz Striker. And there were police everywhere. Everybody was suspicious. He didn't know at first of course who the note was from. She went to see him in his room, laughed at him, threatened him. She was a nasty piece of work, that one. He asked her to give him time to get the cash. Then that night he went to her room. But he wasn't carrying the money in the jiffy bag, he was carrying the iron pipe he'd used on Liz Striker. He killed Rachel too.'

'So his problems were over?' Sally asked.

'Just beginning,' Jane said. 'He was stuck with a blackmail note and a murder weapon. He'd been careful not to leave prints anywhere. And when he was being interviewed, as you all were, by the police, he'd heard they were about to issue warrants. So he took his chance. He slipped the note under the door of a man called Harper-Bennet and smuggled the pipe into the room of a Dr Moreton. To do that, of course, he had to lift the master key to the rooms. A bit of chatting up of the receptionist, I gather, achieved that. He's a clever man, my husband, Mr Maxwell, whatever you may think of him. He did all this under the noses of the police and he walked away scot free.' Her face suddenly darkened. 'Until now, that is.'

'Why did you ring the police, Mrs Wynn?' Sally asked, looking the woman full in the face. 'You know they'll throw away the key, don't you?'

Jane Wynn nodded. 'Yes,' she said, 'I know. It's all got out of hand, Mrs Greenhow. I can't live like this any more. It's ruined so many lives — Liz's, Rachel's, their families; Jo and her children; Michael and our boys, me. Does murder always do that, I wonder?'

'I should think so,' Maxwell said. 'Always.'

There was a silence, then Jane Wynn stood up. 'Mr Maxwell,' she said, 'how did you know it was my husband?'

'I didn't,' Maxwell confessed.

'He thought you were on to him. When Jo told him you'd been to visit. And Father Brendan likewise. That's why he went after you, in the Range Rover. He said Jo's Maestro wouldn't necessarily do the job.'

'There were a couple of things,' Maxwell said. 'Things that didn't quite add up. Everybody told me that Michael Wynn was such a family man. Except that when I visited his family, they said they hardly saw him. And when he showed a picture of his family to someone on the course, he talked about his boys. I didn't see the photo myself, but I'd be prepared to bet that was you, Mrs Wynn. You and your boys.'

'Oh yes,' Jane smiled, 'I know he loves us. That's what all this has been about.'

They heard the snarl of tyres on gravel, saw the headlights fill the hall beyond the open lounge door. The law had arrived.

'Why did you become involved in the first place?' Jane Wynn wanted to know.

Maxwell's gaze had rested on the mock embers that in the harsher winter months would have been glowing, warm and friendly. 'An old flame,' he said. 'An old flame who died a long time ago.'

* * *

The Wiltshire police were waiting for Michael Wynn as he drove into the large sweep of the drive at his second home in Bournemouth. He'd gone there to grab some cash, some clothes and do a Lord Lucan, driving for the coast. He'd contact Jane and the boys later, from South America or somewhere, when the trail had gone suitably cold. St Bede's would have to advertise for another Deputy Principal, of course.

Instead, he felt the cold eyes of the constabulary and someone holding down his head as they tucked him into the back of a squad car. Briefly, he saw the little dying woman he'd married ten years ago, standing in the hallway, crying.

* * *

It was raining the day they buried Rachel King. Sally Greenhow was back in the forgiving, grateful arms of her Alan again and all was nearly right with the world.

After they'd lowered all that was left of Rachel King to the flowers, the little contingent from St Bede's wandered off leaving Maxwell, in his dripping panama, the one the police had found and returned to him, by the graveside. 'Mr Maxwell?'

He looked up from the new flowers, the mock-grass tarpaulin and the ropes. A young woman stood looking at him. He'd seen her briefly in church, but hadn't known her.

'Yes.'

She held out a gloved hand. 'I'm Helen Gadsden. I believe you knew my mother.'

'Your mother?'

The girl nodded at the fresh grave.

'Oh.' Maxwell suddenly felt uncomfortable. 'Helen King as was.'

'That's right.'

'I'm . . . really very sorry,' he said, taking off the panama.

She was shaking her head. 'No,' she said, 'there's no need to be. I came half-way round the world out of . . . what? Duty, I suppose. I didn't think anyone else would be here. Oh, the St Bede's people, I suppose. But children are so naive, aren't they? They didn't know my mother. You did. You know what a bitch she was, but you still came. Why was that?'

'I don't know,' Maxwell said. 'To put out an old flame perhaps.'

Helen Gadsden smiled. 'Thank you for what you did in bringing her murderer to book. That was kind.'

'No,' sighed Maxwell, 'that was justice. You know, you don't look anything like her.'

She smiled again. 'I'm very glad of that, Mr Maxwell,' she said. 'She did her best to ruin my father's life, mine, even Michael Wynn's, the police have told me. If she was an old flame of yours, your fingers must have been burnt too.'

He looked at his bruised hand, still swollen from its encounter with Michael Wynn's Range Rover. 'Perhaps,' he said softly. 'Just a little.'

Under the trees, two or three hundred yards from the grave of Rachel King, Superintendent Malcolm and Inspector McBride sheltered from the worst of the rain.

'Do we move in on him now?' McBride asked.

'No,' Malcolm shook his head. 'Let him go.'

'Let him go?' McBride was appalled. 'Breaking and entering, impersonating a police officer, withholding evidence? You'll excuse me for asking this, Mr Malcolm, but are you fucking mad?'

Malcolm smiled. 'No, John,' he said. 'You've got your man. It'll be a cold day in hell before they let Michael Wynn go — I feel it in my water. And it was Peter Maxwell who gave him to you on a plate. All right, he didn't play by the rules, but then he doesn't have to, does he? That's our little lot in life; the little cross we have to bear. And don't forget, John, our complicity in this.'

'Our complicity?' McBride was lost.

'Miles Warren wound him up. You tightened the key. I pointed him in the right direction. It got a result in the end.'

'But I also warned him off,' McBride defended himself, 'and you gave me orders to pull him in.'

Malcolm laughed out loud. 'Oh, yes,' he said, 'but neither of us meant it, did we, John? Come on, you can buy me a cuppa tea. And an egg and cress sandwich.'

Peter Maxwell watched the daughter of his old flame wander away in the rain. She could, he reflected for a moment, have been his under slightly different circumstances. He looked down for one last time at the carnations and the ribbons, bedraggled in the rain. Then he looked up to the sky. Somewhere, in the miles beyond those trees, was the rest of his life and Leighford High.

'Well, Hectorina,' he said to himself, 'you've had plenty of time in my absence. Now, tell me all about Napoleon's domestic policy. I don't want to frighten you all, but A levels are now only thirteen contact days away.'

THE END

THE JOFFE BOOKS STORY

We began in 2014 when Jasper agreed to publish his mum's much-rejected romance novel and it became a bestseller.

Since then we've grown into the largest independent publisher in the UK. We're extremely proud to publish some of the very best writers in the world, including Joy Ellis, Faith Martin, Caro Ramsay, Helen Forrester, Simon Brett and Robert Goddard. Everyone at Joffe Books loves reading and we never forget that it all begins with the magic of an author telling a story.

We are proud to publish talented first-time authors, as well as established writers whose books we love introducing to a new generation of readers.

We won Trade Publisher of the Year at the Independent Publishing Awards in 2023. We have been shortlisted for Independent Publisher of the Year at the British Book Awards for the last four years, and were shortlisted for the Diversity and Inclusivity Award at the 2022 Independent Publishing Awards. In 2023 we were shortlisted for Publisher of the Year at the RNA Industry Awards.

We built this company with your help, and we love to hear from you, so please email us about absolutely anything bookish at feedback@joffebooks.com

If you want to receive free books every Friday and hear about all our new releases, join our mailing list: www.joffebooks.com/contact

And when you tell your friends about us, just remember: it's pronounced Joffe as in coffee or toffee!

ALSO BY M.J. TROW

SCHOOLMASTER MYSTERIES
Book 1: MAXWELL'S HOUSE
Book 2: MAXWELL'S FLAME

Printed in Dunstable, United Kingdom

66997722R00150